Praise for The Judge's Wife

"A richly woven tale of passion, conspiracy, hypocrisy, and a chilling secret beyond the grave. . . . In a compelling read, Ann O'Loughlin renders her characters with precision, while also revealing the dark side of Dublin society, even in the 1980s."

—*Sunday Independent*

"A passionate, dramatic story . . . deftly written between time-lines and places. A poignant tale . . . many narrative threads are woven in to the rich fabric of the story but at its center are the complexities of love and how to navigate a relationship when all odds are stacked against you."

—*Books Ireland*

"She applies herself with lyrical zest . . . O'Loughlin digs deeper to explore the more tangled knots tying down the wider dramatis personae of her drama and she fleshes them out with compassion . . . she opens the throttles and guns it for full metal melodrama with two huge revelations towards the end."

—*Irish Examiner*

"It is neatly done, and O'Loughlin weaves her tapestry well, with most of the characters coming gloriously, tangibly to life. . . . O'Loughlin's prose in this novel is precise and restrained, almost hauntingly so . . . that the result is great writing. . . . *The Judge's Wife* is essentially an uplifting read, the kind of book you want to gobble up in one sitting."

—*Sunday Times*

"Grace was a rare and memorable character, one I don't think I've read similar to in any other book. . . . Powerful with its emotion and captivating with its storytelling, *The Judge's Wife* is a book that breaks your heart."

—*Reviewed by the Book*

"I'm not normally a very fast reader, but I literally devoured this. . . . There is so much to tell about this enthralling tale of love and deception, but I don't want to spoil the shock and surprise . . . an absolutely pleasure to read, I thoroughly recommend this book."

—*Ampersand Book Review*

"To say that I loved *The Judge's Wife* would be an understatement. I couldn't believe the amount of emotion I felt whilst reading this story. . . . Ann O'Loughlin could not have written a better book. It is full to the brim with emotions and is just as heartwarming as it is heartbreaking."

—*Kelly's Book Corner*

"*The Judge's Wife* is a powerful and moving story, very well written with characters that are fascinating and a central theme that is quite tragic."

—*Random Things Through My Letterbox*

"I absolutely, completely and utterly adored this book from the first page, all the way through every single page, through to the very last. . . . A stunning book that broke my heart, on more than one occasion. It was devastating, it was perfect and it was beautiful. I couldn't stop thinking about the characters and their lives long after I'd read the last page. A magnificent read!"

—*Kim the Bookworm*

Praise for The Secrets of Roscarbury Hall

"A delicious novel, filled with the joys and sorrows only humans can cook up. O'Loughlin has written a tale of sisterhood in all its forms—siblings, nuns, and strangers who appear out of the blue to become your family when you need one the most. Best read with a cuppa tea and warm scone, drizzled with sugar icing, sprinkled with lemon zest. Sweet and sour. Just like the women in Roscarbury Hall."

—Mary Hogan, bestselling author of *Two Sisters* and *The Woman in the Photo*

"A lovely story of two women with the courage to confront the injustices of the past, bringing light to a dark corner of Ireland's recent history."

—Kathleen MacMahon, bestselling author of *This Is How It Ends*

"Warm and engaging . . . I loved journeying through the lives of these fascinating characters. A beautifully drawn, skillfully written, well-researched novel."

—Kate Kerrigan, *New York Times* bestselling author of the Ellis Island Trilogy

"Ann O'Loughlin has spun a masterful tale with *The Secrets of Roscarbury Hall*, a story full of secrets and dark memories. . . . Beautiful."

—Manhattan Book Review

"Unraveled family secrets are rewoven into bittersweet truth in this poignant debut. . . . O'Loughlin metes out revelations, both painful and redeeming."

—*Publishers Weekly*

"A moving tale of loss, love, and redemption."

—*Bella Books*

"Secrets emerge, there's a whopper of a twist, and this unabashed tear-jerker ends with a well-earthed, well-calculated emotional finale."

—*Irish Times*

"Highly engaging."

—*Irish Independent*

"Deftly written, moving, and courageous."

—*Sunday Times*

The JUDGE'S Wife

Also by Ann O'Loughlin

The Secrets of Roscarbury Hall

The JUDGE'S *Wife*

A Novel

Ann O'Loughlin

Skyhorse Publishing

First North American Edition 2018

First Published by Black & White Publishing Ltd in the United Kingdom.

This is a work of fiction. Names, places, characters, and incidents are either the product of the author's imagination or are used fictitiously.

Skyhorse Publishing books may be purchased in bulk at special discounts for sales promotion, corporate gifts, fund-raising, or educational purposes. Special editions can also be created to specifications. For details, contact the Special Sales Department, Skyhorse Publishing, 307 West 36th Street, 11th Floor, New York, NY 10018 or info@skyhorsepublishing.com.

Visit our website at www.skyhorsepublishing.com.
Visit the author's website at http://annoloughlin.blogspot.com/.

10 9 8 7 6 5 4 3 2 1

Library of Congress Cataloging-in-Publication Data

Names: O'Loughlin, Ann, author.
Title: The judge's wife : a novel / Ann O'Loughlin.
Description: First North American edition. | New York, NY : Skyhorse Publishing Inc., 2018.
Identifiers: LCCN 2017043001 (print) | LCCN 2017046308 (ebook) | ISBN 9781510723962 (ebook) | ISBN 9781510723955 (hardcover : alk. paper)
Subjects: LCSH: Family secrets—Fiction. | Families—Fiction. | Man-woman Relationships—Fiction.
Classification: LCC PR6115.L6795 (ebook) | LCC PR6115.L6795 J83 2016 (print)
| DDC 823/.92—dc23
LC record available at https://lccn.loc.gov/2017043001

Cover design by Erin Seaward-Hiatt
Cover photo: iStock

Printed in the United States of America

To John, Roshan and Zia . . . my universe

Acknowledgements

Many years ago, John and I went on a great adventure to the land of colour and spices. We travelled the length and breadth of India, but it was only when we stopped and settled to live in Bengaluru, which was then known as Bangalore, that we truly experienced the delight of this wonderful and diverse place.

There we met the Noronha family, Olga and the now late Tony, and their two children, Nikesh and Nitya, and a huge extended family. They took us into their hearts and their lives, transforming our stay in India into a life-changing and truly life-enhancing experience. We will be forever in their debt for the love and friendship they offered two strangers from the other side of the world. Now is the time to say thank you to Olga Noronha and her family and all our dear friends in that beautiful city of South India for a friendship that has spanned over two decades.

Writing a novel is a long and slow process; it is the writer's family who lives that journey. To John, Roshan and Zia, who were always by my side offering support, my love and thanks. So too must I thank my agent, Jenny Brown of Jenny Brown

Associates, who, with kinds words of encouragement, helped bring *The Judge's Wife* to publication.

The team at Black & White Publishing has, as always, been wonderfully supportive, but special thanks must go to my editor Karyn Millar for her sound advice and rights manager Janne Moller for her constant good humour.

A final thank you to all the lovely readers who took my first novel *The Ballroom Café* to their hearts. My hope is that you enjoy *The Judge's Wife* equally, and to the new readers who have happened on this novel I hope that you enjoy the story of Vikram and Grace as much as I loved writing it.

The Judge's Wife

One

Our Lady's Asylum, Knockavanagh, Co. Wicklow, March 1954

Every part of her ached. The thin wool coat, heavy on her shoulders, scratched across her skin. The powder he had told her to pat on her face made her cheeks bristle. The shoes he had laid out for her were too high; her ankle throbbed from where she had banged it on the last stone step on the way to the car.

Grace dropped her face into the soft silk of the scarf loosely knotted around her neck. Tears swelled up inside her. She wanted to roll down the window and scream, to throw herself from the car when it slowed on O'Connell Street. She scanned the crowd. A woman waiting to cross the street with a male companion took in the wide car with the soft leather seats and gave a haughty look.

Her husband, the judge, had told her to pack a small suitcase. "A time away will do you good."

He had stayed with her while she dressed, his arms folded,

his head bowed, waiting to chaperone her to the car. At the wheel now: a silent hulk of a man.

Judge Martin Moran took the coast road to Wicklow as if on a day trip from the city. She sat beside him, tears coursing down her cheeks, chiselling grey channels through her make-up. Hidden in her hand, inside her glove, was a small piece of white marble pressed to her skin, the smooth chill of the stone giving some comfort. Aunt Violet, tightly clutching her handbag, sat in the back, silent, watching her niece blubber into her scarf.

The shutters were down in Knockavanagh, the shops closed for a half-day. At the far side of the town and past the meat factory, Judge Moran stopped at the gates of Our Lady's Asylum.

Panic streaked through Grace. Tentatively she put a hand out to her husband, but he jerked away. They slid past the tall grey building with the small windows and the water tower set aside on marshy land. At a small stone bungalow, the Morris Oxford pulled into a parking space marked "reserved".

"This is your new home. For a while, anyway." The judge spoke in a firm and matter-of-fact tone. Aunt Violet placed a tight grip on Grace's shoulder.

A man in a suit flanked by two attendants emerged from the house, smiling, arms extended. Grace was gently helped out, her small leather case taken from the back seat.

The suited man, his forehead beaded with sweat, stepped forward and bowed to the judge and Aunt Violet. "Judge Moran, Mrs McNally, we have coffee prepared for you."

"We can't stay long."

Grace pulled hard, tried to turn to her husband. "Martin, don't leave me here."

Her words fell into the pit of the space between them as Martin was shown into the small house.

Aunt Violet waved her gloved hand in the air. "Coffee is an excellent idea," she said.

The attendant nearest dug an elbow into Grace's ribs. "Don't be creating such a commotion. Be a good girl."

Catching her up under the arms, they scooped her so high her shoes fell off.

"My shoes, I need my shoes."

"Where you are going there is no need for fancy footwear."

One of them took out a key and unlocked a thick iron door. "You might be a judge's wife, but in here you are nothing, simply nothing. Get in there, take off those clothes."

Grace stepped in. Pressing her back into the wall, she held her arms tight across her chest.

"Do what you are told, like a good girl."

Her gloves were wrenched off. Her silk scarf slid to the ground. Her coat was yanked from her shoulders and her dress pulled so that the flimsy satin gave way down one side, the sound of the tearing fabric shrieking through the room, echoing the screams in her head. She stood in her cream silk underwear, shivering.

"Take them off."

"But . . ."

The attendant took a step towards Grace. Quickly, she danced out of her slip, unhooking her bra, desperately trying to hide her breasts.

"Knickers off as well."

Grace shivered. "I gave birth only days ago."

"Take them off."

Grace pulled down her knickers, shame flushing through

her. She stood, her legs squeezed together, trying to hold in a pee. Voices, loud and jovial, wafted past: the hurried good-byes, the crunch of gravel, the purr of the Morris Oxford as the judge turned it in the small yard and drove away.

She was steered by the shoulders to the door.

"But I am naked."

With a push to the back, Grace was guided across the corridor to a long, narrow room with five tiled showers. A bar of red carbolic soap was shoved into her hand; the cold tap was turned on.

"Wash yourself, like a good girl."

Grace slapped the soap across her body, the harsh smell making her want to throw up. When the water stopped flowing, she was handed a towel and a blue flannelette nightgown.

"If flannelette was good enough for May Minihan in Ward B, it can be good enough for you."

Rough to the touch, the nightdress had been boiled so many times that the flower pattern had long since faded.

"Look lively."

They marched her down a long corridor. As they approached the steel door at the end, a key screeched in a lock. The door was pulled back from the inside.

"My case, what about my case? Can I please have my case?"

Grace was directed to where a stout nurse was waiting for her.

"Ward E. Walk."

Scuffles of clouds framed by rectangular, dirt-encrusted windows danced overhead. The sound of laughter drifted up from downstairs, where the two attendants puffed on cigarettes and relayed to the staff canteen every detail of the committal of the judge's wife to the asylum.

Two

Parnell Square, Dublin, March 1984

It was a small brown leather suitcase, snapped shut with a buckle to keep it tightly secured. A red-flecked cord was knotted tightly around the middle.

Wedged into a corner between the judge's desk and the window overlooking the back garden, it was as if it had been long forgotten, slipped out of the way in haste, abandoned in a dark space.

Emma reached down. The judge was dead, otherwise she would not dare to investigate. The handle was soupy with dust; the leather creaked when she pulled on it. It remained stuck. She yanked stronger, a determination rising inside her to see what he had hidden away. Leaning forward, she gripped tighter, pulling fiercely, the rigid leather groaning as it gave in to the force, sticking halfway up until she managed to dislodge it, a funnel of dust swatting around her.

It was heavy. An envelope addressed to Judge Martin Moran, No. 19 Parnell Square, Dublin, was attached with brown tape to the flat top. Half ripped open, the envelope had browned with age, the contents missing.

Emma hesitated. He would not like her going through his things, especially because she had only returned once he was dead. Twelve years had passed since they last spoke.

Here, in his room, she had shouted at him, told him he was more like a jailer than a father. He had sat back in his leather-buttoned armchair at his desk by the window, staring at her, making no attempt to interrupt.

Glancing over her shoulder as she stalked to the door, she saw his shoulders stiffen, but he did not call her back. He knew her bags were packed. Deliberately, he hunched over the documents on his desk before slowly picking up the phone and asking the kitchen to send up a tray of tea. In a surge of fury, she grabbed a book from a shelf and threw it. It fluttered by him, plopping like a dead bird onto the windowsill behind him.

She pushed the case into the centre of the judge's wide desk and swiped off a layer of dust with her sleeve. Not bothering to look for a pair of scissors, she tugged at the cord, but it bit into her fingers, refusing to snap. Frustrated, she swiped at it with his letter opener, hacking like a butcher until it gave way.

Unbuckling the strap and easing the clasps back, the case creaked on release, silverfish scattering on all sides. There was a faint whiff of old leather, and the hinges squeaked as she pushed the lid back. The sweet smell of a perfume locked away for too long wafted hesitantly past her. Emma flushed with surprise to see the neatly packed contents: a silk nightgown rolled so it did not crease, a soft brush and a comb, a small bottle of perfume held upright between powder-blue silk slippers and a small vanity bag for make-up. Two coloured cardigans were folded neatly, along with a tweed jacket pressed small, linen ruched skirts, one grey, one red, and a pair of black shoes.

Slowly Emma fumbled with her fingers around the case, scrabbling along the bottom until she felt a rectangular shape. A red notebook. It was tied with a wide ribbon. Inside the cover the name Grace: curly writing in purple ink. Emma's stomach tightened. The writing was even and neat. The first page the only used, as if the writer expected a lifetime to fill in the rest.

March 22, 1954

Martin says I have to go away to recuperate, but he does not say to where. He is so different, I can feel the anger cross in the door in front of him. Aunt Violet is in charge, I know that. She has only said a few words to me, none of them good. She is a wicked woman. How can she be so horrible to her own flesh and blood?

Vikram, where are you? I worry so much. Has anybody told you what has happened? I am so very tired and weary. I should have run away with you, I know that now. This regret will haunt me. Have you gone back to India? Please forgive me, please don't give up on me. Please make contact, please find me. I have written a letter to you and it is stamped, I just have to find a post box to throw it in. Maybe when I am better I can walk to a village or something, or maybe if the people are kind they will post it for me, though no doubt there will be gossip about an airmail letter to India.

Emma scanned the rest of the book, hoping for more. Her head hurt. Grace was her mother: the woman who gave birth to her, the woman who died before she could hold her, the mother she never knew. Grace was the woman she could never talk about. The judge never even allowed her name to be uttered in his presence; he never would let anybody talk of Grace. When she had tried, his face darkened and he snapped, "Don't, please," his face contorted in such pain, she was never brave enough to push further.

Furious at her inability to understand, she threw the note-book. It cleared the room, landing with a thud on the hall floor, a small pink envelope skitting out under the hall table. She made to follow the envelope, but the doorbell rang and she was afraid the caller would hear her in the hall. Turning away, the persistent buzz of the bell pushed through the rooms, but she ignored it. There was a lull when Emma thought the person outside might have given up, but the buzzing started up again in short, sharp bursts, displaying the caller's impatience. The bell *brrring* itched at her brain, making her rush down the hall in anger. She swung the door open so fiercely it bounded back, bumping her on the shoulder. The woman waiting there jumped back, startled.

Emma took her in. Middle-aged, blonde hair whipped up in a high bun. Her angular face was caked with heavy powder, her lipstick was creamy pink, little spots clinging to her two front teeth, her eyelids were heavy with blue eyeshadow.

"Your neighbour, Angie Hannon, from the bed and break-fast. I was sorry to hear about the judge. I helped him out, did a few bits and pieces for him these last few years. I thought I should introduce myself. I brought you a box of groceries, you don't want to be worrying about shopping at a time like this."

"Thank you, Mrs Hannon, but I am all right."

"I don't like to see you on your own here. If you want, you

can stay in my place. The bed and breakfast is not that busy these days. I have plenty of free space."

Angie Hannon reached down and picked up a large cardboard box from the ground. "Shall I carry it downstairs for you?"

Emma stepped back to let Angie into the hall. "Maybe leave it on the table here."

Angie slid it onto the mahogany table, letting it glide a path through the dust. A bottle of wine was tucked in tight beside food in paper bags, showing Mrs Hannon had shopped at more than a supermarket.

"I am just close by, call me any time. I liked your father. He was always good to me."

"I did not get on with my father, Mrs Hannon, we never could find a space where we had anything in common."

Reaching over, Angie squeezed Emma's arm. "That hardly matters now."

Emma did not answer and Angie stepped back out onto the front steps.

Emma closed the door and turned to the judge's library. Switching on the electric heater by the desk, she sat looking at the open suitcase. Slowly, she pulled at the red linen skirt, releasing it from its tight ball. It gave way easily, unfurling in a shiver of wrinkles to stand long and straight, its pleats still pressed in place. A grey cardigan next, the softness of the wool a reminder of when she was a child and the housekeeper soaked her clothes in vats of cold water to loosen the wool and keep it soft. Slowly, she undid the buttons and slipped her hands into the bolero sleeves. The fit was right. As she stepped into the skirt, the linen brushed a breeze across her ankles. In the cabinet at the end of the room was the judge's mirror, installed on the inside of a door so he could check his appearance every morning, before his car arrived for the Four Courts. As she opened the door a puff of sweet mahogany pushed past, the familiar, intense smell of his cigars encircled her. Shaking her head, she tried to avoid it.

As she twirled, the pleated linen spanned out slightly, and she felt at that moment happy, like a young girl who had sneaked into her parents' room to try on her mother's clothes.

Three

Bangalore, India, March 1984

"Rosa, come with me. Just two weeks."

"Uncle, Anil won't like his wife travelling so far. Have you told Mama of your plans?"

Vikram laughed out loud. "Tell? You know how Rhya will react."

"Maybe she is right, it is too soon after the all-clear."

Vikram took off the reading glasses he had been wearing as he glanced over the *Indian Express*. "When will the women in this family realise we men are capable of making our own life decisions?"

"Mama won't be happy – she hates that country. Let's go somewhere with a bit of history. To London. See the queen?"

Vikram patted the cushion of the rattan chair beside him on the balcony. "Sit. I have something to tell you."

Sighing loudly, she slumped down beside him.

"I need to go to that side to visit the grave of the one woman I truly loved."

"What?"

"Grace died. I came back to India."

"Grace? Who was this Grace?"

Vikram hesitated.

"She was Irish?"

Vikram nodded, getting up to finger the lilac blooms of the jacaranda tree. "I must do this, Rosa."

"Uncle, you are beginning to sound as if you are getting ready to expire."

"Quite the opposite, dear Rosa. I want to stand at the grave of the woman I loved. What is wrong with that?"

"Why am I only hearing about this now?"

"When a man comes so near to death as I, there are many things he decides to revisit if given the chance. Grace was everything to me. I have loved her all my life, I want to stand quietly at her graveside. I would be honoured if you felt you could do that with me."

Rosa reached out and took Vikram's hand. "Anil will just have to put up with it. Tell me about this Grace."

"Grace, Grace who?" Rhya padded down the balcony in her cotton housecoat, plaiting her long hair, ready for bedtime. Glancing between her brother and daughter, she stopped threading her hair. "Rosa, you should go home. Won't your husband be wondering where you are?"

"Hush, Mama, with the old-fashioned talk."

Vikram shook out his newspaper elaborately in an attempt to distract the two women from arguing. "We will talk more tomorrow, Rosa. I suspect your mother is going to order me to my bed."

Rhya threw her hands in the air. "Vikram, you were once a medical man. You know rest is so important at this stage of your recovery."

Before Vikram had time to answer, she turned and walked away with Rosa.

"You should have brought him a drink, Rosa, the poor thing sweats so much, still. Poor Vik: life has been so unkind."

"He is not complaining."

Rhya, deftly twisting her long, grey hair, once more swung around fiercely. "Isn't that what was always the problem with Vikram? Too kind, too easy-going."

Rosa put her hand on Rhya's shoulder. "Hush, Mama, he has got the all-clear. No need now for so much worry."

Rhya gave up on her hair, letting it fall loose across her shoulders, as Rosa rooted beside the couch for her handbag.

"You shouldn't have left it there. I do not trust this new servant, you know that," said Rhya.

"I will come by early, bring him his favourite snacks from Nilgiri's."

When she heard Rosa get in the lift and go downstairs, Rhya marched back to her brother. "You are cooking something up with Rosa. Aren't you?"

Vikram put down the newspaper and beckoned to Rhya to sit. "I want Rosa to take a trip with me."

"What sort of trip?"

"A foreign trip."

He hesitated, and an agitation welled up inside her at what she was to hear next.

"I am going to go to Ireland, Rhya. I would like Rosa to accompany me."

"Are you mad, Vikram Fernandes?"

"There is no need to be like that. It is time I went back. I have to find where Grace is interred. I want to pay my respects."

"And how can you do any of that without telling the child the truth?"

He held out his hand to Rhya, but she ignored it. "She is not a child any more, Rhya, maybe it is time she knew."

"And what about me? What is she going to think of me?"

"Rhya, you are her mother. She adores you."

Tears were streaming down Rhya's face. "You can't do this to me, Vik. It will ruin me with Rosa for ever."

"You know that is not true."

"Did she say she was going with you?"

"Rhya, which is worse? To keep this whole thing from her or to tell her at last? Rosa needs to be told."

Rhya pressed her fingers across her brow. "You don't get it, do you? That child has loved me completely all her life. I have loved her and still do, beyond anyone in this place. You can't risk running a knife through it, just because you can't throw away the past. You can't deliberately discard my life like this."

Vikram reached for his newspaper, intending to block out his sister, but Rhya got to it before him.

"You stay and fight me, Vikram Fernandes. I won't let you hide behind that stupid paper."

"I don't think there is anything else to say. I do not want a row," Vikram said, his voice flat.

"Of course you don't, you just want your own way. I am telling you, Vikram Fernandes, if you utter a word of the truth to Rosa, I will never speak to you again."

Rhya stood for a moment on the balcony, afraid she had said too much.

Vikram reached and picked up the newspaper, rustling it loudly before starting to read the cricket match report.

Quietly, Rhya retreated to the side balcony, taking deep

breaths so she could consider what had happened. Her hands were shaking and her head ached. Vikram was good at creating a storm and leaving her to deal with the fallout. Downstairs, she heard the nightwatchman clear his throat and settle on to his cot bed. She should lie down, but her agitated mind would not let her.

Moving to her bedroom, and picking a key from the big bunch she usually carried around her waist, she unlocked her sari cupboard. Whenever she was troubled, she rummaged among her saris: amid the history, bright colours and luscious fabrics, she could find some solace and peace.

Sliding her hand over the shelves, her fingers hovered over the heavy silk saris, many only worn once, for occasions never repeated. Reaching into a small pile at the back, she pulled out the sari she had worn on the night they gathered to send Vikram to Ireland, all those years ago.

Letting the pink silk billow across the bed, the purple and gold border shimmering under the bare electric bulb, Rhya felt a sea of loneliness overcome her. She was too old for such a colour now, she knew that. The servant Rani had helped her dress that night, making sure her pleats were stiff and straight. Her blouse was a slightly deeper purple-pink, the colour contrasting with her long hair swept into a high bun. Her mother's gold drop earrings dangled and glinted in the light. Vikram was going to Ireland, but she was beginning on the road to marriage. The Pintos had been invited to the celebration, so that Mrs Pinto and Rhya's mother, aided by Flavia Nair, who had been called in specially to oversee the match, could discuss future plans.

There were many times she wanted to throw the sari away, but the softness of the fabric and the memory of being young and hopeful for a future, for both herself and Vikram, was so compelling, yet so painful, she had to keep it. She sighed to think of all that happened within a year afterwards, throwing their whole family sideways. Before she married him, she had only known Sanjay Pinto to see, but without him and his steadfast presence, she would never have got through the scandal that crawled through their family.

The night Vikram celebrated his move to Ireland, their mother's sari had been green raw silk with a pink border embroidered thickly in gold. Rhya kept it now at the back of the wardrobe, not wanting to see the folds of fabric her mother had worn to honour a country she would later come to hate.

Quickly, she balled up the pink sari and hurled it back on the shelf, moving to happier times: the navy and gold for the celebration of her daughter's marriage at Bangalore Club, a grand sari for a grand night alongside the diaphanous silk in autumnal russet and green for her son's graduation from medical college. Saris that now made her glow with the beautiful memories of great pride and joy.

This cupboard gave her the freedom to pull up the memories she dared to ruminate over: the happy days at the front, so easily accessible, while others, which raked up the sad and bad family stories, were stored at the back, where they could be easily ignored.

On the top shelf was her mother's wedding sari, laid out flat for as long as she could remember. Every so often Rhya remembered Shruthi in a quiet moment, pulled down the layers of fabric and shook them out to let the air through, the rich silk weave shimmering in the light. The border, in real gold thread, was heavy and wide. Some of her friends had their wedding saris melted down and were left with a tiny gold nugget, but Shruthi could not let hers go. It was a kind memory of a sweeter time. Rhya fingered the heavy silk. What of Rosa? Would she keep her mother's wedding sari so carefully? Would she even want to talk to her when she came back from that place? Vikram was being selfish. It was more than she could bear. This daughter she loved so deeply: even the thought of possible discord between them hurt her to her core. Tears swelled through Rhya. She fingered the heavy gold border. She must remember to hang the sari over the balcony early tomorrow and sweep it back in before the sun bore down too hot.

Four

Our Lady's Asylum, Knockavanagh, March 1954

The blanket was too short. Whatever way she tried, she could not keep her toes covered, and the cold seeped up past her ankles, settling in her knees, slow, damp pains groaning through her. She dozed off but woke with a start shortly after.

The cry of a baby was eating into her brain. She sat up, staring into the half-darkness, the lights of the moon throwing strange shapes of grey across the beds.

The midwife had attended to her for nine solid hours. The shutters at No. 19 Parnell Square were pulled across; if anybody heard the cries of a woman in labour, they ignored them.

She imagined the judge had sat at his desk, his head dipped low over his work.

The midwife chastised her for making too much noise, for calling Vikram's name, for asking somebody to tell him. She strained her hands to reach when she heard those first cries in the shadows of the room. Two women she did not know, lingering at the bottom of the bed, slipped away like ghosts, holding bundles of blankets.

Screaming until her throat hurt, she punched, kicked out, trying to get out of bed. Her legs would not follow, only her pleading and tears.

Summoned to the bedroom, Aunt Violet had come in, standing stiff by her bed.

"Dead. The doctor will give you something to help you sleep."

Grace slipped down her mattress, pulling the blanket over her head.

At the end of the ward, the patient who sang all day now shouted, angry words spilling from her, like she was a channel for all the angst and pain resting deep in the walls.

Grace woke again at daylight, as the woman in the bed next to her tugged furiously at her shoulders. "Quick, get out of bed, stand out."

"Why?"

"Do it."

Grace got up and was standing when a stout woman with a big set of keys dangling at her waist walked down the narrow corridor between the rows of steel beds, calling out names and ticking a clipboard. When she came to Grace, she stopped and spoke over her shoulder to the nurse shadowing her.

"The judge's wife. Make sure she sees Dr O'Neill today," the matron said as the little group moved away.

The woman beside Grace sniggered, digging her in the ribs. "Do I call you the judge's wife or are you going to tell me your name?"

"Grace."

"A nice name. Call me Mandy. Maureen is the real name, but Mandy sounds better, like a secretary in London or something."

The two of them joined the queue at the trolley, for tea and bread.

"You think I am definitely mad, don't you?" said Mandy.

"It is not for me to say."

"You are thinking the doctors have certified me to stay here, so that is the way it is."

"I am sure they do their job."

"And what exactly is that?"

"You ask a lot of questions," said Grace.

Mandy guffawed loudly so that one of the attendants walked back to check the line.

"Move on, we don't have all day," she snapped, clicking her fingers.

Each patient was handed a tin cup of milky tea.

"Go for the buttered bread, the butter softens up the staleness," Mandy muttered as the young woman handing out the food called out in a lilting voice, "Buttered or plain?"

Grace took a thick slice of bread with butter and followed Mandy to sit on her bed.

"It is quite good today. No spots of smelly green mould either," Mandy whispered, examining her slice carefully. "They take the stale bread from Connolly's Bakery in town. My aunt works there, throwing old loaves and currant buns into the cloth sacks for the lunatics."

"The judge's wife: Dr O'Neill will see you now," called out an attendant reading a magazine, without even raising her head.

Mandy pulled Grace close. "A tip: don't let on to hearing voices."

"But I don't."

"That's all right, then."

A nurse snapped at her to tidy herself up before escorting her off the ward and down the corridor to a small office at the end.

"Dr O'Neill, here's the special one."

The doctor pushed his glasses up his nose and took in the young woman. Not even the faded nightgown could take from the beauty of her face. Her eyes were soft and her hair still had enough of a fashionable shape that it framed her face in loose curls.

"Mrs Moran, do you know why you are here?"

"My husband had me admitted. I lost my—"

"Are there voices in your head, Mrs Moran?

"No."

A young nurse walked into the room and began fiddling with the drawers of the filing cabinet. She winked at Dr O'Neill, who turned again to his patient.

"You are not well, Mrs Moran?"

"I am tired. I want to go home."

"What will you get from being here?"

"I don't know."

"That will be all, Mrs Moran. We will review your case again in time."

"What do you mean?"

He indicated to the nurse lingering beside his desk to take the patient away. The nurse, blocking Grace's view of the doctor, called an attendant to escort the patient back to the ward.

"Call me if there is any noticeable change: depression, aggression, anything like that," Dr O'Neill muttered to the nurse, as he quickly wrote out a prescription and handed back the file.

Grace made to say something else, but the nurse remained solid in front of her.

"Come along, we don't have all day."

"I want to go home."

The doctor and nurse laughed. "Don't we all?" the nurse said.

Grace stiffened, not budging when the nurse gently pushed her. "I should not be here."

She heard the doctor sigh deeply as he opened another file on his desk. "Mrs Moran, just give it time," he said, a weary tetchiness in his voice as he called out the name of the next patient.

"Please, I should not be here," Grace said, her voice high-pitched, but neither the doctor nor nurse answered. An attendant came into the room and took Grace by the arm, pulling her roughly away as the nurse swung around to talk to the doctor.

Five

Parnell Square, Dublin, March 1984

The phone was ringing in her head before she woke. For a moment, Emma did not know where she was and a fear rose inside her, only half dissipating as she recognised the judge's study. She had fallen asleep on the purple chaise longue after sashaying around in the linen skirt. The phone jumping on the desk, its ring twirling across the shelves, bouncing between the books, made her rush to pick up the receiver, a strange agitation rising inside.

When she answered, Sam's voice was strong and comfortable, causing loneliness to swell through her.

"How did you get the number?"

"I found it in your desk."

"What do you want, Sam?"

"Em, I am sorry about everything. Your dad . . ."

"No need."

"I have an offer on the apartment, but it will just cover the mortgage. We are not going to make anything extra."

"After five years of marriage, zero."

"I am afraid so. Can I accept the offer?"

"I don't care."

"Okay, but what about your things?"

"Dump it all, there is nothing there I want."

"How are you, Emma?"

"It's bit late for polite chit-chat, Sam, don't you think?"

He sighed, making her feel intensely angry. She banged the receiver down, flares of pain rushing through her.

She saw the judge sitting back, his two hands folded in front of him, quietly watching her. The rows of law books stood sentry over him: rows and rows of books nobody would ever read now. She could feel him here, still cosseted by these laden shelves, this library his haven from the world, a place she only ever entered if she had something important to say.Once, as a young child, she rushed in after tripping on the front steps and grazing her knee. Sobbing, she had hoped to throw herself into his arms, to hear words of comfort, but he put up his hand like a traffic warden slows a speeding driver approaching a crossing.

"Quietly, Emma, quietly."

The tears gushed down her face and she could not articulate her hurt. Relief flooded her as he rose from his desk and walked to her. He reached down. Gratefully, she moved towards him, only to find him placing his hands on her shoulders and twisting her back towards the door.

"I am not to be disturbed when I am working. The sooner you realise that, little lady, the better."

Too young to detect the firmness in his voice, she protested, and he called for Aunt Violet, who ushered her away, whispering fiercely in her ear. "Don't bother the judge. Toughen up."

Now, Emma paced along the straight line of the shelves,

picking with her nails at the books, pinching at the spines until the first, heavy, navy book with gold lettering gave way, toppling to the ground. On a roll, she plucked the others, making them fall like thudding dominoes, the dust rising in bulging clouds around her.

Bundling a pile of books from the top shelf into her arms, she made for the front door. Three doors down, the skip outside a house being refurbished was already full. Emma walked smartly over and tipped five law books in on top of worn-out kitchen cabinets.

She had gone back for a second pile when there was a polite knock on the open front door.

"Miss, I saw what you did. You know, we had to pay good money for that skip. I hope you are not going to dump anything else in there."

The elderly man looked harassed. His wife was standing at their front door, her ears open to hear every word of the exchange.

"I am sorry, I acted on impulse. I want to get rid of the books."

"How many have you? If it is only a few more volumes you are all right, but . . ." He peered down the hallway to the library. "Jaysus, you are not thinking of clearing the room into our skip, are you?"

"Tom Harty, don't be fretting. Emma here is just sorting a few things out. It is a hard time for her."

He turned around to Angie Hannon. "That may be, but not into our skip, please. Somebody would pay good money for the judge's law books: you should flog them," he said to Emma.

She came out onto the steps. "I am sorry, I got a bit carried away."

Tom Harty put out his hand. "We can put it behind us?"

Emma nodded at Tom, and he walked back to his house. Angie Hannon clapped her hands.

"Don't you want to keep the judge's library? It was his life," Angie said.

"Maybe that is why I want to get rid."

"I am sure we can find a library to take them off your hands. I will make a few calls for you in the morning."

Emma made to turn back to the hall, but Angie called her softly. "Time for a drink, I think."

She walked past Emma to the library, tapping her on the shoulder to follow.

"Must let you in on one of the judge's best-kept secrets."

Leading the way, she neatly stepped over the bound law reports and the heavy books on constitutional law.Reaching up to the third shelf, she fingered along until she reached Salmond's *Law of Torts*. Shifting the book to the side, she stretched into the darkness behind, pulling out a silver tray. A bottle of cognac was half full, the tumblers beside it cut crystal.

"Welcome to the judge's private bar."

"My father did not drink."

"There are lots of things you don't know about the judge, my girl. Drinking late at night is one of them."

"What do you mean?"

"Like a fish in the early hours. A cigar in one hand, a brandy in the other."

"I never saw him even have a glass of wine with dinner."

Angie guffawed out loud as she poured the brandy into the glasses. "Judge Moran was an expert at giving off the right aura."

"How come I did not know this?"

"He certainly appreciated the finer things in life," Angie said, raising her glass, letting the light glint through the crystal. "To the judge." She reached over and clinked Emma's glass loudly. "Surely you can wish him well."

"Maybe," Emma said, sitting down on the chaise longue. "I did not say anything at the funeral."

"I noticed."

Emma took the brandy bottle and lobbed more into her glass. "They say if you have nothing good to say, say nothing."

"Emma, the judge had a lot on his plate, maybe you need to get to know him better."

"I lived with him for nineteen years and that was enough. Anyway, it is too late now."

"Never too late, Emma."

"What do you mean?"

"There can be a lot of things that make up a person."

"No offence, but I don't need a lecture."

Angie stood up. "I wouldn't dream of it. We will have to know each other a bit better for that."

"I never knew you when I lived here."

"I have only been on the square ten years. You were gone for twelve."

"You don't think I should throw away his law books."

"It is not for me to say. They might be worth a lot. Wouldn't you be interested in having the collection valued?"

"I just want rid."

"Stay at mine tonight? It might be better than staying in this big old house on your own."

Emma shook her head. "I am not going to let this place defeat me. Not now he is gone."

Angie put her glass down on the desk. "You know where I am if you need me." She leaned down to pick up volumes of the *Irish Law Reports*.

"Don't do that."

"I just thought . . ."

"Please, you don't know anything, Angie. He loved the law, there was no room for anything else."

"I did not mean to upset you."

"I am not bloody upset, I am just tired of everybody telling me what a fine man and judge my father was."

"It is a hard time, but it will get better."

"No doubt the old man will have cut me off and left it all to the gentlemen's club on Stephen's Green."

"I don't think your father would do that. This is your home." Angie patted Emma on the head. "I can let myself out."

Emma didn't answer but poured the dregs from the bottle into her glass and sat at the desk.

Slumping beside the brown case, she picked everything out one by one, rolling each item across her hands before laying it down carefully on the desk. She shook out the second ruched linen skirt, marvelling that the tiny pleats, pinched and creased, remained in horizontal lines. Holding it up to her waist, she found it was almost exactly her size. The lining was feathery soft. Inside the waistband at the back was the designer's name: Sybil Connolly, Dublin. A white blouse with a lace insert had the same label, along with a short black jacket. Quickly, Emma pulled off her clothes. Pulling up the skirt, she almost snagged a line of pleats with the bulk of her engagement ring. Splaying her hand out, she took it in: the big blue rock they had bought on a weekend trip to Sydney, and the small gold band he had first pushed on her finger as they sat looking across at the Three Sisters. She pulled at the gold rings now, slipping them off, not really knowing what to do with them, only that she could not bear the weight of them. She opened the first drawer in the judge's desk and dropped them into a green marble ashtray.

The covered buttons on the blouse were fiddly, the jacket a soft wool. The outfit needed jewellery, quality pieces: not even her rings would have been good enough. Reaching for the small bottle of perfume that had been wedged between a pair of slippers, she read the label: Evening in Paris.

Unscrewing the top, the sweet floral aroma with a hint of apricot floated past her, as if the ghost of her mother had entered the room. This was all she had of her. Was it enough: the clothes, the perfume, the echo of another life lived? Emma slumped into her father's leather chair, her shoulders hunched as shivers of tears pumped through her. She should have gone to a hotel, she thought, but instead she climbed the stairs to her old bedroom, where the mattress was bare and stickily damp, the air musty. Huddling under an old school coat, she was too exhausted to worry about sleeping in this big old house on her own.

Six

Bangalore, India, March 1984

Vikram stretched out on the balcony, waiting. Soon Rhya would send his coffee. He closed his eyes, listening to the city breathing. The sweeper families on the street called to each other as they readied for the day, their chat wafting slowly upwards from a canvas overhang thrown between two trees for shade. The lilt and softness of the talk of the younger ones and the rasping pitch of the grandmother weaved their way to him, their words distorted on the journey. The fish seller lingered, singing out his wares, waiting for the women to send down their baskets. The watchful caretaker hovered, ready to shoo the man and his basket of fish away.

The rising clamour of the city encircled Vikram, sapping his energy. How he longed to be back in Chikmagalur, where the air was heavy with stillness and workers concentrating stooped low; where the mountains, high and strong, held up blue umbrellas of mist to the sky. The orange flash of a rat snake flitting across a path, the sound of chopping and pans on the fire in the kitchen as the cook prepared the food for the day, the low, far-off hum of conversation from the line of stone dwellings where the workers lived.

The family estate house was old and battered-looking, with stone walls and floors over which rugs were strewn to take away the sharpness of the cold in winter. Built to service the hectares of the coffee estate, it had changed little over the decades. The only obvious luxury was the early-morning coffee ceremony, after Vikram had gathered his workers and sent them off for the day, his instructions ringing in their ears. Thick black coffee and steaming-hot milk were poured into small china cups from tall silver coffee pots. Vikram's father had insisted on this ritual and his son saw no reason to change it. The china cups, first brought to the house by his mother, had seen better days and were chipped in places, but Vikram never had the heart to throw them out. Instead, he ordered his servants to handle with care, and they did, because nobody wanted to upset the boss.

How he wanted to be in his big old chair on the covered porch at Chikmagalur, where he could look out over the drying grounds and terraces, past the tall trees giving pools of shade, to watch the hills and clouds fight for the sky. This was where peace dropped slow. Whether the sun baked the ground or the monsoon rain spattered or tore down on top of them, Chikmagalur was his place apart.

His favourite spot in the bungalow was the sitting room, where he could sit quietly, the green hills on guard. The furniture was dowdy, the circular brass table in the middle gone green in places from old coffee stains, where he had spilled his cup too many times as he reached across for his newspaper. In one corner was a stack of weeks-old newspapers about a foot high, on the walls were photographs, worn, creased in places and sepia-brown.

He wanted to be there when the white flowers in the Robusta coffee plants unfurled, putting on a show, breaking into the mist, which clung in gossamer swirls to the trees. There was nothing as lovely as when the first blossom revealed itself: a reminder of the frail beauty of life, before the monsoon rains battered the hills, flooded the roads and cut off the mountains from each other.

"Uncle, your coffee."

Rosa stood in the doorway holding a tray with a steel beaker, steam curling away from it.

"You were deep in thought?"

"I was thinking of the flowers in bloom at Chikmagalur. I long to breathe them in, fill my nostrils with their heavy scent. You never liked it there, my Rosa."

"Uncle, there was nothing to do."

Vikram settled himself deeper in his chair. "Boredom, the affliction of the young. Loneliness, the affliction of the old." Blowing on his coffee, he paused for a few seconds before noisily slurping it.

"I have definitely decided I will go with you." She fiddled with a stray piece of wood and let out a nervous laugh.

He took in her dark eyes, black hair and the delicate features that came from her mother. The way she pushed back her hair from her shoulders, her laugh tinkling until it had faded like a fog on a summer morning: so like her mother.

"Let me tell you about Grace."

Twisting her long hair into a bun, she sat back to listen. Vikram gulped his coffee.

"Not even death could stop me loving Grace . . ."

He went quiet as the servant, bending low, pushed a broom

under their chairs, before moving away further down the balcony, sweeping her pile of dust as she crouched.

"She died. It was too painful."

"Uncle, I am beginning to feel I don't know you at all."

Vikram's face softened. "You know me best of all: only this part of me, I kept secret until now."

Taking a slow, deep breath, he began again.

"Grace was beautiful in every way. When I met her it was in such an ordinary, routine way. Who could have predicted that she would capture my heart for ever?"

"Uncle, this is too much." She frowned, making Vikram smile.

"I was a young doctor in a big hospital in Dublin. Grace accompanied her aunt Violet there, a cranky, stubborn woman. Violet was in severe pain, she had slipped on the stairs and sprained her ankle badly, but the crotchety woman would not even let me examine her. 'I am not letting any foreigner put a finger on me. How do I know his hands are clean? Get me a home doctor, please,' she shouted at the top of her voice.

"Grace was very embarrassed and tried to placate the woman, but she was having none of it. In truth I was quite used to it. I smiled, bowed and retreated. Every hospital there in those days had at least one Indian doctor. They did not have enough people themselves with such a high qualification, but try explaining that to Violet McNally. The matron calmed her down and left her for quite a time in excruciating pain, until Dr O'Connell could see her himself.

"I was writing up reports when Grace approached the desk.

"'I wanted to apologise for my aunt; she really is up the walls over what happened.'

"'Up the wall?'

"Her laugh tinkled like the bells at a temple.

"'High with stress. She is due to visit some gardens in Wicklow on Sunday and is afraid she won't be able to walk.'

"'I doubt if it is that serious. A few days' rest only.'

"Her eyes twinkled. 'Maybe it is best that you did not see her. Do you think it would be dreadful of me if I left the price of my aunt's taxi home with the nurse? I have to be at a fitting with Sybil Connolly in ten minutes' time.'

"'Sybil Connolly?'

"She rapped me lightly on the knuckles. 'Sybil Connolly: only the best dress designer in the country and, someday soon, the world.'

"I laughed. 'A ballgown, is it?'

"'Good lord, no: a linen day dress, quite simple.'"

Vikram turned to Rosa.

"I thought I would never see her again. Her warm laughter haunted me. It was only a week later when we literally bumped into each other. I had taken to wandering through St Stephen's Green during my break. I loved the way the wind wheezed in the trees; it reminded me of Chikmagalur. I saw her sitting alone on a bench. I was not sure if I should disturb her. I decided to walk by and greet her only."

*

When Grace looked up and smiled, he noticed she had been crying.

"Doctor, how nice to see you."

He paused in front of her, not quite sure what to say next.

"You like this quiet section of the park as well," she said.

"It reminds me a little of the coffee estate back home: the tall trees, the thick vegetation."

She laughed. "I think I would rather be in India than damp old Dublin." Getting up from her seat, she stood beside him.

He noticed a black smudge under her right eye and he reached into his pocket for a handkerchief, pointing to the mark as he handed it to her. Slightly embarrassed, she accepted it and wiped the smudge away.

"So kind of you, doctor. I am so sorry, I don't know your name."

"Dr Vikram Fernandes, Bangalore, at your service."

"Grace. Grace Moran," she said, stretching out her hand.

He took her hand tightly. It was as light as a feather and he bowed again before her.

"I hope you made your dress fitting."

"How kind of you to remember. Yes, in fact I am wearing it today. I am due to meet one of the judge's wives for tea in the Shelbourne."

She pointed to where her coat was open and he saw a flash of turquoise linen.

"Most beautiful. A brightness of colour more associated with my side of the world, I think."

She giggled, nervously twiddling with the buttons on her coat, and he felt himself wanting to stay there, beside her on this damp pathway through a park.

"How long have you got in Ireland, Dr Fernandes?"

"One year. I am from Bangalore, in the south of India."

"You are so far from home! We must do everything to brighten up your days. We are having a drinks party on Friday evening. My husband, twice a year, likes to open up the house and invite all his friends. I am sure everybody would love to meet you. Please come along."

Vikram smiled, but, noticing a sparkle in her eyes, was not sure how to answer.

"I will send around an invitation to the hospital tomorrow," she said, gently touching his arm.

"That is most kind, I will look forward to it."

"I have to go. It was lovely meeting you, and please come on Friday," she said before scurrying off for her appointment.

Halfway up the path, as if she knew he was watching, she turned around and waved, and he felt a sense of belonging to her, a fact that made him intensely happy.

⋆

Vikram stopped for a moment, swirling the dregs of the coffee in the beaker.

"Rosa, she mesmerised me. I saw only her, I cared only about her. There was a magic about Grace. I pined for her attention, because only then did I feel one hundred per cent complete. When she flashed a smile, my heart gladdened. When she frowned, I worried. When she showed her displeasure, I was ashamed.

"I loved every bit of her. She was never afraid. I fell in love with her that day in the hospital as she fretted over her fitting. I was completely hooked after I met her in the park."

Rhya stuck her head around the door. "Rosa, enough of the talk with Uncle. You surely have things to do."

Rosa slowly got up, kissing Vikram goodbye.

Seven

Parnell Square, Dublin, March 1984

"There is a lot more in the attic: boxes mainly, light enough, clothes probably. What will the men do with all them?" The foreman overseeing the clear-out of the house waited on the landing for an answer.

"Isn't that why I got a skip? Chuck them."

"Are you sure? It could be the family silver you are throwing away."

"Knowing the judge, I very much doubt it."

The workman stepped into the room. "All the same, it couldn't hurt to have a quick look."

"No, thank you."

"You might be sorry, when there's a crowd around the skip."

"I doubt if anybody would be interested in my father's old legal files."

Shrugging his shoulders, the workman backed out of the room.

Emma could see the judge, hunched, leaning into the pool of

light from his desk lamp. On a rare occasion, he would motion her to sit. Holding his place with his finger on the document he was examining, he would look over his glasses and ask what did she want.On edge, she would garble her words, he would snap at her to run along. She remembered the time she had spent days composing the sentences she needed to tell him she was unhappy and hated school. Shuffling her feet, she had knocked over a small pile of folders stacked near his chair.

"Mind where you go," he said, not raising his eyes from the papers in front of him.

She spoke so quietly she was not sure if he heard her.

"Not liking something is no reason to give up."

Underlining a word on the text, he clicked his teeth in annoyance, scrawling his comments in red at the margins. She slipped away. If the judge heard her leave or the thud of the door when she shut it, he did not let on.

Emma turned away as the workmen trailed up and down the stairs to the hall. Edging her fingers down the piped line of the linen skirt, riding the pleats, she watched from the window as Angie Hannon sidled past the skip several times before stopping to examine a coffee table.

When one of the workmen threw a pile of files on the rubbish heap, she stopped him, persuading him to lift down the table and carry it to her door. Emma threw up the sash window and called out, "Mrs Hannon, do you want to come in and see if there is anything else you want? I am having a clear-out."

"I suppose I could. I have a few minutes before my Mass." She made for the door and the stairs. "My God, are you moving in or out?" Angie peered around a stack of boxes in the hall. "What's going on?"

Boxes and boxes were piled high, with the name Grace

scrawled in thick black marker. Stumbling, confusion clouding her face, Emma hit against a high stack of boxes, making it shake.

"Where did these come from?"

The foreman stepped from behind a tower in the front room."I told you."

"Don't touch them."

"You said—"

"Don't touch them."Tremors hurled up her body, buckling her knees and gripping her stomach. When Angie ran to her, she let her pull her gently into the library.

"You need to sit down, dear. Something has spooked you, for sure."

"These are my mother's things. I never knew any of it was in the house."

Somebody called out that everything was down from the attic and Emma jumped to her feet.

"Now, now, these boxes are going nowhere. You catch your breath," Angie said gently, pressing Emma back onto the chaise longue.

A man carrying a wide box stepped into the library and placed the box beside her. "A pretty fancy box. I would open it first, if I were you. We are moving to clear out the old kitchen in the basement. Will you want to inspect anything there?"Emma shook her head.

The box took up the width of her arms. Once white, it was now covered in a layer of fine dust, the string faded a green-grey. Behind the dust, the name *Sybil Connolly, Dublin* was set in plain black print.

"I had better scoot along." Angie Hannon stood and watched Emma for a few seconds. "Will you be all right?"

Emma nodded, walking to the hall with Angie. "It is just a shock, I hardly know where to start."

"The box in your hands is as good a place as any."

Angie looked at her watch. "I had better get going or I'll miss the first collection." She whipped out the door, stopping only briefly to berate the workmen. "Will you quieten down a bit? They can hear you cursing in the city centre."

Glancing into the front sitting room, Emma looked around. Stacks of boxes like a child's playing bricks everywhere, four abreast on the upholstered couch, spanning the width of the window.

Placing the outsize rectangular box on the floor, she eased the top off gently, her hair tumbling down, blocking out her face, her hands trembling. A cloud of dust blustered up around her as she pushed back the cover and pulled on layers and layers of white tissue paper, which piled up and crumpled around her.

A dress, ivory, ruffled with lace and inlaid with satin ribbons, was folded neatly. Emma lifted out the dress, standing up so it unfurled to the ground in a hurried whishing whisper. Layers of pleated frills were topped with lace and interwoven with pale-blue ribbon. The skirt spread out in tiny pinched pleats, a series of Chinese fans fluttering their messages. It was heavy to hold, the taffeta underskirt setting the pleated ruffles in place. Emma held it to her, swaying from side to side. The whoosh of the linen as it swept across the carpet made her swing faster and faster, the room twirling until she felt dizzy. Falling between two boxes on the couch, the linen spread around her as if it owned her.

She felt at home here, probably for the first time. All the times she had dreamed of her mother, wanting to feel her comforting presence, her soft touch, all the times she imagined it. Passing her hand over the linen, she disturbed the fabric and a faint hint of perfume waved around her. Pulling the nearest box on the couch, she nudged the cardboard flaps open. A bundle of silk scarves lounged like sleeping snakes.

Placing her hand into the well of colours, she heard the *klssss* of the silk as it moved, disturbed after years locked away. Not checking what she was picking, she pulled, latching on to one long scarf. It slithered out in a haze of royal blue, green, purple, the colours bouncing in the light, throwing bars of colour at the mirror over the mantelpiece. Crumpling it to tame it around her neck, she pushed the linen dress aside and jumped up to look in the mirror. Settling her hair on top of her head, the scarf complemented her long, graceful neck. Then, abruptly, she let her hair fall down.

There was no going back to Australia, but what life could she make here among the forgotten treasures of a long-dead woman? Opening two more boxes, she tumbled out the contents, sifting through the clothes and losing track of time, only stopping when she heard the chat from the people standing at the bus stop outside the window. Peeping out, she saw a man finish his bottle of Coke before leaning over the railing and letting the empty bottle smash to the basement.

Cross, Emma ran to the door, but the man was already boarding a double-decker.

"You will have to put up some sort of netting. They don't care about anyone."Angie Hannon, on her way home from Mass, was carrying a small white box. "I stopped off at the Kylemore and got you some cream slices: they go lovely with a cup of tea." She hopped up the steps and placed the small box in Emma's hands. "Don't worry, I won't be imposing myself. I am off out with the women's club today."

Emma smiled and made to go back inside. Angie called out softly, "Your skirt: it is a Sybil Connolly, isn't it?"

Emma spun around. "How did you know?"

"Anyone with an eye for fashion could not miss a Sybil Connolly. Sure, didn't she bring linen from the bog to the city?"

"I found it in the house."

"Look after it. A vintage treasure, it is."

"I didn't realise."

"I always heard your mother was a right looker and stunning in Sybil Connolly."

"I wouldn't know."

Emma's throat tightened and pain flared through her that so many knew her mother and she did not even have a faint memory: a favourite name or nursery rhyme, a touch, a look. Anger swelled inside her at her father and she wanted him to be alive so she could cross-examine him, demand answers.

Angie Hannon called out to Tom Harty's wife and Emma, taking advantage of her distraction, slipped back inside her front door.

What good was it opening these boxes and rummaging through the life of the mother she had never known? She should lock up this place, run away, but where would she go? There was no home back in Australia, just a lot of other possessions she did not care about and a husband busy playing house with another. She kicked a box, so light it skidded across the tiles in the hall. It hit a stack piled too high and the top box toppled over, the contents spilling across the floor.

Not bothering to pick up the items, Emma climbed the stairs, stopping on the fourth step to look back down the hall. The black and white tiles glinted in the light spilling in from over the door. It was the judge's house. It still had his smell, and she expected him to call out from his library, to hear him clear his throat as he read his files.

Her hand on the brass knob of the first-floor drawing room, she hesitated, pulling in a deep breath and automatically checking her clothes were straight, as if she expected somehow he could still be there.

No doubt he would have had something to say about her choosing not to speak at his funeral. It was, she knew, the final cut: the public show that she could not speak of her father, even in death. He would not have liked either that she wore grey: a lightweight colour to display the depth of her grief.

Turning the knob, she swung back the cream door. The walls were painted a sage green, the ceiling and its plasterwork, once brilliant white, now tinted yellow. The couch, deep mustard velvet, spanned the width of the faded rug, which had flowers picked out in blue, green and burnt yellow. Two fireside chairs upholstered in embossed gold stood on guard either side of the black marble fireplace. A low mahogany table ran between the tall windows. There were no curtains, but the shutters were half across.

Tentatively, she walked to the window, her eyes on the distant mountains. Pushing back the shutters, light fell into the room. She sat on the mustard couch, the stillness walling around her.

A bar of sunshine crossed over the room. Two pigeons patrolling the windowsill pecked and cooed. Somewhere on the street, a man shouted across the road to a friend. A double-decker bus revved up the hill out of the square. Emma sat in the corner of the velvet couch, at peace for now amidst the city bustle.

Eight

Our Lady's Asylum, Knockavanagh, April 1954

A blue-black magpie rested on the branch of the small tree in the front garden, tipping back and forward with the bounce of the wood in the wind. It caught the flash of Grace's purple top and stared at her. It stalked her, never giving her the satisfaction of being able to count two for joy. She wanted to rap on the glass and make it fly away, but she could not, for fear of drawing down the attendant on top of her.

She saw the Morris Oxford as it slowly trundled around the bend after the security gates. Weeks she had been here, and now they had come for her. A giddiness grabbed hold of her and she pulled Mandy to the window.

"I told you he would come back for me. Martin would never leave me." Grace tugged at her hair. "I have to comb it properly. I will need my clothes. They haven't given me my case yet, so I have no make-up."

"Don't lose the run of yourself."

"I am leaving."

"If you say so. I will save you some bread from lunch. If

you are here when I get back, so be it. If you're not, you're not."

Grace, her eyes shining, began to fuss, flattening her hair and pinching her cheeks to raise a bit of colour.

One of the attendants called out her name. "Grace Moran. You have a visitor. Smarten yourself up."

"Can I please have my case and my own clothes? I am going to need them."

"Whatever for? You were supplied with perfectly good clothes. Now get them on, we don't have all day."

Mandy put an arm around Grace. "You can have my lace collar." She reached under her mattress, pulling out a cream collar tarnished with rust spots, unravelled and frayed at one corner.

Grace licked her finger and rubbed a stain from her plaid skirt. "What will I do if Martin won't sign me out?"

"Come back here and eat the bread I saved for you." Mandy caught her by the shoulders. "If he is taking you away, don't forget me." Her eyes were staring, spit pressing out of her mouth.

"How could I?"

"It would surprise you how quickly a memory can be wiped, once a person realises they can get through those gates."

The attendant beckoned to her. Grace slipped on the shoes stored under her bed.

"No funny business – follow me to the visitor's room."

Grace nodded, smiling at the other patients as they watched her leave.

Teresa, who sang all day and cried all night, ran up and hugged her, whispering loudly in her ear. "Run for it, dearie, when you have a chance."

Roughly pushed back by the attendant, Teresa cried out, "Get your hands off. I've been assaulted."

The nurses laughed. "Assaulted? Calm down, sweetie, or a nice cold bath is on the cards," one of them snapped.

Violet McNally was standing looking out the window when the attendant opened the door. She moved across the room, catching the young woman's hand to press a crisp banknote to it.

Grace edged into the room, perching on a straight-backed chair. She took in her aunt, who was settling into an armchair, unbuttoning her red-wine tweed coat, which had a circular red rhinestone brooch at the lapel. Carefully Violet took off each black glove and placed the set in her handbag before shutting the clasp with a loud snapping noise.

"Would you like tea?" Violet gestured to the small table with a lace tablecloth where a silver tray was laid out with china cups and a big pot of tea covered with a knitted cosy. "So kind. They even thought of biscuits."

Grace, tugging at her cardigan sleeve, shook her head. "Where is Martin? Why isn't he here?"

If Violet heard the question, she ignored it. "It is cool out. Hospitals are always warm. You probably don't feel the cold." She smacked her hands together, reaching over to the tray to pour tea into a gold-rimmed china cup.

"I want to go home. Why isn't Martin here?"

Violet, who was shovelling her second spoon of sugar into the tea, stopped what she was doing to look directly at Grace. "You are mightily interested in your husband all of a sudden." Violet finished ladling the sugar into the tea and, picking up her cup and saucer, stirred slowly. She gazed at the picture of the Sacred Heart on the wall above Grace, as if she drew some strength from it. "Martin Moran is a judge and a good man. He did not deserve what you did to him. He has left all this unpleasant business to me."

"I want to come home."

"Why? So you can carry on with another man and heap more shame on us all?"

"I love Vikram Fernandes. You can't take that from me."

Violet placed her cup and saucer carefully on the table. "How dare you even mention his name? Have you no shame?"

Grace jumped up. Agitated, she paced to the window, momentarily distracted by a young woman outside rummaging in her handbag, a cigarette hanging out of her mouth. The woman scrabbled in the bag before giving up and running along the path. She was laughing loudly, calling out to a man who was standing there smiling, holding a lighter in his hand.

"Martin would never leave me here."

Violet sat back, stretching her legs out in front of her. "My dear, nobody is leaving you here. You are not well. It is up to the doctors."

Grace swung around. "See what they have done? Look at me."

"I understand you have resisted the therapy, so ably prescribed."

Grace did not answer.

"It is entirely up to you when you leave here. Do as the doctors say and you are halfway there."

"Am I? I don't know what they are telling you, but there is nothing wrong with me. I want to come home."

Violet McNally poured a fresh drop of tea into her cup. "Start being a good patient and you may find things are different."

"I will go mad if you leave me here. I hear mice scurrying at night under the beds. Doesn't Martin care about me? I am his wife, after all."

"He is your husband. Did you ever care for him?"

"You were wrong to get me to marry him."

"Nonsense. You did not resist."

"Vikram will find me."

"The Indian chap? Bolted like a greyhound from a trap. Married to a good Indian girl by now, I should think."

Pain streaked across Grace's chest and a loud ringing burrowed into her ears. "You are telling lies."

"Why would I? He has skipped off, nothing more, nothing less."

Grace stood, squalls of anger bursting through her. Violet was still talking, but she only saw the smug set of her lips, the indifference in her eyes, heard the icy tone of her voice. Grace lunged, her fists clenched.

Violet was too fast for her, catching her tightly by the wrists, squeezing her so tight her nails dug into Grace's skin as she screeched for help.

When the attendants burst in, they grabbed Grace from behind, smartly navigating her out on to the corridor. She saw Aunt Violet feign weakness and an attendant ease her gently into a chair, calling for a glass of water.

"You have done it now. No more visits for you," a nurse hissed.

Two male attendants dragged her away. She kicked, called them names, threw punches into the air, and they laughed, pulling her so hard her knees grazed along the floor. At a running pace, they swished her down two long corridors to a landing with a steel door. They did not say anything but pushed her roughly inside, quickly slamming the door shut. She heard them chat briefly before one of them pulled back a tiny hatch in the door. "Four walls and a floor. This place should help you cool off."

In the shaft of light from the hatch before it was slammed shut, she saw the room was bare. Sliding down the wall, she put her hands out to feel around her. The stone was rough, clammy-cold and damp. The floor lino was thin and she could feel a chill seeping up through her already. She must have got halfway around when the hatch was swiped back again. A shaft of glaring light banded across the room. Grace shrank back, afraid.

"Not as feisty now, are we?" The woman outside scuffed her shoes against the door, making it shudder. "Cool your heels for a while."

Sliding down to the floor, Grace heard a woman call to another in the garden. "A pleasant day for this time of year, Geraldine."

*

It was the evening when they took her from the room and walked her to the ward.

Mandy, crocheting a doily, did not look up at first. Her fingers deftly threaded the hook, making the stitches. She waited several minutes before speaking.

"Thought you had gone home. They put some things in your locker."

Grace pulled open the door of the steel locker. Her gloves, hat and scarf were in a small pile in the corner. "Who put these here?"

"Matron."

Grace lifted the baby-blue hat and scarf, feeling the softness of the wool. "A present from Martin last Christmas."

Bertha, the woman newly admitted, smiled. "My husband brings me flowers every Friday evening."

"Can I have a go?" Mandy whirled the scarf over her shoulders and walked jauntily along the narrow corridor between the beds.

"You can have it."

Mandy spun around like a model at the end of the catwalk, jutting out her hip. "Never. Are you sure?"

"Yes."

As the others clustered around to admire and touch the scarf, their fingers lingering on its rich softness, Grace pushed her hands into the gloves. Feeling the soft cold of the hidden piece of marble, she sat and stared ahead, his voice running in her head, telling her his story. She did not hear the two attendants scattering the gaggle around Mandy. She didn't see them look to each other and mutter that a few hours in isolation had knocked the spirit out of the judge's wife. Neither did she hear the prediction she was going to be one of the quiet ones from now on.

She only heard his soft, lilting voice tell the story.

"This is my grandfather's story, a man who also loved big.

"He was assigned to Agra for four weeks. He had a habit of writing every day to my grandmother. One day, he sat and wrote his letter at the Taj Mahal. Workmen at the rest house were restoring the delicate paintwork on the ceiling and replacing little inserts of marble in motifs along the walls. The works foreman called out to my grandfather and asked what he was scribbling. A little taken aback, grandfather said he was writing only to his wife.

"'Is she kind, wise and beautiful?'

"'She is all those and more.'

"'Do you love her?'

"'Beyond imagining.'

"'You are a lucky man.'

"The foreman reached into his pocket and took out a small piece of white marble. Perfectly cut, the translucent white marble glistened as he held it up to the sun.

"'Take it and give it to her, so that she may know the feel of the Taj Mahal,' he said quietly, before moving away to climb the scaffolding. Grandfather followed and put his hand on the man's shoulder, before he swung himself on to the bamboo rod bars.

"'Brother, this means a great deal to me.'

"'I know,' he said climbing up the bamboo scaffolding like a monkey springing from branch to branch."

Grace knew the next bit off by heart.

"I give you a small piece of this symbol of love, Grace Moran, to show you I love you beyond anything. My grandparents were only separated by death. My ambition for us is no less."

Mandy shook her shoulder.

"You know they are all saying you are properly doolally now." She pushed her face into the scarf. "It smells nice."

"Evening in Paris."

"I would take an evening in Knockavanagh, never mind Paris," Mandy said, throwing the scarf over her shoulders in an extravagant fashion.

Bertha, in a state of intense agitation, screamed, “My roses have been stolen.”

“Now, now, you are imagining things. What would a man be doing buying flowers every Friday evening? Sure, there would be no money left for the groceries,” the attendant snapped, as she pushed her back into her chair.

Bertha fell back to one side, mumbling into her chin.

Nine

Bangalore, India, March 1984

Rhya was watching television, the sound blaring from the apartment, bouncing off the idle heat lurking outside. A squirrel scampered past, its tail high, before scuttling under the blooms of the jacaranda tree. Vikram, his morning's work done, sat in the shady section of the marble balcony. He had promised Grace to show her the jacaranda in flower, but he never did keep his word.

Anger rose up inside him that it could have been so different. The day they met, she had showered one hundred thousand blessings on him, though it did not always seem that way. When he told her that much later, she reached over, pinching him on the cheek, her laugh tinkling upwards to the cloudless sky.

"I mean it: if a trumpet bloom falls on you, you are truly blessed. You will be favoured by fortune."

"Tall tales, Dr Fernandes, but so pleasing. I must see this jacaranda and claim my good fortune. I will gather up a bundle. It will take more than one flower to wipe out my sins."

"It will be my honour to show you the jacaranda."

Vikram sighed. The trumpet blooms, mauve to lilac, mocked him. She would never stand here, the jacaranda a backdrop to her simple beauty.

The invitation to the Parnell Square party had been the start of it. He should have politely turned her down. Yet how could he? He was helpless against her requests.

⋆

He could not bow out: it was unthinkable to let her down. The battleaxe landlady begrudgingly let him have his weekly bath on a Friday rather than a Saturday. She made him feel like a beggar, eventually forcing out of him the reason he needed to wash. She said nothing at first, waiting until he was halfway up the stairs to spit out her opinion.

"What they are doing inviting somebody like you is beyond me."

He continued his trudge to the third-floor bathroom he was told he could use.

The landlady rocked back on her heels and shouted after him. "Let's see if himself is happy with the situation."

He wore his finest silk kurta and waistcoat. The house at Parnell Square looked very grand: lights on in every room, the curtains drawn back, as if the occupants wanted the whole of Dublin to stop and stare. He was sure he heard the tinkle of her laugh punctuating the buzz of conversation growing around the house. A worry gripped him that she might not remember him, that she was trifling with him. He loitered at the front steps, thinking of passing the house by. Somebody opened the front door a gap and threw out a cigarette butt. It rolled at his feet as the door banged shut and the shrill banter deadened. He stubbed out the last spurt of fire from the cigarette with his leather shoe before quickly walking up the steps to the door. He was sure of one thing: if he disappointed her, she would never forgive him for his cowardice. He pressed the bell quickly before he could doubt his decision. It was several minutes before the door was swung back.

The housekeeper kept the door half open as she peered at him. "Yes?"

"I am Dr Fernandes."

"So?"

"Mrs Moran invited me."

She looked past him and her face opened in a wide smile. "Mr Justice Fitzpatrick and Mrs Fitzpatrick, do come in. I will tell the judge you have arrived."

They pushed past Vikram, the woman wearing a thick fur coat, the strength of her perfume making his nose twitch. The housekeeper made to close the door behind them, but he stepped closer so she could not avoid his gaze. She gave out a deep sigh and muttered, "Stay there, I will check."

The door banged shut. The house vibrated with talk and laughter as he looked over the smoky city and wondered if, after all, he should leave. The chill wind blowing in from the River Liffey made him shiver and he was already down three of the front steps when the front door pulled open again and the housekeeper motioned him to step into the hall.

"Stay here, she will be down in a minute," she said, going upstairs, casting glances back at him every few steps.

Vikram moved from one foot to the other, anxiety coursing through him. Those passing through from the library to the upstairs drawing room pushed past him. He moved back into the shadows, out of the way.

"Don't hide, Dr Fernandes, you are my honoured guest."

She called out from the top of the stairs so that everybody turned around and looked at her. With a whip of her shoulders, Grace bunched up a handful of her dress in her hands and danced down the flight of stairs.

He had never seen anything so beautiful: a silver-white butterfly fluttering about him. Her dress fanned about her in a concoction of delicate white ruffles.

More than anything, he wanted to grab her hand and run out the door and down the street, where they could sit together and just be.

Grace beckoned and Vikram walked towards her, following as she took the stairs slowly, stopping to exchange words with friends. At the top of the landing, she turned to Vikram. "You look very fine this evening, Dr Fernandes. You put all these other men to shame."

He coughed to hide his embarrassment, but she had already grabbed his hand and pulled him into the room, announcing at the top of her voice: "Dr Vikram Fernandes, Bangalore, India."

Those nearest the door stopped in mid conversation, stepping back to allow the guest more space. The women, noting the girlish excitement in Grace's flushed-pink face, felt a spear of jealousy.

Judge Martin Moran was deep in conversation with a constitutional lawyer when the room suddenly went quiet. He swung around to see his wife advance towards him, her arm linked with an Indian man's.

"Judge, please meet Dr Fernandes. I told you about him. He saved Aunt Violet's life."

"Saved might be too strong a word, doctor, don't you agree?"

"Yes, sir, I do. The credit for Mrs McNally's recovery lies with Dr O'Connell. But your wife is most kind."

Vikram extended his hand. The judge gave it a limp shake.

"You are welcome, Dr Fernandes. Help yourself to some food and drink."

They stood, an awkward silence between them until the judge, spotting somebody else, smiled, indicating he must circulate among his guests.

Grace caught Vikram's hand and led him to the far end of the room, where a long table pushed up against the back wall was laden down with silver platters of sandwiches, cake stands holding small bites of apple tart, sweet cake lined in a row and a wide tray holding small glass bowls of sherry trifle. In the centre, a silver candelabrum gave off the heat of twelve candles. At the far end Violet sat, her eyes watching him, her mouth set at a tight line of disapproval.

"Never go for the sandwiches under the candles, unless you like a wax garnish," Grace whispered in his ear. "We really put the Shelbourne to shame," she giggled, as she piled up his plate high with ham-and-salad sandwiches and fruit cake. She motioned to Aunt Violet, who looked elegant in a deep-red silk dress, her hair swept up into a neat bun. Vikram bowed to the old lady, but she looked past him.

"You know Dr Fernandes, Aunt Violet. He was kind enough to accept my invitation to the party."

Violet placed her sherry glass on the serving table. "Grace, I would like to speak to you in private, please."

"Maybe I should leave?"

Violet stared at Vikram. "That would be a sensible course of action, Dr Fernandes."

Grace stood in front of Vikram. "Dr Fernandes is a good friend of mine and will be treated with courtesy in this house. The judge has already welcomed him."

Violet guffawed loudly, so that people around them stared at her. She lowered her voice appropriately. "Just because that husband of yours does not know what you're at doesn't mean I don't. You have some cheek."

Vikram stepped in between the two women. "Thank you for the kind invitation, Mrs Moran. I must go."

He turned on his heel before Grace or Violet could say anything. Depositing his plate of food behind a large punch bowl, he slipped by revellers on the landing, going against the flow down the stairs. In the commotion, he found himself pushed into the library. Lined with books on all sides, there was a wide desk in front of the back window where sturdy brown files were stacked high. At the far end, the judge was deep in conversation with a tall man in a grey suit. Embarrassed, Vikram made to back out of the room as the judge swung around.

"Dr Fernandes, you found my hiding place."

"I am very sorry, sir, I am afraid I lost my way."

"Not at all."

He bowed and made to leave as the man in the grey suit swept by him and up the stairs. Judge Moran called out to Vikram. "My wife seems rather taken by you. I hope you intend to respect her as a married woman."

Vikram spluttered in his surprise. "Of course, sir, Mrs Moran has been more than kind to me." He backed away, making for the front door.

He was already on the top step when Grace caught up with him. She looked distressed, her brow furrowed, a glint of tears in her eyes. She stepped out on the front steps with him and he was not sure what to say to her.

"You should go back inside. You don't want people to gossip."

She shrugged her shoulders. "They will gossip anyway."

He made to leave and she called him back. "What do I call you? If we are to become friends, we have to move past the polite titles."

He grinned. "Vikram."

"Call me Grace."

He bowed. "Goodnight, Grace."

She giggled and blew him a kiss.

*

Grace skipped in front of him along the path, laughing. It was months on and they knew each other so well. It was a squally day and they were the only ones rash enough to be on Howth Head. Seagulls surfed the air, caterwauling as they were buffeted from side to side. He stopped to look at the ferry ploughing the Irish Sea and she came up behind him, leaning on his shoulder.

"You are a silly dreamer," she whispered in his ear. He turned around and kissed her. She pulled away, laughing, skipping ahead. He called to her to wait for him, but she did not hear, dancing up the hill, her skirt billowing around her, her laughter whipping up across the gorse bushes. When she turned around, she threw her arms wide and he raced to her.

★

"Vikram, what is wrong with you, man?"

Rhya was clicking her fingers in front of his face, which annoyed him intensely. Four months ago, some character on television had done it and Rhya had adopted the practice as a suitable mode of communication. He regularly had to suffer this intrusion, though he voiced his disdain on many occasions. This time, he pretended not to notice and woke slowly from his reverie.

"I was far away."

He felt the gentle touch of Grace's kiss now, her perfume enveloping him.

Vikram closed his eyes to draw up this vision who so captivated him. It was this moment he conjured up most often, when she had stepped off the last step, the dress swishing into place around her, her smile wide, searching for him in the half dimness of the hallway.

Had he ever seen her so beautiful?

Ten

Parnell Square, Dublin, March 1984

Emma rushed along the east of the square. The bluster of cold spring air whipping up the tunnel of O'Connell Street pressed around the judge's residence. A high red-brick Georgian building dulled by city fumes and dust, it had once been a fine residence with a bird's-eye view across the city to the mountains beyond. Now it was a faded high house warding off the biting air streams channelled from the city centre down below. Wind squalls made the windows around the square rattle and those walking by shiver and button up their coats.

The pavement was pocked with chewing gum, the stone steps filthy in the corners with faded, stained, water-blotted chocolate bar wrappers. A man in a business suit leaning on a railing took out a cigarette before letting the packet drop to the ground. Emma clicked her tongue in disapproval, but he did not notice, folding his newspaper neatly into his pocket before striding smartly away.

Stepping quickly into the wide hall of No. 19, the door pressing heavy against her, the gloom of the day followed

Emma in, turning the stacks of boxes into pillars of shade. She pulled open a large box full to the brim with clothes, tumbled in a hasty hiding-away. Clutching a bunch of light dresses to her, she ran up the stairs to the front bedroom.

For as long as she could remember, the blue bedroom had been an empty, cold room. The big, heavy mahogany wardrobes were bare. The brass-framed bed's base and mattress had long since been discarded and never replaced. Set in the space between the long windows was a dressing table, the drawers half open, the delicate blue on the walls and the gold silk of the curtains replicated in a deep frill covering its four legs.

It had been her mother's room. In the past, she avoided the room because it was chill and still. Running her hand along the top of the dressing table, the dust puffed up, making her cough. Accidentally whisking one of the dresses across the surface, she swiped off more loose dust. It clouded until it was grey and she had to push up the windows quickly to air out the room.

A shiver of sunlight lit across the room and Emma set about opening the wardrobe doors, a heavy, musty smell seeping around her. A jizz was on her to preserve the memory of a life that had been so brutally cut short. The wooden hangers were still in the wardrobe, so she took them down to arrange the dresses, covered in tiny, delicate, faded flowers. Their Peter Pan collars in simple white cotton dipped down from tight bodices to A-line skirts. Excitement pulsed through her that she might piece together a collage of the mother she never knew.

In the basement kitchen, she found cloths, a bucket and disinfectant under the sink, and an electric kettle she filled with water. When she got back to the bedroom, it was cold. The sound of the traffic down below creeping in the open window made the room seem a part of life once more. She switched on the kettle, standing and waiting for it to boil. She had always been so afraid of this room, afraid of its emptiness, the chill that curled around her ankles when she stepped in. A lonely, uncluttered room. Any time she had ventured in as a child she was so overcome by the fear of being found out that she could only stand and take in the blue wallpaper, garlands of flowers patched across the walls, before her back began to prickle with perspiration, making her bolt down the stairs.

Swirling the water into the bucket, some spilled on the floor, making patterns and channels through the decades of ingrained dirt. Squeezing out a steaming-hot cloth, she wiped across the centre of the dressing table, cutting a path through the grime set down over years of deliberate neglect. Circling across the dressing table, she worked until the dark hue of the walnut broke through and the ring-pull knobs on the drawers showed a dull gold. The mirror clean, she blew her breath on it and polished it with a dry cloth until it gleamed. Propping up the sash windows, she leaned out to splash water on the outside panes of glass, stretching to scrape away stubborn stains. Her arms aching, she retreated to the hall, stopping to rummage through some more boxes.

A large cardboard box, Jacobs Biscuits printed on the side, caught her eye. Dipping in, she took out a square blue gift box. A whiff of perfume snaked past her as she lifted a cobalt bottle from its satin bed. The label read Evening in Paris and the bottle with a silver top promised romance, though it might, after all this time, be just tar.

She had to put an effort into unscrewing the top, which was

tight with age, then gingerly dabbed out a drop on her wrist. The sweet, woody aroma clouded around her. The perfume was brown-black, the smell strong and sweet. She sniffed again, the jasmine hinting at something exotic. There was a comfort about it, making her somehow feel satisfied.

She rummaged some more, taking out a wider box that looked like a gift set. The lid was stiff at first, but when she lifted it soft music flowed through the room. A small perfume bottle in the middle had been half used up, but the eau de cologne appeared not to have been touched and the midnight-blue tins of talcum powder were still heavy to hold.

When the music stopped, Emma pushed the lid down. She scooped up some more of her mother's dresses and bundled the gift set into the crumple of silk, before tramping back up the stairs to the blue room. Carefully, she placed the boxes and the bottles on the dressing table. Sitting down, she thought she was sad, surrounding herself with the forgotten bits and pieces of another woman because she had nothing of her own and too much wounded pride to go home and even throw a few things in a case. Twisting hard on the perfume bottle, she used the dauber to stroke some more of the sweet scent with jasmine down the line of her neck. How many times had Grace done this, before going downstairs?

A sharp buzz of the doorbell interrupted Emma. She surveyed the room: the hint of perfume surfing the air, spots of sunlight lighting the faded blue wallpaper, the stool pushed back at an angle from the dressing table. Already it felt as if Grace had moved back in. Reluctantly, she went downstairs.

"I brought you a bit of hot lunch. I know you don't want to be in that basement kitchen of yours trying to pull something together." Angie Hannon was standing, a tray bunched with foil in her hand, a line of steam puffing across her face from a slight break in the silver cover. "I do the best coddle this side of the Liffey. I have never heard anyone say anything else."

Angie's face expectant, her eyes wide, Emma thought she looked like a child given free rein at the sweet counter.

"I did not realise it is gone lunchtime."

Angie made to step into the hall, her face more relaxed now that her offering had been accepted. "Hope you don't think me too forward. It is just . . ." She swung awkwardly from one foot to the other, unsure of what to say next.

Emma softened to the older woman, closing the hall door gently so that they were left standing looking at each other in the wide hall, surrounded by pillars of boxes.

"Don't mind the mess. Would you like to stay a while?"

"I would love to and don't mind any of that. Sure, it has to be wrong before it is right."

Emma led the way to the upstairs drawing room. "What about a brandy?"

Angie beamed with pleasure. "Unusual at this time of day, but don't let that stop us."

Emma wiped the crystal glasses on the sideboard with a clean cloth and poured from another bottle she had found the previous night behind the judge's law books. Angie stood by the drawing room windows, taking in the view as if it was her first time watching from the first floor of Parnell Square. She beckoned Emma to join her.

"You see that man sitting down there in the park? John McDermott goes there every day to remember his wife. She loved that garden, she did. They used to sit like lovers, holding hands. Poor chap sits now and talks to her in his head. Says it is better than going to a cold graveyard where you can't even put up a chair to rest your bones. When they built that park, they never thought Maisie McDermott would be the one remembered the most."

Emma handed her the brandy. Angie raised her glass, so that the liquid inside glinted in the sunshine streaming across the square.

"To you and this place."

"I may have taken on too much. We'll see."

Emma opened up the coddle, dipping into the stew, attempting to fight the fatty meat and confine herself to the vegetables.

"A Dublin dinner in the bowl. It is my most popular dish when I do an evening meal special."

"Have you always run the guesthouse?"

Angie's face clouded over while Emma, a little distracted, scooped up a bigger spoonful of coddle. "Moved here about ten years ago. I will have to give you the recipe. I have never seen anyone tuck in with such gusto."

Emma raised her brandy glass; they connected loudly, like two men with pints after a successful horse fair.

"Are you planning to stay, Emma, or are you just getting the place ready for sale?"

Emma hesitated. "I am not sure. I split up from my husband so there is not much to go back to in Australia."

"Take time out here, lick your wounds, maybe find a man to keep you company for a while."

"I rather think I've had enough of men at this stage."

Angie giggled. "Never turn down a nice meal and good company, I always say."

"How about yourself?"

"Forever on the lookout. Tell me, do you have a job to leave in Australia?"

Emma noticed the deliberate change in conversation, but let it go.

"Super exciting, working in a bank, but I am not sure there will be many opportunities here."

"Once the will is sorted you may not have to worry too much in that regard. I know the judge had property all over the place."

"You seem to know more about him than I do."

Angie flustered and giggled. "It is not as if he opened his heart to me or anything, but I think I was somebody he trusted. He told me once he had an apartment in Paris. Funny thing was he did not know why and he had never even seen the inside of it. It was purely an investment, I suppose."

"That sounds like my father."

Angie got up and walked back to the window. "Have you met Andrew yet?"

"Andrew?"

"Andrew Kelly. He was a good friend of your father."

"He introduced himself at the funeral. He was kind."

"He was very good to your father, stayed with him at the end."

Emma got up and began to tidy away the glasses, her head down so Angie Hannon would not see the tears pinching at her eyelids. She fussed, straightening the pile of books on the table.

"You think it was bad of me, that I did not come earlier."

Angie Hannon swung around. "I never said such a thing, never even thought it. Besides, it is not my place to make such a judgement. You were the only one who could make that call."

Emma put the tray down on the sideboard and stood beside Angie, taking in the city.

"Andrew was a bit upset. He could not understand it," Angie said quietly.

Two phone calls and one letter and still she had made no effort to book a flight, instead taking a day out on the Hawkesbury River, pretending he was not dying. Andrew Kelly wrote her two letters, the first two months before. He made it very clear, diagnosis and prognosis: six weeks maximum, and doctors, he said, were never out on their accuracy on such important pieces of information. Four weeks later, the second letter arrived: more formal, with the warning that she was in danger of making a decision she may later regret.

Did she regret it now? She didn't know. When Andrew Kelly had introduced himself at the funeral, he made no reference to the correspondence and for that she was grateful. Neither did he ask why she had made the journey home when her father had passed away. She was not sure she had an answer to any of the questions he was too polite to ask.

Angie Hannon clapped her hands loudly, making Emma jump.

"I had better get along. I have a party of German businessmen staying with me tonight. I can't imagine why they picked my little place when they could have had the best of any hotel. Either they are pocketing a lot of the expenses or the people they work for are cheapskates." She reached over and put an arm across Emma's shoulders. "I will give Andrew a ring. He will know exactly what to do with those law books."

Emma nodded, walking Angie to the door.

Andrew Kelly had been so supportive at the funeral, beside her every step of the way. Before they closed the coffin at the funeral home, he had asked her if she wanted to spend a last few moments with her father alone.

She shook her head, so instead he waited until everybody had left and took his own private time with the dead judge, emerging many minutes later, his face grey with grief.

He was beside her too as she stood in the church the next day, when the whole of the Law Library queued up to shake her hand and offer sympathies for her loss. He introduced the judges to her, steering her clear of those who wanted to linger longer, causing a bulge in the queue, as words that meant nothing to her were enunciated with such earnest conviction.

He had also arranged a reception in the Gresham Hotel, so that after her father was buried they all went there, where plates of sandwiches covered a table and waitresses walked about with big kettles of tea. When she stole away to get some quiet, he followed her.

"Emma, would you like me to drop you home? You don't have to stay until the bitter end, you know, everybody understands. Grief is a strange thing, it affects us all differently."

"I don't know any of these people. I never knew my father had so many friends."

Andrew Kelly laughed. "I would not call them friends exactly, but a judge of his standing has a certain following. He probably would have had a lot to say in private about the majority of those here."

He went out and stood with her on O'Connell Street, the wind whipping their ankles and forcing him to dig his hands into his trouser pockets.

"I can call a taxi for you or, if you like, I can walk you up to the house." Dancing lightly from one foot to the other in an attempt to offset the chill, his cheeks and nose were blotched red.

"I can go on my own. I need to clear my head."

"Are you sure?"

He looked relieved when she insisted she could walk on her own. She was surprised when he kissed her on the cheeks.

"I will stay on with this crowd and see the last one gone."

They made no arrangement to meet again and she had wondered whether he was just a funeral buddy or somebody who would hover at her shoulder, as if he knew more of her father than she.

He did neither, sending a handwritten note the next day to say he had, as per the judge's wishes, settled the bill with the Gresham Hotel and was forwarding the receipt to the solicitors handling her father's estate. He was, he said, going to be out of the country for a few days but would, if she did not mind, call on her on his return. She liked the old-fashioned tenor of the letter, but believed his intention to call was more a polite comment than a direct intention.

Emma hoped she was wrong, because for some reason she found the company of this man comforting. That he was a friend of her father made it more surprising. She liked him; there was something reassuring about Andrew she could not quite put her finger on.

Eleven

Our Lady's Asylum, Knockavanagh, April 1954
Mandy was pulling a comb through her hair. "Curse these knots. I have to get them out."

"Tell him to give you flowers," Bertha said, and Mandy's face reddened.

"How is it that that mad old bat always knows what's going on?"

"You are not meeting somebody, are you?" said Grace.

Mandy gripped Grace's arm and pulled her close. "What if I am?"

"Where? How could you?"

"In the kitchens. Why do you think I volunteered to do the bin work down in that dark basement?"

A scowl came across Grace's face. "Who is he?"

Mandy pulled away. "I know what you are going to say: to be interested in a girl in an asylum."

"I didn't say that."

"He is a man who likes the look of me and I like the look of him. What is wrong with that?"

"What do you plan on doing?"

Mandy threw her hands in the air. "Have tea and talk about the weather."

"Mandy . . ."

"Don't you miss it, Grace? The appreciative look of a man, the feel of his hand, his body."

"But what if you get caught?"

Mandy jumped up. "Oh, oh, oh, oh, they might put me in the asylum, call me a lunatic." She laughed out loud and one of the attendants looked their way. Mandy moved closer to Grace and whispered, "We are going to slip through the stile down at the holy well: there is nobody around there and there is a fair bit of cover."

"Don't go."

"He says we can run away together once he works out a plan to get me out of here."

She rummaged through her clothes.

"I am looking for something to match my pink blouse. Could I wear your red skirt?"

Grace pulled out the poplin gathered skirt she was given on her first week. "Are you sure about this?"

Mandy snatched the skirt and stepped into it. "What's the worst that can happen? Hasn't it happened already? You know why I am in this place?"

Grace shook her head.

"I went down by the river with a nice lad when the circus came to town and I ended up having a baby. They took the baby from me, I never saw her again, and my father drove me from the hospital to here. That was five years ago. I was just eighteen."

Mandy shrugged her shoulders.

"If I am not back in time, will you sneak a slice of bread for me?"

"What do you mean, not back in time?"

"He is friendly with the night porter. I can come back a bit later. Cover for me, won't you?"

"Dance till your feet give out," Bertha shouted.

"Oh, shut up," Mandy said.

She straightened her skirt and did a twirl, laughing with excitement as the fabric spanned out.

"How do I look?"

"You look lovely." Grace reached over and straightened the blouse collar. "Are you sure?"

Mandy giggled.

Grace stood in the middle of the ward, watching her friend as she reported to the nurses' station to be accompanied down to the basement.

"For someone doing a dirty job you are very dolled up," the head nurse said, as she unlocked the ward door and called an attendant to bring Mandy to the kitchen.

Grace sat on a straight chair by the window. From here she could see the curve of the driveway past the grassed lawn and the monkey puzzle tree in the middle, its thick branches stuck at angles, as if it was boxing the wind. A grey stone wall blotted the view of the road and planks of timber nailed across the gates obscured any other view.

The noon bus from Knockavanagh to Wicklow, only its roof visible, slid past. Somewhere down below, a member of staff kicked the ground and dragged on a cigarette. An awful loneliness seeped through Grace, so she took out her sewing kit and threaded a needle. A pile of linen handkerchiefs lay in the basket. She picked up one and began to hem it, concentrating on the neatness and the tightness of her stitches. If she got money for all the hankies she hemmed and the labels she sewed on saying "Made in Ireland", she would be rich. Sometimes she worked too hard and her thumb chafed from pushing the needles through the double thickness of cloth. Her finger joints pained her because the hankies were fiddly and her back was sore because she had to bend over to get the best light near the end of the day.

Once she held a piece of linen back and left it stuffed in a ball in her pocket for days before she dared take it out, when there was quiet and the attendants had their feet up, gossiping. Flattening the fabric as best she could, with the blue thread she had pulled from the old blanket on her bed she stitched their initials, intertwined. Vikram and Grace: first the V and then the G, as they should be, husband and wife.

He would never use it, he did not like handkerchiefs, but he would never tell her that and would carry it in his pocket all the time because it pleased her so.

It was much later that night when the hunt was on for Mandy.

"Do you know where she is?"

An attendant was standing over Grace.

"Who?"

"Maureen McGuane, that is who."

"You mean Mandy?"

The attendant walked off, grumbling to herself.

"A man was going to give her flowers and they were going dancing, just like Barry and me," Bertha shouted out.

The matron, who had arrived at the station, walked over. "What did you say?"

One of the nurses stood between the matron and Bertha. "Take no notice of her, she is always full of that talk."

The matron, wearing a navy dress, pointed at Grace. "Are you friends with Maureen?"

"Yes."

"Do you know where she is?"

"In the kitchens, working."

"I hear she was very dressed up for a woman going to empty bins. Would you know why?"

Grace took up a bunch of linen handkerchiefs. "I did forty today. Do you like my stitching?"

"I was asking about Maureen."

"In the kitchens, working."

The matron stamped her foot. "A dead loss. Conduct a search of every ward and tell Paddy O'Brien to look around the grounds and alert the gateman," she snapped to two nurses standing at her elbow. The matron picked up one of Grace's handkerchiefs. "It is nice stitching. If you play your cards right, make yourself better, we might be able to get you work in a local factory."

She looked to Grace's face, expecting some sort of gratitude, but she was staring off into space. The matron turned on her heel and told the attendant to alert her as soon as the patient was found. Using a key from a big bunch around her waist, she unlocked the ward security door and left.

"She has run for the hills," Bertha said, and Grace looked to her in surprise, but the old woman was picking her nails and muttering to herself.

Grace lay down on the bed and closed her eyes. Vikram whispered in her ear, his arms enfolding her. He had rented out a room in a small hotel in Bray. It was a small room, washed up and forgotten, overlooking the railway line, but the sheets were clean and the proprietor willing to take cash and ask no questions. When Grace first went there, she was nervous. Vikram held her close, whispering in her ear, slowly unzipping her dress. They made love, laughing when the mainline train thundered past, making the room shake and the pictures on the walls shudder. He liked to stroke the top of her arms, all the time whispering his love for her, so that she felt loved and safe. Feeling his touch, she drifted away, imagining they were far away on the coffee estate, locked in by the heavy monsoon rains.

★

It was much later when she woke up. She knew by the way the grey light on the ward threw up shapes on the far wall. Bertha's heavy snoring punctuated the air: she had fallen asleep, sitting on the chair by the window, her head dipped into her chest. Teresa was beginning to shout for her supper and other women were also grumbling.

"They are very late tonight. Don't they know we are starving?" the old lady at the end shouted.

Another woman pulled on a coat and stood at the door, as if she wanted to be top of the queue for the dining hall. As the attendant pushed her roughly back to the beds, the door opened and a man with a trolley walked in. First they were quiet, then someone let out a screech and another pulled up her skirt to show her heavy stockinged leg. The man's face went fire-red as he ladled out bowls of soup and handed out bread.

"Sonny, you can stay and entertain us, we could do with a bit of cheering up," the old woman shouted, and the others laughed.

A young woman still in her nightgown sidled up to him, making to touch his hair. One of the ward attendants slapped her back. "Behave and let the poor fellah do his job."

"Why aren't we in the dining hall?" Grace asked.

The attendant spun around. "Always the questions. If your friend ever comes back to this ward, you can ask her that."

"Mandy – has she been found?"

The attendant didn't answer but sniggered, whispering something to the man doling out the food, which made crimson seep up his neck.

"Is she all right?"

"Let's just say she won't be worrying about whether the bread is speckled with green tonight."

Some of the women stopped to listen. Mindful she had an audience, the foolish attendant continued.

"Best to keep the rules: remember that and you won't end up discarded at the well. Must have been gone in her head to think any man would look at a woman in an asylum." The attendant laughed heartily at her own joke. "Not right in the head, sure, ye are all wrong in the head, ye poor things."

"What happened?" Grace asked.

The attendant pulled her aside fiercely. "Five men, that is what happened to her, and her wearing a red skirt. The skirt was found down the holy well. She was only barely alive. You did not hear any of this from me, understand? Or I will have ye."

The attendant clapped her hands, shouting, "Time to bed down."

"Did he bring her flowers?" Bertha asked.

"Faith, it wasn't flowers she got," the attendant sniggered, putting her hands together loudly to move the women towards their beds.

Grace climbed in. She was shivering, but not from the cold. Teresa was singing at the far end of the ward, over and over, the same line: "Mandy fell down the well. Mandy fell down the well."

Grace, not caring her feet would get cold, pulled the blanket over her head and shut her eyes tight, afraid to think of what had happened to her friend.

Twelve

Bangalore, India, March 1984

Rosa seemed on edge, fidgeting with the strap of her handbag.

"There is something wrong, my Rosa?"

"Anil is not happy that we travel next week." She shook her head. Her lips curled and she sighed deeply, the arch of her shoulders tightening. "I am afraid what will happen if I go away, Uncle. Anil is womanising, I know it."

Vikram checked the servant was not throwing an ear into their conversation. "How can you know such a thing, Rosa?"

"I heard talk."

"Talk counts for nothing. Have you spoken to Anil about it?"

Rosa jumped up. "Uncle, he is never home."

"It is still only talk, Rosa. How have you been getting along?"

She turned away and began to finger the hibiscus, brazen-red in flower. "We used to enjoy being together, Uncle, but now . . ." Her voice trailed off.

Vikram, embarrassed, coughed loudly and cleared his throat.

"Maybe your mother is right: you should not be turning up here so much and should spend more time at home."

"Why? He is never there. He comes in very late, and when he is home there are all sorts of phone calls. I answered the phone the other day. A girl was giggling on the line, until she realised it was me. I hate going anywhere, because I know everybody feels sorry for me." Tears were flowing down her cheeks, but she did not appear to notice.

Vikram held out his two hands and she grasped them.

"Grace was a very lucky woman, Uncle, to have a man like you on her side."

"Was she? I don't think so." He squeezed her hands tight and changed the subject. "You still love Anil?"

She flopped on to her knees on the marble floor beside Vikram and lay her head in his lap, like she used to when she was a young girl and had fallen out with her friends. "I love him more than anything, but when he is at home I am on edge. I pick fights. He likes to argue, because if we do he does not have to love me."

Vikram released one of his hands from her grasp and stroked her hair. "Marriage is a difficult contract at the best of times. It often requires renewal and further negotiation."

"That I would not mind: it is the constant telling me I am in the wrong when he is running around the whole of Bangalore with girls half his age."

"Do you want me to talk to him?"

"No offence, Uncle, but he is not afraid of you." Rosa laughed. "I think Mama would be a better bet. Would you ask her for me? I can't bear the interrogation she will put me through."

Vikram smiled and nodded. "My sister is a wonderful woman, but a High Court judge would be hard pressed to match her in cross-examination. Much preferable to have Rhya on side."

Rosa got back on her chair. "Tell me more about Grace."

She was smiling, and it gladdened Vikram's heart to see a softness return to her eyes.

"You would have liked her, Rosa. She was so sweet and gentle. We had arranged to meet at the park a few days after the Parnell Square party. I was a bit late arriving at the Green. She was sitting on the bench her shoulders hunched."

*

Vikram stopped and took her in: the smart suit and cape, a cloche hat to match the fleck of the suit. She did not see him at first and he noticed she was drumming the bench lightly with her fingers. When she turned and saw him, a smile curved across her face.

"I am sorry, but the ward was so busy this morning I am afraid I can only stay about twenty minutes."

"So there are people who let you treat them."

"Some are so sick they can't voice their objection."

She laughed.

"Shall we walk?" he suggested.

"I thought you may not come after what happened at Parnell Square."

"Nothing was going to stop me."

"I like your company, Vikram, I am not going to let anybody like Aunt Violet spoil it."

He detected a firmness in her voice, though she looked at him shyly and they walked on. When they got to the far corner of the Green, he said he had to rush back.

"I have a day off tomorrow. Maybe we could meet again and have a cup of tea after our walk."

She nodded enthusiastically and stood watching him as he pelted across the road back to the hospital.

The next day, he was the one who was early. Grace arrived fifteen minutes later, her cheeks rosy with exertion.

"I was afraid you would not wait. Aunt Violet insisted I accompany her to the dentist. It was as if she knew of our plans. We met Claire Fitzpatrick, the judge's wife, there and she wanted us to have tea with her. I had to tell a lie to get away from them."

"What did you say?"

"I told them Miss Connolly had scheduled a last-minute fitting and I had to go, as the judge wanted me to have a new ballgown for the King's Inns dinner. But enough. I want to hear all about India and the coffee estate."

"You would love the plantation, Grace, it is the one place in the world that brings such peace to my heart. There are times it is so quiet you fancy you can hear the plants grow and stretch to the sun, the snakes slide across the paths. There are other times, the peacocks are crying so loud it feels haunted. The wind among the trees high and hoarse, the birds settling into their nests, the sweet scent of the flowers of the Robusta plant, they are all dear to my heart."

"I would love to go there."

"I will bring you to where the river widens, where the elephants lie about waiting for their mahouts to scrub them after a day's work."

She clapped her hands in excitement. "I have to go, Vikram, I just have to."

They crossed to the top of Grafton Street and down the street to Bewley's. He faltered and she turned to him.

"Are you worried to be seen with me?" he asked.

She looked insulted, her eyes sweeping across him anxiously, trying to read his face. "I rather hoped you had a better opinion of me, Vikram."

"I just worry for you. In India this would not be acceptable unless we were related."

She stood and looked Vikram in the eyes. "People gossip in any language, Dr Fernandes, and good luck to them if they do. Now, let us have tea."

*

"Rosa, I was caught in a whirlwind. It happened to both of us, within a short time."

The sound of the front door banging made both Vikram and Rosa jump.

"Oh my, what a squall there is today. Rosa, come help unpack the marketing bags."

As Rosa got up to help her mother, Vikram reached out and took her hand. "Stay tough, Rosa, stay brave. It will all work out, one way or another."

"That is what I am afraid of, Uncle."

Out of the corner of her eye she saw Rhya, so tugged away her hand before her mother began to question her.

Vikram watched her help her mother and he wondered how Anil could look anywhere else. Not only was Rosa beautiful, with a lovely tip nose, but she also had her mother's warm heart.

Closing his eyes, he felt Grace about him. The lovely, warm-hearted Grace. Sitting in Bewley's after their tea, she had started to cry.

★

"Grace, what is wrong?"

"Everybody has been so awful to you. I don't know what you make of us."

"I don't think badly of you, Grace."

She pulled a handkerchief from her handbag and blew her nose. "I have to leave. I don't want to arouse Violet's suspicions."

She made to open her handbag, but he put his hand up to stop her. She blushed and giggled, then, flustered, called the waitress for the bill.

★

The breeze surging past the jacaranda tree ruffled his hair. Grace whispered in his ear, her breath warm against his neck, her perfume enveloping him, and he felt young, felt a sense of excitement to be in her presence.

When Rosa returned to the balcony, she thought he was asleep, so she slipped quietly away to go home and talk to her husband.

Thirteen

Parnell Square, Dublin, March 1984

Emma, a wool blanket thrown over her and another rolled up as a pillow, slept on the library chaise longue. She woke up stiff and cold down one side. At first she thought she was in her apartment near Sydney Harbour, that she heard the neighbours noisily pass on the outside corridor to go to work. She lay there cramped with cold, wondering why she could not hear Sam in the shower. They had married in an enthusiastic rush, but she had no inkling he was not happy. Grumpy, unkind, inattentive of late, but she had thought she had nothing to worry about, until he came home one day and told her he had a new partner. A child with a nice-sounding name was also mentioned and Emma ran from the apartment. Two days later she returned while he was at work, snatching some clothes, her passport and her mother's necklace, three strands of aurora borealis stones with a silver clasp. The judge had given it to her when she turned eighteen. Reaching into a drawer on his desk, he had taken out the bunch of stones, sparkling in the afternoon sun. He let them drip from one hand to the other as the necklace uncoiled.

"This was your mother's favourite necklace. I hope you look after it well," he said. No other explanation was offered.

Now, the curtains were not drawn in the library, so she lay in the gloom of the wet and cold morning looking out over the back garden, which was so overgrown it was hard to see where it ended. She creaked off the chaise longue, pressing on the lamp at the judge's desk, her eye travelling down the room. When she was very young, she had thought he was a prisoner here, only visiting the dining room when they had company. More often than not he had supper on a tray as he worked. Sometimes, she heard him climb the stairs late and would duck under the covers, pretending to be asleep. Once, she moved too fast and he spotted she was awake, stepping into the room and telling her off sternly, so that she shut her eyes, afraid to open them even when she heard him continue to his own room, across the landing.

Angie had arranged for Andrew Kelly to come later in the day to oversee the transfer of the judge's law books to the Four Courts. When the *Irish Law Reports* were taken away, the last vestiges of the judge would go out the door with them. There was nowhere else in the house that held the judge's spirit.

She shook her head to push thoughts of the judge away, wishing she had a room that would so neatly tidy away her life with Sam.

★

Andrew Kelly rang the bell early. Wearing jeans with an open-neck shirt and cardigan, he looked very different.

"Mrs Hannon got in touch, said you needed the law books moved. I have brought along a few people to help with the lifting, if you don't mind us doing it now."

Emma pulled back the front door as about ten young men and women traipsed in.

"Martin never set it down on paper, but he often said he would like his books to be donated to the Law Library."

"You knew my father well, Mr Kelly?"

"Please call me Andrew. Yes, your father was a very good friend over the last ten years . . ." His voice trailed away and he turned to direct the operation.

Emma watched as each student was assigned a set of books, lifting them carefully from the shelves and placing them in cardboard boxes. Slowly the grey shelves were revealed, naked without their heavy load. Rows and rows were packed together, box sets of the law to be treasured now by others. With the books gone, what had been Judge Martin Moran would be gone as well, in this place at least. A desk, a chair and a few bent folders would be all that was left to sum up the father; precedents laid down in bound law books to sum up the judge.

"Is there anything you want to keep as a reminder?" Andrew asked gently.

"Maybe Salmond's *Law of Torts*. Even the judge had secrets."

He looked oddly at her, letting the book slip through his fingers.

"Apologies, I am all thumbs this morning," he said, and she smiled, crouching down to pick up the book. Spying a small pink envelope under the hall table, she reached for it, tucking it into the book as she stood up.

"Do you need me here? I thought I would go upstairs, continue on the rooms there," she said.

"You go on, it is just heavy lifting here."

She slipped up to the blue room, sitting at the dressing table to read the letter, the morning light pooling through the window. Using the teeth of a small comb, she unpicked the gummed flap. Carefully, she pulled the paper from the envelope. With age it had become dry and flimsy. There were brown crackly creases, as if it had been read and reread, folded over and carried around.

August 31, 1953

My dearest Grace,

They say there is no greater place in the world to show the love of one man for a woman than the Taj Mahal. I want to bring you there, to hold your hand and whisper my love for you in your ear. Please let me take you away. I can see the two of us in front of the great monument.

Grace, know that I love and adore you: nothing can change that. I hope in the future you will learn to accept that as a given every day.

Shah Jahan was able to commission a great edifice to show the love for the woman he adored. I can only tell you and tell you again how much I love you, and reassure you that we will be together. You, Grace, are everything to me. Please believe me when I say it. I can't build great monuments to show you. I can only go on my knees before you and tell you I love you.

I don't need to tell you how beautiful, how powerful the Taj Mahal is, but I can tell you how I feel, thinking of us standing in the shadow of such a dream in marble. I know our love is strong, and if wishes could be granted I would wish to sit in the shadow of that great monument, to hold your hand and just be. Stay strong, my love, and we will find a way to be together.

All my love,
Vikram

A furrow of pain barged between her eyes and tears pressed down her face. The sun was rising high in the sky, sliding into the room. Loneliness consumed her, sitting here at Grace's dressing table: loneliness that no man had ever written to her in this way.

When Andrew Kelly called up the stairs, she rushed to wipe her eyes. Hastily, she opened Grace's make-up and patted some decades-old powder across her face, rubbing it in with her fingers. Red lipstick she dotted on, spreading it with her middle finger.

"Sorry I was buried deep in a box," she said as she came down the stairs.

Andrew took in the pink blotches near her eyes, the powder streaked into ridges under her neck. "It is not too late to change your mind."

"I want to see the library empty." She peered into the room, taking in the length of the shelves, the desk alone at the end of the room, the light seeping in to fill the entire space.

Andrew gave the keys of the truck to the last man out the door and closed it behind him. He walked into the library and picked up a blackthorn stick in the corner.

"That was not Martin's."

Emma stared at it. "It was Aunt Violet's. She lived here when I was young."

"A tough woman by all accounts. Do you want to keep it?"

Emma shivered. "I hardly want to touch it, but I know what to do with it."

"No time like the present."

Emma snapped up the stick. She could hear Violet's voice. "You might think you are high and mighty, girl, but believe me, you are nothing. Just because the judge calls you his daughter, that does not mean anything these days."

Emma marched outside to the skip and fired the stick so that it swished through the air, landing with a clatter on top of an old fridge, the door half open.

Andrew was pacing the library, his hand lightly fanning the shelves, when she returned.

"It does not feel the same without his law books. He could not bear to have them moved before he passed away."

She did not say anything and, sensing an agitation in her, he made to leave. "Call me if you need me, Emma," he said as he went out the front door, pulling it hard behind him.

Taking Vikram's letter from her pocket, Emma walked down the library, her steps echoing, the room no longer insulated by his books. The empty shelves stood sentry on a life lived and now gone. Marooned at the end of the room, his desk no longer dominated. Now the suitcase sat on top, Grace's presence prevailed.

She sat at the desk and opened up the letter again. The house was still around her, the sounds of the city far off. Grace should have run, run, run to Vikram, that is what Emma knew, but there was nothing to show she had.

She read slowly each line again, her shoulders shaking, the tears rolling down her cheeks, some dropping onto the paper, and she wondered would anyone ever come to love her so.

Fourteen

Our Lady's Asylum, Knockavanagh, April 1954

Teresa was crying, but nobody bothered. She snooked loudly, complaining so bitterly that Grace moved away from her to sit by the window. A clump of yellow primroses bloomed bright, wedged between the cracked concrete at the top of a window on the floor below. Sometimes a bird came and swiped at the flowers or a bee flitted between the petals, making the stems spring forward. Grace picked up a white linen handkerchief from the pile beside her chair, folding it over as if making pleats. Sybil Connolly got such perfect tight pleats in her linen dresses, enduring even after being balled into a suitcase.

"That won't be worth sending out to the tourist shop in town if you don't quit squeezing the bejaysus out of it," an attendant called over. Grace released the handkerchief, letting the pleats fall away, puncturing the fabric with her needle.

She had hemmed four handkerchiefs when she saw the judge's car come through the gates. He stopped the car long enough to talk to the gateman, rolling down his window and handing something to the old man, who beamed with gratitude. The Morris Oxford pulled in front of reception and the judge got out, stopping to flick some fluff from his trousers before striding to reception.

She shut her eyes, letting the sunshine dance on her eyelids, feeling the swell of Vikram's kisses, the sea breeze chilly and red on their cheeks, making their eyes shine with water. They should have hopped on a ferry that very day, or any one of the days after that. The word *dead* pounded in her head. *Dead*: four letters carrying an eternity of heartbreak.

Violet had used the word so easily. Grace heard again now the cries echoing down the corridor. Never allowed to touch, to whisper in an ear, to reassure before life ebbed away. She was never even allowed a glimpse. It tormented her thoughts now, the only memories left of pain and loss. When Aunt Violet had come to her, she pleaded for a moment to say goodbye.

"Out of the question. There will be no handling of the dead."

"Just to say goodbye."

"Have some respect for the dead and the job the women here have to do, preparing the innocent for burial."

"I did not get a chance to give a name. Something for the headstone."

"Names don't matter at this stage."

Fear clamped across her. She had tried to get out of the bed, calling at the top of her voice, but Violet pushed her back in, telling her to quieten down.

"Don't wake the whole street. You are not the first woman to be in this situation and you won't be the last."

A finger jabbed into Grace's back.

"He is a saint of a man to come to see you, that judge is,

but he has. Look lively. Get some shoes on and tidy up your clothes, you can't meet a judge looking like that."

Grace slipped on her shoes and closed up her cardigan so the stain from last night's stew at the front of her dress did not show.

The judge, standing by the waiting room door, reached out with his gloved hand and guided her to a chair beside the empty fireplace. An attendant sat to one side.

"I am afraid after what happened the last time, the director is insisting on somebody staying with us. How are you?"

"Okay."

"Grace, it breaks my heart to see you in here. Is there anything I can do to make it better?"

"My friend Maureen McGuane, I want to know what happened her, when she is coming back to the ward."

"I cannot interfere in hospital policy."

"She was attacked by men down at the well. She needs help, not to be locked up like a dog."

The attendant coughed and looked severely at Grace.

The judge stood up. "Aunt Violet suggested I come here. We all only want what is best for you, Grace. We will be guided by the medical people."

"Was there a burial, prayers?"

"Grace, only you can make yourself better. Violet says you are being too stubborn. That is not going to help anything."

"Where is the grave?"

"Let the past go: you concentrate on getting better."

"I am not ill."

The judge gave a sympathetic look to the attendant and smiled. "I know that, darling, you just rest."

He made to walk from the room, raising his hand in a signal so the attendant sidled over. Thanking the small, wiry woman for her patience, he slipped a crisp note into her overalls pocket.

Grace ignored his leaving. There was a cold grave and he was not going to tell her where. Was there even a wooden cross? Neither was there anybody to visit and place flowers. Primroses: the grave needed primroses, sweet and delicate and fleeting.

The attendant beckoned to her and gave her a gentle push as she trudged up the steel stairs to the landing, where a long window held up one end. Her eyes lingered on the boggy fields, spreading away from the well to the farmhouse in the distance. She took in the grey sky, the crows flying low, the sound of a tractor in the field beyond the well, before she was ordered to move on. This landscape was her whole world. An ache of loneliness flushed through her, passive acceptance strangling her. Martin was content to let her stay here, she knew that, and Aunt Violet would make sure of it.

⋆

Three days later, Mandy was escorted onto the ward and told to take up her usual bed.

Nobody spoke as she paced like a ghost down the narrow corridor between the steel beds, her head down, darting quick glances at some of the women she knew.

Teresa danced up the row, singing, "Mandy fell down the well." Grace made to hush her but her voice only got louder.

Mandy crawled into bed. The attendant stopped and looked at her, a tight bundle on a small bed, before leaning over and whispering in Grace's ear. "You got what you wanted, her back beside you, but you will regret it. That one is damaged goods."

Grace sat on the edge of her friend's bed. Mandy, her head under the grey blanket, did not say anything, but the cover twitched, agitated by the storm of sobbing underneath.

Laying a gentle hand on her, she hummed the only tune she could remember: "Rock-a-Bye Baby". Slowly, the crying stopped and Grace thought Mandy must be asleep, so she pulled her chair to the window and picked up her sewing.

Outside, children walking home from school dared each other to climb the asylum wall. One boy, his face pulsing with exertion, his spots bulging, got to the top, but the caretaker saw him and shouted.

*

Mandy ignored everybody for a week, barely eating and hiding under her blanket. Some of the other women walked up and stood at the end of the bed, staring at the mound that was once her. Some whispered to each other in huddles. Others did not even notice the unspoken tension on the ward.

Grace talked to Mandy almost nonstop, any words, so that this shrivelled young woman knew somebody cared enough to be around her. Sometimes she reached out to touch the blanket, making her friend shudder.

"Mandy fell down the well," Teresa sang and Grace knew better than to try and stop her. At first the attendants laughed, but they too soon tired of the one-line ditty. "It is old news, sweetheart, pick another event to crow about," one of them sniggered.

Grace did not think Mandy much noticed her loitering at her bedside, until one morning she fiercely pushed her hand away. "For fuck's sake, why can't you leave me alone?"

"I only want to help. I know what happened."

Mandy jumped up. "Do you? Do you know what it is like to be raped by one man while the others stand around smoking cigarettes, talking football and waiting their turn? Do you?" Grabbing Grace by the wrist, she squeezed hard. "What the fuck would you know about a bunch of men, fat and balding, young and smelly, pushing into you like you would stuff a turkey? Don't tell me you want to help." As quick as she had grabbed Grace, she let go, making her stagger backwards.

Gingerly, Grace reached out. When Mandy felt her hand, she snatched it hard, falling into Grace, sobs coursing through her.

"They ripped off your lovely skirt and threw it down the well. I think they thought I was dead because I stopped fighting and screaming after a while."

"Shhh . . . shhh . . . shhh."

"The bastard caretaker found me and did not even come near me. He ran for the boss man, who would only touch me with his shoe, like I was a dead dog on the road. 'A pity she is not dead. Not a word about this to anyone,' he said, and ordered I be brought to isolation."

"Shhh . . . shhh . . . shhh."

"They told me to clean myself up, pushed me under a cold shower. Three days they left me in a tiny room by myself, handing food trays in the door. Nobody could bear to even look at me."

"Shhh . . . shhh . . . shhh."

Grace got up and walked to the window. Below, she saw a

fox slip across the grass. At the gate, the caretaker was reading his newspaper.

Mandy stood beside her, watching the sunlight making patchwork of the front lawn.

"Wouldn't it be lovely to run over that grass in our bare feet?"

"Run away from here altogether."

Neither of them spoke again. The fox, sensing their eyes, quickened its pace, disappearing through the hedge.

"Maureen McGuane, you have a visitor." The nurse beckoned to Mandy to hurry up.

"Nobody comes to see me."

"Make yourself presentable."

Mandy waited until the attendant was out of earshot. "The last time I did that, look what happened to me."

"Maybe it is the Gardaí," Grace said, handing her a brush.

"Why should I bother?"

The attendant threw a pair of shoes at her. "Hurry up."

"They are too big for me."

"Pardon me if you left yours at the well, young woman. Hurry up, we can't have the visitor waiting all day."

Grace reached over, squeezing Mandy's hand before she left. The shoes clopped noisily as she walked.

One of the tea ladies trundled her trolley slowly down the ward, collecting cups. "If I were you, I would stay away from that one."

Grace pretended not to hear. A basket full to the brim with linen handkerchiefs was plonked down beside her by an attendant. "The chief said to tell you they want more. The Yanks are lapping up the linen hankies."

"Waste of good material. Why can't they be like the rest of us and use cotton?" the tea lady snorted.

Grace pulled the basket to the chair by the window. A robin flew in, dancing sideways on the windowsill. He dipped his head, his eyes darting in every direction, until, with a shake of his fluffed feathers, he rose up, flying away into a sheet of mist shrouding the marshy land beyond the high walls.

Vikram was speaking softly to her.

"We will go to the Taj Mahal, my sweetheart. We will have to wake up extra early to see it peep through the mist. When the morning mist from the Yamuna is down, it is like the gods with giant erasers rub out the dome, the minarets and all traces. The morning haze rolls in to throw a protective cover over the big, cold monument to love.

"Another hour it will be before the sun's rays tweak at the corners of the misty cover and playfully tug the blanket of fog to reveal, if only fleetingly, some of the magic underneath. As the sun builds up its heat, the mist is pushed around each layer and slowly pulled away, as if the cover is made of several rolls of the finest parachute silk. The dome, in all its eerie aloneness, is the first to be uncovered, sitting on top of the light fog like a water lily floating on a pond.

"Next, each of the minarets punch through, finding a weak spot in the silk layers and managing to escape. In a dash, the cover is thrown aside, the silk rolls effortlessly cast away. The monument, yet again, presides over the city. At that moment, everything appears so right with the world."

The tea lady, who was showing a new girl the ropes, pointed at Grace. "That is a perfect example of how to ruin your life over a stupid man. She had everything: looks, clothes and a judge for a husband, and what did she do? Throw it away for a fling with a foreigner. Silly girl thought she was going to run away with him. Keep it under your hat, but that is what I heard the nurses say anyway. I will tell you, once he heard of the pregnancy he skedaddled and the poor husband was left to pick up the pieces. Let her and all these poor creatures be a lesson to you. There is no such thing as love, just a lot of silly women who think there is. Look at her by that window every day, mooning her life away, thinking that foreign chap will come for her. May the Lord bless her stupid heart."

Grace did not show she had heard but continued to watch the front garden, where a man was talking to the director. Agitated, the man threw his hands in the air before jumping in his car and driving off, turning so fast out of the asylum his car tyres left skid marks on the road.

Mandy was back on the ward ten minutes later. She lay on the bed, curled up in a ball. Grace knew to leave her alone. After a while she sat up.

"I suppose you want to know who it was."

"If you want to tell."

"It was my father."

Her voice was trembling, but she concentrated on tracing a pattern on her blanket as she spoke.

"They heard about the attack."

"He was worried."

"About his own good name, more likes. Asked me what I did to lead those men on."

"I hope you told him the truth."

Mandy stopped, her finger smarting from the coarseness of the blanket wool. "Would it matter? People like that like to believe the gossip."

"Surely if he knew … "

"He does know, he chooses not to know. Says if I am pregnant I am on my own. I said I was on my own anyway. He said the family did not want anything more to do with me, that I was not to expect anything from him in the future."

"What does he mean?"

"I am stuck in this godforsaken place until I die. It is not just the shame any more; he is afraid I will want his no-good wet fields."

"Surely your mother . . ."

"My mother is heartbroken and has taken to her bed."

"I am sorry."

"I know."

Fifteen

Parnell Square, Dublin, March 1984

Andrew Kelly asked Emma to lunch at his house. Even if he was only being polite, she still felt a twinge of excitement at the invitation. A handwritten note, the summons was as old-fashioned as the man who extended it. He had followed it up with a phone call offering to send a driver across town to take her to his home in Rathgar. When she told Angie Hannon, she said that was his way: Andrew Kelly was a gentleman through and through. It was Angie who also told her to dress up, that a lunch invitation to Rathgar was an occasion to be relished.

Reluctant to pick something to wear just yet, she sat at the dressing table watching a pigeon hunched on the windowsill, the wind rippling its feathers, before rising to the windows, making them rattle gently. Flicking through a leather-bound notebook, she stopped rustling the pages when she saw a heading "Met the judge today".

December 5, 1952

Martin Moran is a tall, smart man and thankful-

ly he is not too old. He was very polite and formal. Aunt Violet is very taken by him. We walked by the canal and I think he proposed. He is not a man of great emotion, I can see that, but Violet said kindness is the most important thing. That and money, and he has both. I still don't want to marry him, but Violet says I have no choice. If I can get to America, I won't have to marry anyone I don't want. I can't say anything. Violet says if my mother was alive she would be so proud I had the chance to marry into the best stock in Dublin. It makes me sound like a Hereford cow.

Emma heard the clock in the sitting room chime noon as she opened the door of one of the mahogany wardrobes. Angie had helped out for an hour, filling Grace's wardrobes with the clothes from numerous boxes. Evening gowns, fur stoles and fur coats were all pushed into one section. Three shelves of colourful boxes held exquisite little hats. The second wardrobe had skirts, blouses and a number of dresses. Emma chose a peacock-blue dress and a cream bolero cardigan.

She paid particular attention to her hair, sweeping it up high. Clipping a tortoiseshell slide at the back, she reached for the hairspray Angie had placed on the dressing table. Shielding her eyes, she sprayed until the fumes choked the back of her neck and her hair was stiff. Checking her reflection in the mirror, she ran her hand down her dress: it was a perfect fit. Fixing the small cardigan over her shoulders, she fastened the top diamanté button. The pair of black slingbacks she found in a box at the bottom of the wardrobe were a snug fit. Standing in front of the mirror, she wondered what Grace would say, that her clothes could so easily be worn by this imposter.

When the doorbell rang, she jumped. The *brring* bounced through the empty rooms of the house.

Swiftly, so she would not change her mind, she opened the door, sweeping it back too far. The driver had already got back into the car and was sitting waiting for her. After a polite introduction, he did not speak again but concentrated on the heavy city traffic. At Rathgar he pulled into the driveway of a two-storey over-basement red-brick house. The garden featured strong architectural plants. Andrew Kelly came out onto his front steps, wiping his hands with a small towel. Beaming, he lightly tripped down the steps and extended his hand.

She thought he seemed nervous, but she did not know why. He stepped to the side to let her go first, indicating she should turn right when she lingered at the doorway.

"I am not huge into formality, there is enough of that in the day job, so I am afraid you may find the room a little untidy. Lived-in, I like to call it."

It was a large room lined with books, with a huge desk spanning the wide front window. Thick wool rugs were thrown over leather couches and small tables once designed to carry elegant china cups were heavy with books and newspapers.

"Martin always complained about the disarray, but I quite like it, though I am probably in danger of being found dead under a sea of books one day."

He plumped up the cushion on the armchair nearest the fire and invited Emma to sit down. Without asking, he opened a bottle of champagne and poured her a glass.

"I thought we could drink a toast to Martin."

She took the glass, reluctantly clinking his.

"To Martin, a man of honesty and integrity who tried

his best. A true friend. May he rest in peace." He did not comment when she barely sipped the champagne but instead asked her to follow him to the kitchen. "Come and sit, while I get my hands into making the crumble."

She followed him downstairs to a room dominated by a large table, which had been laid at one end for two.

"I was a very good friend of your father, Emma. I would like to think we could be friends too."

She loitered by the table, not sure what to say. Andrew turned around to her.

"I know you had your ups and downs with Martin. I am not expecting happy families or anything."

"Are you on the bench as well?"

"Good Lord, no, they would be afraid of what I would do. A senior counsel making more money than the judges, that's me. Martin and I were on the same beat for years, but I did not get to know him until after he went on the bench."

"You sound disappointed he did."

Andrew Kelly stopped crumbling the pastry and slugged some champagne, streaking the outside of his glass with pastry fingers.

"Your father had a huge sense of public duty. He worked way too hard. At least when he was a senior counsel he was getting paid for all the hours; on the bench they took advantage of him, gave him all the heavy cases."

She sipped the champagne as Andrew fussed around the kitchen. On the mantelpiece was a photograph of her father and Andrew standing, mountains and lakes behind them.

"Four years ago in Italy. Martin went over for a judge's conference, but I persuaded him to spend a week on Lake Garda. We had a great time."

Andrew took the salmon out of the oven and transferred it to two plates. He was about to say something else, but he stopped himself, instead lashing the mashed potatoes and peas on the plate beside the fish and placing it in front of Emma.

"Rough and ready, but I hope you find it tasty." He filled up two wine glasses and they sat eating, each wondering what to say next.

Emma was the first to break the silence. "Would you by any chance know where my mother is buried, Andrew? My father was interred with his parents, according to his wishes, but I have no idea about my mother."

"Don't you have family who can help?"

"The judge was an only child and Aunt Violet was the last surviving relative on my mother's side. She died when I was young."

"Surely Martin's solicitor would know."

"I spoke to her on the phone, but she said she didn't know."

"Did you not visit the grave as a child?"

"My father would not even let my mother's name be mentioned in the house. When I was older and asked about her grave, he said it was in Wicklow somewhere."

"I remember Grace, a very beautiful woman. I saw her once at one of their parties."

Emma laughed out loud. "My father would never have had a party in the house."

"There is where you are wrong. Martin loved a good party, good wine and good conversation. It was quite a thing to be invited to Parnell Square. I had moved down from Northern Ireland and I was glad of the entrée to Irish legal society. I think that was the last party in the house. It was not until years later that I got to know Martin properly, and by then your mother had died."

Emma put down her fork and knife. "Everything in my life goes back to the death of my mother. I just wish I could meet somebody who could tell me more."

"Martin was not able to talk about it to anyone, but he loved you, was devastated when you went to Australia."

Emma jumped up, her chair screeching across the kitchen floor tiles. "Mr Kelly, you have been very kind to invite me here, but I am not going to sit and hear what a great fellow my father was and how I ruined his life by going to Australia. He is the reason I had to travel so far away. He was a good man, no denying that, but unable to express any of that so-called love you and others say he had for me."

Andrew Kelly placed a hand on Emma's shoulder. "I am sorry if I sounded critical, it was not intended. I invited you here today so we could get to know each other and I suppose the only thing we have in common is Martin. He asked me if I could look out for you after he died. I have to honour my promise to him."

Emma rushed to the hall door. "He is dead, what does it matter?"

She had opened the door and run down the front steps before Andrew Kelly caught up with her. "Come back in, eat some crumble. We can talk like two strangers trying to get to know each other."

There was something reassuring about him, so she reluctantly agreed, following him up the steps and taking his advice to sit and sip champagne by the fire while he threw a dollop of cream on the pear crumble. When he returned, they talked and she found it easy to tell this man the same age as her father about her marriage breakdown and her plans for the future, which revolved around the boxes from the attic.

She found it strange to think her father must have sat here too, sipping brandy, talking his troubles away, and that Andrew could listen to the daughter like he had listened to the father and not come to any judgement.

As the light outside began to fade, she got up to leave. Andrew telephoned his driver and, when he arrived, accompanied her to the car, opening the passenger door for her.

"I am here to help if you need me, and even if you don't. We must find time to sit and chat again," he said, kissing her on the cheek.

She left, mulling over Andrew's stories about the judge, like the time he persuaded him to go to Connemara for a weekend, fishing on Lough Inagh. Martin Moran had nearly capsized the boat when he tried to pull in what he thought was a fish but turned out to be a piece of an old car. Andrew's words swirled around her head. "We laughed and passed the hip flask until neither was able to control the boat and a local man had to come out alongside us and put a boy on our boat to row us in."

When she got to Parnell Square, she went straight to sit at her father's desk. For so long she had been afraid to even enter this room. If he was on his own, he was busy, poring over documents on his desk. It was the only side of him she knew. And now this space, their only meeting ground, was an empty space where the judge's desk lay abandoned at the bottom of the room. She had only ever known him here. He had never allowed her into court. She did not know him in any way outside of this room.

Once, she had waited up for him to return from the Four

Courts, where he was sitting on a late-night court. She had fallen asleep on the chaise longue, only waking up as he bundled her into his arms and carried her up to her bed. "Emma, there is no need to wait up for me. Next time, I promise I will have to get cross," he said as he made a half-baked attempt to tuck her in.

Now, placing Grace's suitcase on the floor, she set about examining the contents. Every one of these things spread out on the desk was important to Grace. For the first time, she noticed a long, pale-gold box concealed inside a shoe. Carefully she prised the box from where it had been stuck so long, and opened it. The gold and pearl necklace shivered to be uncovered. Gently, Emma lifted it out. It was a vintage piece, bars of gold holding two pearls each in a sequential pattern, like peas in a pod connected to each other, until it reached the hook-and-chain fastening, which allowed it to be worn as a choker or longer. Turning it over in her hands, Emma spotted it was signed Trifari on the inside of the hook. Holding it up to her neck, she liked its elegant feel.

As she placed it back in the box, she noticed a small card.

Like two peas in a pod, a memory of our wedding day.

Martin

Fingering the card, she traced the writing, which was in fountain pen. Never in a million years would she ever have guessed her father could have presented her mother with such a beautiful gift.

Sixteen

Bangalore, India, March 1984

There was an agitation about Rhya, and Vikram could not avoid it. He had not even sat down for breakfast when she began to fret and fuss, calling out to the servant that she was to wash and swab with extra care this day, calling up the caretaker to instruct him to go back to the milk stand and tell him he was only to give her the bags of fresh milk. Vikram wanted to ignore her, but he knew to do that would only mean a prolonging of the nattering and the intrusion into his thoughts.

As she marched up and down the balcony, watching the caretaker make his way to the milk stand, he put a hand out to stop her.

"Rhya, what is it?"

"You know my daughter arrived here shortly after dawn and is asleep in my bed. Next that girl of mine will bring shame on us, by moving back in here. There is something wrong, but the silly girl won't tell me."

"All in good time, Rhya. Couples need time to work out their differences."

Rhya let a cushion she was straightening fall onto the couch. "She has spoken to you, hasn't she? Are you telling me there is something wrong with the marriage?"

Vikram shook his head fiercely. "I said no such thing, Rhya."

Rhya made to say something else, but the servant called and she scurried off, complaining bitterly at the top of her voice that she had to do everything in this household.

Vikram sat down at the far end of the balcony. When Rosa stole out to sit beside him, he did not question her.

"Distract me, Uncle, and tell me more about Grace."

"She had missed a few days at Stephen's Green and, frankly, I thought she was tired of me. One day, I was on Grafton Street when she came along."

*

"Dr Fernandes, how lovely to see you."

"Mrs Moran, are you well?"

"Call me Grace. I have been ill and I had no way of contacting you. Did you wait on the Green for me?"

"I did, but don't worry. Are you better now?"

He saw a snuffle of tears shiver through her and he took a step towards her.

"Grace, what is the matter?"

She looked anxious, wringing a handkerchief through her fingers. "I am really sorry about last week."

He was about to answer when he was pushed from behind,

making him fall heavily against her. Two young men in tweed blazers and slacks laughed.

"The country's been overrun by the wrong type," the one wearing glasses called.

"Who said you could talk to one of our Irish girls anyway?" the other man shouted, and they both laughed loudly.

The one with the glasses turned to Grace and asked, "Is this man bothering you?"

Grace did not say a word but held her handbag up high and swung as hard as she could, hitting the younger man in the face.

The other, astounded at her reaction, remained rooted where he stood, allowing Grace to aim with better precision and hit him whack on the nose.

"Get away from me, you good-for-nothing bastards. How dare you attack my friend?"

Their hands up to stop the handbag raining down on them, they shouted and ran up the street. Grace hollered after them, her handbag still held aloft. Suddenly, aware that others were watching her, she shook her shoulders and straightened her coat with her hands. Vikram's eyes were full of pride, that this lovely woman should so ably defend him.

"I have ruined a perfectly nice handbag over you, Vikram Fernandes."

"So dreadfully sorry. Thank you for coming to my defence."

"Did you see the way they ran off? One idiot lost his cap."

"Please, you should not have put yourself in such danger. This type of stupid behaviour is really quite common."

"Let's go to the Shelbourne." Gently, she tugged him and they walked together, hand in hand for a few paces until he pulled free. They continued side by side, not needing to say much.

In the Lord Mayor's Lounge in the Shelbourne, the waitress recognised Grace, asking if she preferred her usual seat. Grace nodded and they moved to the end of the room and two armchairs beside the open fireplace.

"I like to sit here on a winter's day and have tea, before taking a taxi home," Grace said, taking off her gloves and coat and indicating to Vikram to sit down.

"It is a very grand place."

"My wedding reception was here."

"What a fine location."

"Unfortunately, not a fine marriage."

"Please, you don't have to explain."

The waitress came and Grace asked Vikram to choose the tea. He picked Darjeeling, because it reminded him of the mountains and faraway hills where his coffee estate lay hidden.

Grace did not return to the previous topic of conversation until the silver pot of tea had been placed in front of them, along with a small plate of shortbread biscuits.

"You know all about arranged marriages, I imagine."

He was pouring the tea and he did not know how to answer. "Our countries and cultures are different," he said, replacing the silver teapot carefully on the tray in the middle of the table. It was only then he detected her tears. "Grace, what is the matter? Is something wrong?"

Delicately, she reached into her handbag and took out a white linen handkerchief edged in lace. Dabbing her eyes, she turned more towards the fire, so that the rest of the room could not see beyond her shoulders.

"And what if the arranged marriage does not work? What happens then?"

He felt uncomfortable. As he was forming an answer in his head, she began to talk again, almost as if she had forgotten she had asked a question.

"You think I am spoilt, don't you?"

Flustered, he made to pick up her hand, but she pulled it away.

For a moment she looked so uneasy he thought she might take flight, but instead she turned to him and smiled, so that he felt the warmth of it over the heat of the fire.

"You are very patient with me, Vikram – too patient, I think – but these are my troubles and I must learn to live with them. Please, happily divert me: tell me if you are settling into this damp city at all."

He went along with the shift in conversation and happily began a long story of how everything was so different. He frequently told this story, because Irish people wanted to hear the same drab likes and dislikes. But Grace was different.

"Dr Fernandes, are you on stage with the set ambition to amuse me? I want to hear from the real you, please."

He faltered, but liked her even more. "You don't want to hear about the loneliness in my heart for my family and my home. I miss when the coffee estate is heavy with the scent of the coffee plant flowers, how I love to stand on the terraces and breathe in deeply. I swear you can feel it permeate through the body, renewing each cell as it goes."

Grace leaned forward. "Tell me more."

"It is the one place in the whole world where my soul is at peace. Nowhere do I feel closer to the sky and the clouds than at Chikmagalur. Somehow the day passes differently there; it has a natural flow. When they are laying out the coffee beans on the drying terraces, I love the hum of activity, the buzz of conversation. As the coffee beans dry and crack, there is a quiet expectancy as the sun beats down hard.

"My favourite time is at twilight, when the plantation is still, the mountains like giant elephants protecting us and the night sky later pushing down the stars to light our way. The wild animals are on the prowl: you can feel they are there, but all you see is a shadow or maybe the frightened squawk of a chicken in its pen or the dog on the veranda suddenly sitting tall, on alert. I miss it all. The bulk of elephants passing by on ancient rights of way."

She reached over and took his hand. "It is one of the great pleasures in my life to know you, Vikram."

He looked in her eyes and, at that moment, he knew he was falling in love.

"So why are you a grand doctor, if you love the plantation life so much?"

He laughed. "Indian mothers, don't you know. My mother had this great ambition for me. My father is a specialist in our city hospital. It was a given that I would also go for medicine, it was not my place to go against it. It is hoped I will get a position in the new Bangalore hospital when I return."

"You won't have much time for your coffee estate then. My God, what was I thinking? We should have ordered coffee."

Her face was so stricken he laughed out loud. "Coffee in this country I will not drink. Some day you must have the coffee from our estate, then you will know what it should taste like."

"I will hold you to that."

She was fidgeting, following the rim of the china saucer with her finger, and he asked her what was wrong.

"My husband likes me to be home when he returns from the Four Courts. I had better go."

He called for the bill and she let him pay.

The doorman jumped in front of them as they left. "Taxi to Parnell Square, Mrs Moran?"

"Yes, Tim, please." She turned to Vikram. "I so enjoyed hearing you talk of India. Could we maybe meet another day?"

"I would like that. Thank you for defending me on Grafton Street."

"How about some Sunday? Martin spends all day in his court chambers preparing for his week's work."

"I will look forward to it."

Bowing, he waited until the taxi had pulled out into the city traffic, before he turned away.

★

Rosa was fidgeting, moving her feet across the tiles.

"I have gone on too long, my Rosa."

"No, Uncle. Maybe I should talk to Anil."

"A good idea. I am tiring of spouting on anyway."

She kissed him lightly on the cheek and slipped out of the apartment, shouting goodbye to her mother, giving her no time to corner and cross-examine her.

"Why did she leave so early?" said Rhya.

"She has gone home. Maybe it is for the best."

"I hope she knocks some sense into that husband of hers. People are beginning to chatter, I just know it."

Vikram closed his eyes and pretended to be snoozing, so Rhya, with a sigh, left him on his own on the balcony.

Grace loved India from the stories he told her. How he wished he could have brought her here. So many places he wished to show her, so many promises he could not keep. His body felt heavy, his head thumping. He closed his eyes to blot out the painful memories, to conjure up when they could walk freely hand in hand. In these moments he liked to think of what it could have been like for them both in India, walking hand in hand, the heat pulsing about them, the air heavy, her hand in his.

★

Grace's fingers were long and she liked it when he stroked her, like a child would a kitten.

"Can I bring you to Sikandra? It is quiet there and very beautiful. It is not far." He saw the tears wet her eyes and he brushed his hand gently on her cheek. "You will like Sikandra."

Sikandra, where deer and squirrels roamed freely in the grass. It was the Great Akbar's tomb. Vikram had visited this great monument and the tumbledown stone buildings, at the far corner of the compound, before travelling to Ireland.

She fluttered past him, bringing him back to the red sandstone buildings, the pavilions reflected in the water channels, the glistening marble. He felt his body relax. Before them was the front gate adorned in abstract patterns of white marble, with arches, pavilion towers and three-storey minarets. Two children pointed at the monkeys swinging from pavilion roof to pavilion roof, as if it was their private playground.

"Why don't we walk, follow the water channels, watch the squirrels. Maybe the deer are up close," he said softly, as he fell into step beside her. They paced up the steps together.

Observing Grace closely, he wished she would stay there, in the shadow of the Great Akbar's tomb in her turquoise pleated linen dress. When she heard his step, she turned, and he saw her face was soft and happy.

"Thank you for bringing me here," she said, and he did not answer, because he did not need to. They walked in silence, taking their time to peruse the little details in these cluttered buildings. He sometimes caught her hand, to show her something she had passed by. When she missed the bees' nests, ten of them hanging in the high point of one ornate arch, he told her to close her eyes and turn her face upwards.

"Now, open your eyes," he whispered.

Suddenly, becoming acutely aware of the low, consistent hum of the bees, she toppled back in fright. He had to steady her and hold her. He did not let go and she did not pull against him. They stood together watching the bees, unaware that the sweeper women who regularly brushed out the pavilions had stopped their work to watch.

Vikram could smell the sweetness of her perfume. He slipped his hands around her waist and she did not object. Slowly, he tipped her back on her feet, but she swung around to look him in the eye before he could release her. They were so close. He felt the softness of her lips as his glanced against hers.

"We should go," he said.

"You promised to show me the deer."

Vikram bowed and they walked on.

★

He must have nodded off. Rhya was beside him, shaking him furiously.

"The boy from the travel agent is here."Her voice was cross, but her face was soft.

Vikram shook himself awake. The boy handed him an envelope. Vikram nodded, pointing to the kitchen. "Go to the kitchen, get some water," he told him. The boy bowed in gratitude.

"Vikram, I beg you to reconsider. The boy can take back the tickets."

"Nonsense, woman, it is all arranged."

"It is not fair on Rosa either. And what about me?"

Vikram sat down at the table to open the envelope. "I have to do this, Rhya. Can't you even try to understand?"

She huffed loudly, marching off to the kitchen to shoo away the boy, who had begun talking loudly to one of the servants.

Seventeen

Parnell Square, Dublin, April 1984

Emma had been awake since before dawn. Her feet up on the couch in the first-floor drawing room, she had watched the light creep across the city. If her father had been here, he would have offered his advice in his deliberately slow manner, ready to stop if she indicated he should butt out. She was not sure, but, bleak as it looked here, to stay and start a new life in this city was probably her best option. But first she had to lay to rest the agitated past, by standing at the grave of Grace Moran and saying goodbye.

There was a lot of chat downstairs on the street, the words wafting upwards losing shape and form, broken by the time they reached her. How many times had she stood inside this window in her nightdress trying to listen as her father said goodbye to one of his friends in the dark of the night? If he later heard her scampering back to her bed as he made his way upstairs, he did not say anything

It was Violet's voice that sent shivers of fear through her.

One night she had woken up to hear Violet arguing loudly with her father.

"That young girl needs to be sent away to boarding school, to be among those from whom she can learn how to behave. That one will go wild, mark my words. Just like her mother and grandmother before her."

Her father's tone was low and firm, and while she could not make out the words, she knew he would defend her against Violet. He was not to know what fun she had roller skating along the square with the boy from the flats near Sean McDermott Street. They were seven and carefree. She heard Violet guffaw loudly, before banging the library door, sending vibrations shuddering through the house.

The next day, when Emma could not find her roller skates, Violet told her rolling along the streets like an urchin holding on to railings and frightening pedestrians was not the way to behave and she would not be seeing the skates again.

Emma had cried herself to sleep for three nights, but Violet told her to buck up, that she was lucky because her stupid father did not want to send her to boarding school.

"If I had my way, you would be somewhere where the nuns could knock sense into you, but the great judge sees things differently," she said, thumping her blackthorn stick loudly off the wooden floor.

When the doorbell rang, Emma jumped, but thinking it was children messing she ignored it until it rang again, making her run downstairs.

Andrew Kelly was standing there, an embarrassed look on his face.

"So sorry to disturb you, but a friend of Angie Hannon

rang me. She is worried about her. Would you by any chance have seen her in the last two days, or know where she is?"

"Did you call to the house?"

"Not a dicky bird. Did she say if she was going out of town?"

"No. She came around last week, doling out advice about men."

"Men? Angie?"

"Why?"

"There was only one man in Angie's life. Hang on, what date is it."

"April 18, 1984."

"I bet she has gone back to the old place." Andrew shook his head. "No doubt she gave you a lot of codswallop about being footloose and fancy-free."

"Something like that."

"The truth is Angie was once married and had a boy. He was about eight when he and his father died. Angie had a lovely house in Greystones, beside the sea. She left there and moved into the city. In her worst moments, she goes back there to sit. I bet we will find her there."

"Maybe she wants some privacy."

"Maybe she wants somebody to share the burden."

Emma sighed. "I wouldn't like to intrude on her grief. I don't know her very well."

"I would rather chance a cold shoulder than have her face old ghosts on her own. Come on, it is a nice drive."

Emma relented, running upstairs to get dressed while Andrew sat at the judge's desk in the library.

*

Angie Hannon was dressed up. She flattened her skirt with the palms of her hands and straightened the front frill on her blouse. Folding her arms over her chest, she slumped into the seat. The upholstery, roughed by dirt, scraped the back of her legs. A cool breeze from the open window pushed what was left of the net curtain in a whispering billow and she relaxed a little, the sweet smell of the wild young fennel in a front bed curling about her.

She sat in this cold empty shell of a house and remembered.

The two of them were so noisy getting ready for the boating trip, laughing together, making sausage sandwiches, stealing bottles of ginger ale from her hiding place under the sink. It was not a first trip, they did it every week, come hail or shine, and this day was spring-like and sunny.

When they were ready, they both came and kissed her and said to wait until they were out of the harbour to wave the red flag from the top window. She laughed at them, calling them her idiots, but she did not know if she said goodbye. She heard them on the shingle path, the boy skipping ahead, his father stopping to light a cigarette: the snap of his silver tobacco box before he smacked his lips in satisfaction around the cigarette, puffing out small clouds of smoke.

In the kitchen, she threw a teabag in a mug and poured in boiling water. She knew it would be a long time before she had to go upstairs to wave the flag. Her husband, Christopher, was a meticulous man who checked every last detail before they cast off from the small harbour. Stretching her feet under the table, she luxuriated in the quiet of the house, the dog outside digging a hole in the back garden, the cats lying out on a warm windowsill.

When she went upstairs, she tut-tutted that the boy had not made his bed like she had told him to and she would have to pretend to be cross about it later. The sea was blue-grey like the sky. She saw their boat, the sail high to catch the wind, zipping out of the harbour and making for the open seas.

She had her back turned to reach for the red flag when she heard a bang, muffled by the distance, absorbed by the weight of water. Freezing, as dread coasted through her, she turned back to the bay window. Where the boat had been, a ball of fire wheeled across the ocean, debris bobbing up. Ripples caused by the explosion surfed to the shore. Sirens sounded and people ran to look. She did not join them, she could not move, she did not need to know. The expectation, the life, the comfortable familiar had been whipped away, taken by the ball of fire that fought the waves and continued to burn. When they came banging at her door, she did not answer, so they had to come around the back, fighting off the dog and walking past the lazy cats to find her watching the sea, holding her flag, not knowing what to do, not caring what came next.

Angie still liked this sitting room and the kitchen: they were all in the before. But upstairs was tainted by the after, as was the wide view of the harbour and the sea, which only days later yielded up parts of their torn bodies. She trudged up the steps past the boy's room, where the door had been closed many years ago, and into the big bedroom with the wrap-around bay windows, where the sea rolled into the room, taunting her, causing an explosion in her head. She felt her chest tighten and the tears push up in her eyes. Defiantly, she picked the red flag from the bed and opened the window, wedging the rod of the flag so that it did not fall but was held aloft, signalling to the ghosts that she knew they were there and she loved them, still loved them insanely.

"Always wave it, Mam. I know you are there when you put it out the window."

She could not look across the wide sea, so instead looked down the hill to where the town went about its business, unaware that another year had passed, making it a decade since her life and their lives had been blown apart.

It didn't matter that the wrong boat had been blown up by the IRA. How could an apology and an explanation bring back their lives, bring back the life settled and happy with her family. She told those who tried to apologise to go to hell, and she meant it.

When she saw the car pull up at the bottom of the driveway, she smiled. It was a lovely late spring day, and even in this dejected state, the house looked well.

The only visitors, if you could call them that, were on sunny holidays, when couples in big cars drove out from the city and saw the dilapidated house on the hill, a beacon in the sunshine. If she was here, she never opened the door but retired upstairs, watching them from behind the heavy brocade curtains in the spare bedroom. She would sit and fan herself cool as they strolled along the driveway, once gravelled and wide, now narrow and blanketed in moss and grass, calling out to each other, building dreams, silly vagaries, in the heat. Often she had to rap on the window and point a finger, to let them know they should not attempt to cross the threshold.

When she saw Andrew and Emma, she wasn't pleased and neither was she displeased. Emma's light jacket caught by the briars, ripping a thread, the fuchsia pressing in on her, trepidation on her face as Andrew led the way to the front door. Angie could let them knock and look through the letter box like everybody else, but she didn't.

Opening the top window, she called out to them. "Go around to the side and push the wooden door. You can come in the back."

"Are you all right, Angie?" Andrew asked.

"What do you think?"

They disappeared out of view. She sat quietly, waiting.

She wished she could blame the sea than have to always address in her mind the type of person who had watched and celebrated as the waves played with the ball of fire, before it dawned on them that the British ambassador had moved his yacht to Dún Laoghaire three weeks before.

Andrew shouted up the stairs. "Angie, will we come up?"

"Sit in the sitting room. I will be down in a minute."

Andrew and Emma walked to the front sitting room, a wide room with high ceilings that was permanently in the shade, because the rose bush had climbed over the window and obscured the glass. The only daylight came from a side window that overlooked the front door, the light pooling in a little group of armchairs that looked as if they had been gathered there for that reason. Andrew gestured to Emma to sit down and they did, gingerly. The chairs smelled of damp. Cold had crept into the emptiness of the room, curled now around their ankles, across their shoulders, making them shiver on this warm spring day. Shafts of light danced on layers of dust and mouse droppings. The damp smell of a house left undisturbed through too many sunny summer days invaded their nostrils.

"You found me out." Angie stepped into the room, looking overdressed for her surroundings.

"We thought there might be something wrong," Andrew said, getting up to give Angie a hug.

"Is there ever anything right? Come on, the kitchen is brighter," she said, turning on her heel.

In the kitchen, she reached into a cupboard and took out a bottle of whiskey. "The only thing that does not go off. Damp can't penetrate the taste of a good whiskey." She washed three glasses and placed them on the table. "I come here every now and again and drink to my boys." She stopped midway through pouring and turned to Andrew. "I take it you told Emma."

Emma leaned forward to rub Angie on the arm. "I was very sorry to hear it. I had no idea."

"My boy would be almost a man now, and me and my husband would be an old couple, maybe not even on talking terms. Life has a way of messing everything up." She handed out the glasses. "To life and the memories of those we have lost."

All three sipped their drinks.

"Don't be so polite. I am not going to get drunk. Maudlin, maybe, but not drunk."

"It is such a lovely house," Emma said, anxious in case the mood dipped.

"And a constant reminder of what I lost. And yet I can't get rid of it." Angie slumped down on the big chair at the end of the wooden table. "I am a sad case, hiding out in the city, pretending to be this eccentric broad when really I am a woman ground down by grief, with no idea of what to do next."

Andrew got up and went to the window. "You would get a grand price for this place. Angie, you need to let it go."

Angie knocked back the remainder of her whiskey in a fast gulp. "I as good as buried two empty boxes. There was little left of my boys. While I have this house, I can, when I want to, pretend there is a possibility they might come back, there might be the chatter, the laughter again, days so ordinary I thought they were boring. What I wouldn't give for an hour from one of those days now. If I sell up, I am abandoning those dreams. They are all that keep me alive."

The three in the kitchen were quiet. Outside, they heard a man call to his dog. A child screeched in frustration he could not have a lollipop. A wagtail landed on the kitchen sill, poking at the cracked paint before suddenly twitching into the air and flying off.

"I can pick up Timmy's toys and lie in his bed. I get the smell of him still. With my finger I can trace where he wrote his name on the wall, where he thought I would not see it. I can lean back in Christopher's leather chair and hear his soft voice in my ears. I can feel him take my hand and kiss it, like he used to sometimes, when I passed him by. I can't get any of that at the graveyard."

Emma took one of her hands. "We understand."

"I can't live here, yet I can't let it go. My life stopped here and yet it is where I can find some part of it. I am in limbo, set down forever. This place is where I am in turmoil yet can also be at peace."

Andrew mooched to the window. "You could cut back the garden. It is taking over."

"Don't worry, Andrew, I am not going to ask you to do it."

He laughed. "Once a city lad, always a city lad. Cutting grass is not my thing."

"I love the city. I hide under its anonymous cloak."

"You are hiding wherever you are, Angie."

"You can always depend on Andrew to say it as it is," Angie said to Emma.

"A spade is a spade and I don't mind saying it. Angie, it has been ten years."

At first Angie did not answer. She got slowly up from the table to the dresser and rummaged. Pulling out a framed photograph, she propped it up in the middle of the table. "Look, that is what I had: a husband and a son, happy out. Don't tell me to move on like you would tell a child snivelling after being caught pinching flowers from the neighbour's front garden."

"Christ, I didn't mean to insult you. I was only trying to help."

Emma examined the picture: Angie, her hair flowing down her back, her husband wearing a ridiculous canvas sun hat, a boy, maybe near eight, between them, squinting into the camera, leaning into his mother, a hand holding on to his dad's trousers.

"Taken two weeks before. Mr Garry down the road was trying out a new camera. It took him a year before he had the courage to show it to me. He framed it up lovely, but I keep it in the drawer. It hurts too much to look at our faces, to see such innocent happiness reflected back at me. How is it we only know what happiness is when it has marched on?"

Andrew wandered outside and Angie followed. Emma stayed in the kitchen, where the clock did not tick and the fridge sat unplugged, its door propped open so mould did not take hold. On the walls, still, a child's drawings, faded, the writing in some places obliterated by time. In the far corner a hurley stick and sliotar thrown to the side, as if the boy had thought of something better to do but could be back any minute to swipe them away and start pucking the ball.

Outside, she heard the muffled tones of the two friends and she saw them embrace.

Angie stuck her head in the door. "What are you doing hiding out in the kitchen? We thought we will have a nice lunch together before I bring you both back to Parnell Square." Angie swept past her as Emma pushed her chair out from the table. "I will follow you out to the car, I will just say goodbye to the ghosts and lock up the house."

She pounded upstairs before Emma had time to answer.

"We will give her a few minutes. Wait in the car," Andrew said and they pushed their way down the shingle path, the briars whipping at their legs, the bindweed trying to trip them up. They were quiet in the car on the way back. As Andrew dropped them off at Parnell Square, he declined an invitation to tea. Angie dithered but then decided one cuppa would not hurt.

They sat in the first-floor drawing room sipping their tea, for a while lost in thought. Angie was the first to break the companionable silence between them.

"I suppose you think I am a bit mad, hanging on to things."

"Nobody knows how they will cope with loss."

"I feel myself it might be time to move on, but maybe I don't know how."

Emma caught her hand. "I am sure if the right person comes along you won't even have to think about it. It will just feel right.

"I hope you are correct," Angie answered, putting her teacup carefully down on the saucer. As she got up from the couch, she leaned over and kissed Emma on the head. "Thank you to you and Andrew for making this day easier," she said, before making for the door.

Eighteen

Our Lady's Asylum, Knockavanagh, March 1955

Grace buttoned up her cardigan to shut out the cold draught from under the window. Outside, a family were walking up the driveway, one girl, one boy skipping ahead, stopping only when their mother called out to them. The melody of the children's chatter weaved its way to the second floor, luring the women on the ward to crowd at the windows.

They gathered and watched, the little girl bending low to pick up a small stone. Nobody said anything out loud, but each of the women nursed a sense of loss in their hearts, a deep longing for a life not lived.

An attendant barked at the group to get away from the window, before stopping herself to glance at the family walking towards reception. "Making a holy show of yourselves, standing watching those innocent creatures."

"Are they coming up or will I go down?" Bertha asked

"What would they be doing visiting anyone on this ward? Never you mind what they are up to." She held her hands wide to cover the span of the window. "Sure, it is like trying to herd sheep," she laughed.

Grace picked the chair at the end of the corridor, where she could view the far fields, shining green after two full days of sunshine following a long spell of rain.

Vikram had gone back to India and she did not blame him. How could he have found her here? She did not even know the address of the place herself until Mandy had told her. How could he come back? Did he know about her tragedy? A dull pain creaked through her body, making her bend over so nobody would see the tears plop down her face.

"Whoever put us in here has a lot to answer for." Mandy was standing looking at Grace.

"It is my fault, every bit of it."

"Never ever think that. Otherwise you will end up here forever." She gripped Grace's shoulder, shaking her hard. "My girl is five now." Mandy outlined the figure of a girl in the condensation on the window glass. "I wish I could buy her a dress with flowers so pretty the butterflies will queue up to land on her. We will run by the sea and paddle and laugh."

"Wouldn't it still be too cold to get in?"

"I didn't think of that." Mandy, upset that a flaw in her plans had been highlighted, drifted up the ward to the nurses' station to tell the nice nurse from Aughrim about her daughter.

Grace could not get Violet out of her head, and the marriage of convenience she had so quickly engineered and executed for her. The justification she had grandly put forward was that Grace's mother had behaved in such a way that no right-thinking man would look at the daughter. Grace knew well what her mother had done: Violet had told her often enough.

"Your mother ran off with a Pakistani and then had the

audacity to come back and marry your father when she knew she was already pregnant. How you were not born dark, I will never know. All I know is it was a mercy. Things could have stayed that way but for your mother taking up with that oily Pakistani again. Once that happened, nothing could stop our family catapulting into a shameful tragedy, which unfortunately became everybody's business."

Grace was weary of being reminded of the night her life changed utterly. She had been four years of age. When she fell asleep in their small red-brick terrace house in the Liberties, her mother was getting ready for a friend to come over while her husband worked the night shift at the Guinness brewery. Grace heard nothing. She was gently woken up by a Garda in the middle of the night. Her head covered, she was transferred to a patrol car and brought to Aunt Violet's. It was several days before she was told a version of the truth: both her mother and father were dead. It was many years before she knew the full story.

"Your mother brought untold shame on all of us by continuing to carry on with that Pakistani who ran the shop off Meath Street. Your poor father was sent home early from work because he was feeling poorly and he walked in on them. The man snapped. He had had enough, and who could blame him?"

Violet held back nothing.

"Your mother had reignited the affair. Your poor father should never have taken her back in the first place. That was his fatal mistake. Unfortunately, Bert stabbed Aileen and the shopkeeper. The Pakistani managed to make it out onto the road for help, but by the time anybody was brave enough to look inside the house your mother was dead and your father had stabbed himself in the heart and was dying. You slept through it all."

Grace remembered everybody was busy at Violet's, huddling and whispering, and it remained that way until after the funerals. Violet, whose husband had died in a freak accident a year before, when he slipped and fell in the canal, was glad of the company. But as the years went by, Violet worried about the future of the young girl with such a troubled history.

She got her niece a job in Clerys department store serving at the jewellery counter. Grace wore smart dresses and began to talk about training to be a secretary. When Violet suggested it might be time to settle down, Grace laughed and asked if she was serious.

"Why would I bring up the subject if I was not deadly serious? To be frank, it is necessary that you start paying your way, young woman. My George left me with a very small amount of money and it is nearly all gone."

"We could sell the house and move to something smaller."

Violet snorted loudly again. "You would not ask me to leave my home, would you?"

Grace did not say anything, so Violet continued.

"I had a visit from Martin Moran, an eminent senior counsel who expects to be appointed as a judge of the High Court before this government goes out of power. He must get married. If he is to progress in his legal career, he needs a wife. I suggested you. Thankfully you have your mother's good looks and that is sufficient for Martin Moran to consider you. You also have good enough manners, which I have vouched for."

"I surely have a say in this."

Violet, who always had her walking stick by her side, swished it high to emphasise her point. "My dear, it is simply business.

If we have to carry on another month, we will go under. Martin says after the marriage I can live at his house in Parnell Square and can rent out this old house, so I may have some income. He is a kind, good man with excellent prospects, and quite willing to overlook your past. I can't see you doing better. You won't have to work another day in your life."

"I am not taking part in this charade. You can't make me."

Violet pulled herself up to standing. "Girl, you owe me. Do you think I wanted to take you in, that I wanted a brat around my house, to feed and educate you? It is payback time and I need you to do this."

"You are asking me to marry a man I have not even met."

"You are overreacting. I am asking you to marry a perfectly nice and wealthy man who is about to become a judge."

"I am not doing it."

Violet sat down. "I suppose you are going to give me some nonsense about love and all that."

Grace walked out of the room before Violet could say more, but her aunt followed her.

"I am the only family you have got. This is as good as it gets and you will take this offer," she shouted after her as Grace rushed upstairs, too angry to even cry.

After about an hour, she heard Violet's step on the stairs. She knocked lightly on the door before walking in. "Grace, I am doing this for your own good. Surely you know all marriages end up being marriages of convenience. The only difference for you is that it will be that from the start and you will have financial security for life. It is a good thing I am doing."

"You are asking me to marry a man I don't even know."

"You can get to know him. He is coming for Sunday lunch and I expect you to show off your impeccable manners."

The next day Violet had the Clerys ladies' fashions department send out a selection of dresses. She picked a gold colour, a smart dress with a full skirt, a bodice leading to a Peter Pan collar where a small ribbon was tied in a bow. She told Grace to wear a white cardigan with the sleeveless dress. Violet said it was sophisticated-looking.

Martin Moran arrived promptly at one and shook hands politely. Grace noticed his height and how straight he sat at the table, his long slim fingers and his gentle voice. When he asked if she cared to go for a walk by the canal, she agreed.

"You know why I am here?" he asked as they were walking.

"I know Aunt Violet has a plan for me."

"Is that such a bad thing? She has looked after you all your life."

Grace did not answer.

"I could give you a good life. You would never want for anything and I would not ask anything else of you, only to be my wife."

"I have a job I like."

"You would never have to work again, Grace. I earn more than enough."

"But I don't love you. I don't even know you."

"Love complicates everything. If we can have respect for each other, it will do for starters."

"I need time to think about it."

He picked up a stone and skimmed it across the glassy water in the canal.

"You know, it is also a financial arrangement that your Aunt Violet badly needs, so I would advise you not to take too long."

They walked back along the canal path, neither feeling the need to have any further conversation.

Mandy came over and tapped her on the shoulder, so that Grace jumped.

"You are far away. Nurse Gilmartin says she might be able to arrange for us to stroll in the gardens tomorrow."

"It would be nice to get some fresh air."

"I told her if there is any work that needs doing, we will do it. What were you dreaming about? Your young man?"

Grace did not answer and Mandy prattled on.

"Best to remember the good things only. It makes the here and now better."

Grace walked over to the window. "Had you a name for your girl?"

Mandy turned away. "They made sure she was taken from me the minute she was born. I only heard her cry. I will never forget that cry."

Grace made to put a hand on her shoulders, but Mandy shrugged her away.

"We had better get in the queue for the dining hall," she snapped.

Bertha ran over, her face full of excitement. "My Barry has come and brought the girls. I can go home today. Look, I am wearing my best dress." She twirled in front of them in her faded nightgown, a pink cardigan buttoned over it. On her face she had patted some powder and she had slicked lipstick across her lips. "Don't I look nice?"

"You look lovely," Grace said.

"Mad as a hatter, that one. She is lucky," Mandy mumbled, and Grace nodded in agreement.

Nineteen

Bangalore, India, April 1984

Rhya had only just got up the next morning when Rosa arrived.

"What time did you leave home to get here so early? Vik is still dozing."

"I couldn't sleep, so I got my man to drive me."

"What is wrong, girl? No marriage is without its difficulties, you know."

"Has Uncle told you?"

Rhya, who was sorting through the post, stopped. "Told me what?" She saw a hint of tears in Rosa's eyes and went to her. "What can you tell Vikram that you cannot tell me?"

"Mama, I don't want to talk about it."

Rhya drew her to the sofa. "Do you think I can leave it like that? What has this husband of yours done?"

"I think he is going to dump me."

Rhya straightened in her seat. "He can't and won't do that. You must tell me everything."

Rosa shook her head. "I am here to see Uncle. We leave in

four days and there is a lot to discuss. Mama, I don't want to talk about it to you. I may not be able to go away."

"What has happened?"

Rosa shook her head.

"How can I help if I don't know what we are dealing with?"

Rosa jumped up. "Anil is off every night partying with other women."

"What sort of women?"

Rosa made to find Vikram. "The sort of women who don't mind being seen out with a married man."

Rhya threw her hands in the air. "Come back here and talk to me, girl."

"Mama, I am finding this so difficult."

"And you don't think I do? This has the potential to pile a heap of shame at our door. You listen, Rosa, it is not easy when a wife is constantly leaving the house. Maybe if you give him more attention . . ."

Rosa slumped down in a chair. "I doubt he is jealous of Uncle."

When Vikram walked into the living room, he felt the tension straight way.

"Uncle, I want to hear more about Grace. I have packed already."

"Four days we have until we leave for Delhi and you have packed," he laughed, trying to avoid eye contact with Rhya, who had a scowl on her face.

Rosa caught her uncle by the arm, intending to go to the balcony, but Rhya stood in her way.

"She is not telling you she may not be able to travel because of this stupid husband of hers. You have to do something about this Anil, Vik."

Vikram pulled away from Rosa. "I don't think I can make this journey without you, Rosa. When were you going to tell me? Everything is booked: flights, hotels . . . Everything is finalised. The boy brought the envelope around. We can't go back on it now."

"Mama, you had no right to say anything. I am going, I was just upset Anil is being so . . ."

She started to cry and both Vikram and Rhya made to comfort her.

"Why do we have to concentrate on it so? I come here for a break from all this trouble. Please, Uncle, I want to hear more of Grace."

Vikram indicated to Rhya to leave them to it and, though upset, she retreated to the kitchen to give out to the servant for not filling the filter jug to the brim. The servant smiled. She knew Rhya was snapping because she was angry at her daughter; she should not take it out on her. Rhya, feeling cross, retired to her room to rummage through her saris and calm down.

On the balcony, Vikram let Rosa catch her breath before he started his story. Her eyes were still wet with tears and every now and again a shudder ran through her, but he continued in the hope of distracting her.

"Things moved quickly between myself and Grace. I knew after the Shelbourne tea that she was such a lovely girl, but so troubled.

"On the Saturday morning, I was on O'Connell Street and found myself walking towards Parnell Square. I knew I would meet her and, sure enough, she was at the front door. She had just seen the judge off for a weekend legal think-in, somewhere or other."

*

"What luck your good friend Violet is away as well," she said, pulling him in the door.

In the basement kitchen she took out a stool from under the table and climbed up to the top shelf of the dresser, taking down a McVitie's biscuit tin. Prising open the lid slowly, the smell of rich fruit cake laced with poitín slipped through the room.

"Just one slice or we will be drunk and Violet will know we have been mooching around. Aunt Violet is more than a match for your battleaxe landlady."

"Surely, never that bad."

"Do you miss home?"

"Every day."

"I can't imagine why you would want to be in Ireland. Life here must be so dull in comparison."

Vikram laughed. "It is certainly different."

"Do you mind if I ask a personal question?"

"Go ahead."

"Will you have an arranged marriage?"

"Always the same question in this country, I notice. If my mother has her way. A doctor is a good catch."

"A judge was a good catch too."

"You are happy, Grace?"

She got up, twirling with her hands outstretched across the kitchen. "Look, Vikram, I wear the finest clothes, live in this wonderful house. I have not been on a bus in a whole year; I take taxis everywhere. I should be happy. I am married to a judge."

He did not know why, but he bowed and asked her would

she like to dance. "I am not very good at waltzing, but I would love to dance with you."

She took his hand and they glided for a few seconds in the same direction before he stumbled across her toe.

"We will have to practise more, Dr Fernandes."

He could smell the perfume on her neck, feel the softness of her hair against his cheek. He reached over and kissed her.

She did not pull back but responded, leaning in to him. He held her close, until she pulled away.

"You want to know why I married the judge, don't you?"

"Only if you want to tell me."

"I had no choice. My mother and father died when I was young. I was taken in by Aunt Violet. She gave me a roof over my head, but when I reached eighteen she said I should marry a man with money. Conveniently, she knew such a man. Martin is much older than me and has always been kind, but I don't love him and he certainly does not love me." She stopped suddenly. "I don't want your pity, Dr Fernandes. I am just giving you the information."

"I am sorry, but it is not pity." He took her hand and kissed it and he saw the smile come back into her eyes.

"Let's get away from here. I have heard there is a newfangled passport machine at Heuston Station. Wouldn't it be fun to go there?"

"But we must go by bus, Grace."

She clapped her hands in delight and ran off to get her coat. He waited at the top of the front steps for her. A few people who passed by looked oddly at him and a Garda on the beat shot him a suspicious look. When Grace came out the front door, the Garda approached.

"Is this gentleman with you, Mrs Moran?"

"Yes, is there a problem?"

"No, ma'am, just doing my job. May I speak to you in private?" He stepped into the hallway and made sure the door closed behind him. "I wanted to ask you if you are all right. Do you know this character? Does the judge know him?"

"That fellow, as you call him, is Dr Vikram Fernandes. I am astounded, Garda O'Mahony, at your attitude."

The Garda reddened around his collar and began to stammer. "I was only doing my job. You can't be too careful."

"Of foreign men. I get your message, and yes, my husband has met Dr Fernandes and even had him here at his drinks party recently. Will that be all?"

The Garda mumbled something she thought was an apology and opened the door. Grace swished out, her perfume curling after her. Snapping her handbag shut, she walked down the road, the large pleat of her swing coat swishing from side to side, highlighting her indignation. Vikram followed two steps behind as they moved towards O'Connell Street.

"Quick, there's the bus that passes Heuston. Hurry," Vikram shouted, racing past her towards the bus stop. The bus was pulling away when Vikram jumped on the back, swinging on the bar and pushing his hand back to pull up Grace, who was giggling uncontrollably.

"I hope after that spectacle you are going to pay a fare. One of these days somebody is going to get killed pulling one of those stunts," the bus conductor said as he clinked his bag of money and prepared his ticket machine.

Vikram paid the fare and they went upstairs as the bus throttled down the quays and the stench of the Liffey bit into their nostrils.

*

"Rosa, my voice is going. We had such fun there. Afterwards, we knew I would stay the night, and I did, in the judge's house. From then on, I cared about nothing else, only Grace. She was my soulmate in every way. What can I say? I loved her completely and I know she loved me. Would you like to see a picture of her? Reach into my desk and I will instruct you."

The photograph he had hidden in a small silver box so long ago because he could not bear to see her face. Now, he knew he wanted to look in her eyes. The box was under a pile of envelopes. Carefully, Rosa took it out and studied the woman's fine features, her wide smile, the sparkling eyes.

"It was taken on the most perfect weekend. We were so happy. We did not know what was to come."

Rosa made to say something, but he hushed her.

"We felt free, silly and happy, a good way to be. I doubt if either of us felt that way again. We spent the rest of the weekend together, happy in the moment. We had such fun together. Now I only have the precious memory and that photo-booth picture to remind me of blissful days. Looking back on it now, I am so glad of that day. So often we can spoil the good things of the present with worries about either the past or the future."

"You look so happy."

"We were, but that was a long time ago." Vikram let the tears splash down his face. "Everything got serious from then on. Tomorrow, I will tell you."

"Thank you for not cross-examining me, Uncle."

"The day may come when I will have to deal with this Anil."

"For now, I think I can handle it," she said, and bent down

to kiss Vikram on the cheek. She got up and left the apartment quickly, before Rhya had time to demand conversation.

For his part, Vikram disappeared into his room, so that he would not get caught up in useless and excessive mulling over of the possible troubles in Rosa's marriage with her mother.

On days like today, he liked to think of the good times with Grace. It gave him the strength. She was in front of him now, frisking down the street, telling him to hurry or they would be late for Sybil Connolly.

★

"You hardly need me there when you are trying on a dress you will only wear for your husband."

She laughed because he sounded cranky, his cheeks swelling in the upset of feeling sorry for himself.

"You silly man, I could wear a sackcloth and that man would not notice. I value your opinion. I can't even bear spending an hour in Miss Connolly's fitting room without you."

"I am not sure Miss Connolly will approve of you bringing a gentleman friend to a fitting."

"What if she doesn't? She will never dare say it. I want you to see me in this gown: it will be the most exquisite thing I own."

He could not refuse her, her eyes shining, her look defiant. She giggled, pulling him by the hand towards Grafton Street. Hastily, he snatched back his hand.

"What if the judge or somebody you know sees us?"

"You worry too much. The judge is either in chambers or at home in his library with his head stuck in a law text."

Vikram, though worried, was in awe of her fighting words.

Sybil Connolly greeted him with a nod. He sat tapping a tune out on his knee with his fingers while Grace was taken away to try on the dress. After about half an hour, she burst through from the dressing room, a swirl of gold pleated linen. Spinning in front of him, she laughed like a child on a merry-go-round until she slumped awkwardly against him, her head reeling.

When he put his arms around her, he felt the softness of the linen pushed and kept into place by bunches of taffeta underneath. The bodice, covered in thick lace, ran down to the waist, where a myriad of tiny pleats fell to the ground. The gold-bronze of the dress accentuated the hazel flecks in her eyes and he felt tears well inside him that she could be so lovely.

She stood and walked slowly across the room as if it were her catwalk, the rustle of the taffeta complemented by the soft sweep of the linen. Suddenly she stopped, swinging around.

"You don't like it."

He put his hands out to her and she took them. "I have no words for how beautiful you look, because you take my breath away."

"But do you think it suits me?" Her head to one side, she looked like a doll twisted into a funny shape.

"What greater compliment can I give, Grace? I am left watching this vision in gold and words strangle in my throat because all are inadequate."

She placed her hand on his shoulder and kissed him lightly on the cheek. "I think I love you, Dr Vikram Fernandes."

He did not move, a swirl of emotion racing through him. When he looked up at her again, she was smiling and he smiled back.

"I know I love you, Grace Moran."

They stood, too afraid to touch, too afraid to kiss, even too fearful to talk.

Miss Connolly's assistant came to the door, stopping for a moment to take in the room before stepping inside.

"The dress will be ready for tomorrow morning. Is that all right?" She hesitated, looking slightly away, when she saw they were holding hands.

Grace pulled away quickly, knocking Vikram momentarily off balance. He watched her and he knew he loved her beyond anything. He looked at her again, her head down, her long hair tumbling down the lace bodice. She was busy discussing whether the pleats should stick out so far, so preoccupied that she did not notice him slip away further and further, until she was, to him, a slick of gold against the black.

Twenty

Parnell Square, Dublin, April 1984

Andrew Kelly drove out to the sea at Sandymount. He needed to walk, so he could think. The wind buffeting in from the Irish Sea shoved him sideways, but he pushed on with a steely determination. He had a decision to make and not even the gale-force wind was going to stop his journey to that destination.

Rain sheeted across the strand, but he ignored it, too busy fussing in his head, worrying about her reaction. Why he hadn't told her when she came for lunch? He did not know. He could not tell her in the car either, as Angie had been there and he did not want a three-way discussion.

Digging his hands into his pockets, Andrew paced back towards his car, stopping to lean on the strand wall. A woman hunched against the rain and wind, pulling her dog along with her, looked oddly at him. Further down, she stopped and retraced her steps, peering closely before enquiring if he was all right. Embarrassed, Andrew did not answer but scuttled back to his car.

Worse not to tell Emma, he thought, turning to the city centre, water from his wet clothes pooling at his feet.

When he pounded on the front door, Emma was in the library. He stood soaking wet, shivering. She did not know what to say.

"Can I come in? I apologise, but what I have to tell you has to be done in person."

She pulled back the door. "You could still have phoned, Andrew."

"I have important information about your mother."

"What do you mean important? Let me get you a towel."

She saw Andrew's face change as she put out a hand to guide him onto the landing and into the drawing room.

"Sit down, Emma."

"It is bad, isn't it?"

"Your father told me a little of your mother. He asked me to keep it confidential. I did, but now I feel in my heart it is something you should know about. I also feel that to tell you is not exactly breaking the confidence." He paused, as if he was trying to carefully pick his words.

"Please, Andrew, what is it?"

"Grace didn't die at the time of your birth but was committed to an asylum. It was all hush-hush. Seemingly your father was devastated, a broken man as a result."

"My father would not do such a thing. This can't be true."

Andrew shifted uncomfortably, not wanting to sit down for fear of staining the furniture with his wet clothes. "It tortured him all his life, from what I could see. He told me the poor thing was not well at all. He acted on the best medical advice." He cleared his throat. "Her spell in the asylum seemingly did not work very well for Grace. It all took longer than anyone intended at the start. He said she died there."

Andrew stopped and walked to the window.

"Emma, you have to look at this from Martin's point of view. All the doctors said she needed it and Aunt Violet was more than insistent, so he put her in the asylum. He said afterwards that it was a decision he would regret past his dying day, but, at the time, it seemed the only thing to do. It was heartbreaking."

Emma sank deeper into the chair. "He loved her so much he put her in an asylum."

The silence of the room closed in around her, gripping at her throat, so she felt as if she may choke. She noticed Andrew's trousers were wet up to his knees. On the mantelpiece, she saw the wedding photograph of Grace and Martin. She wanted to fling it out the window, to hear it shattering on the city street below.

"Emma, are you all right?"

Andrew's voice was far away, stabbing through the fog enclosing her. She wanted to speak, but she could not. She felt him place her feet on a chair, put a pillow under her head. He fretted over her.

"Emma, are you all right?"

She looked into his anxious face. "Tell me everything, please."

"Emma, I don't know what happened. It was clear it had all so devastated Martin. It was the past, a painful one, and I left it there."

Emma put her hand up to stop Andrew placing a rug around her. Pushing her head into her hands, she dragged her palms down the length of her face. "What do we do next?"

"We find out what happened: that is what we do. I will be right there with you, don't you worry."

"Why was she committed? Why did he do that?"

"I don't know, Emma. I had to tell you. It is your right to know the truth. Who knows what Martin had to deal with?"

Emma sat quietly, the pain of not knowing seeping through her, tightening across her heart. The next step: did she want to take it?

She did not even know Andrew was still in the room and, realising that, she turned to face him directly. "Do you think you can help me find out what happened to Grace? I can't decide to stay or leave until I know."

Reaching across, Andrew picked up her hand and rubbed it gently. "The first thing we should do is go to Knockavanagh, Wicklow. There was an asylum there and your father mentioned your mother was buried in the county. It makes sense to make it our jump-off point."

"Isn't there a central place to get a death certificate?"

"We don't have a date and sometimes the local area will give us more information. It is just a hunch, I am not saying it will turn up anything. Knockavanagh in Wicklow was the nearest and the best asylum at the time."

"Does it matter if an asylum is good or bad? It is still an asylum."

Andrew hugged her gently. "We won't know anything until we go there. I should go now and let you take this in, but let's head out there whenever you are ready."

Emma waited until she was sure he had left before she padded downstairs to her father's study.

The law books were gone. Maybe she had been silly to think she could throw out what was precious to the judge and, in the process, banish him from her life. The physical reminders of him were gone, but the questions remained, as well as threats of secrets so bad that maybe they were best left uncovered. Why after her birth had there been a need to commit Grace to an asylum? How long was she there, unaware that a daughter had loved her and missed her all these years?

Was that why the judge could barely utter Grace's name, why he had had every memory of her mother cleared to the attic? Was that why he was so impatient, distant and dour as she grew up?

Fidgeting, she picked up Grace's case from the floor, making room for it on the desk. She did not know why, but she felt compelled to repack it, as if it had been some desecration to take out the personal items, so carefully chosen.

She folded the cardigans, wound up small the narrow belts, stuffed in the silk slippers with the tight balls of silk stockings and the shoes. Looking for a space to secure the boxes of talc, which she was unable to squeeze back into the gift set, she pulled out the elasticated pouches at the case's sides. As she stuffed in the box of talc, an envelope squeezed out the bottom, crumpled from its hiding place. Light blue in colour and addressed to Vikram Fernandes, Emma recognised the flourish of Grace's handwriting.

Quickly, she snipped it open with a pen from the top drawer.

March 23, 1954

My Dearest Vik,

I wish we could go back to the happy days when it was us and our lovely plans for a life together.

It has all come to nothing. I have failed you. I know that.

I know your heart is breaking many times over. I have brought such terrible times on you and I am truly sorry. Aunt Violet has relished telling me all the lies uttered against you and I believe none of them. You were cursed the day you met me and I was so blessed. I cherish, no matter what happens next, the seconds, minutes, hours and days we spent together. I love you so completely.

They say at the end you should regret the right things. I regret the pain I have caused you, what you have had to suffer, the awful lies told about you. I regret that my belief and trust in you did not manifest itself earlier and let me run away with you, away from here, from this place. I should have been brave, Vikram.

That is my one regret.

Know that I love you. If you have gone back to India, I understand. I hope some day you will learn to forgive my cowardice and that some day you will look for me and I will welcome you. I know you will if you can.

Know I love you: that is a constant, though all about me is change. Find me, Vik, that we may be together in India.

Your Grace

Written in purple ink, the script appeared hurried. The envelope was addressed but the letter never posted.

Emma stood in the vacant and empty room, not knowing what to do. Her hands were shaking, her stomach sick. She wanted to throw up, but nothing came. She wanted to cry, but the anger inside her, the sadness, made her stay in that one place beside his desk and his empty shelves.

She had to stand at Grace's grave. Otherwise, Emma knew she would be left with one terrible regret.

Twenty-One

Our Lady's Asylum, Knockavanagh, July 1955

Mandy slipped out of her shoes and pulled off her socks before the attendants saw her.

"Feel the grass between your toes."

Grace looked around to make sure nobody could see her and did the same.

"It tickles and it is damp," Mandy whispered.

"Do you think if we run, they will panic?"

"Are you mad? Walk slowly, let's trudge, and they won't know the difference."

"Why are we even doing this?"

Mandy lifted up her skirt, like she had just walked into the sea. "Because we can. There is so much, girl, we can't do. We might as well get any snip of pleasure we can."

Bertha was standing at the central flowerbed. "My husband is visiting on Friday," she mumbled, yanking the tight pink rose blooms and tapping the spent flowers so that the petals scattered across the ground.

The caretaker rushed over. "Missus, can you just stop doing that? You are making more work for me."

Bertha looked at him. "My Barry buys the biggest bunch of flowers."

"Don't be touching the roses, please."

"They are my flowers and I will touch them if I want." Bertha took a swipe at the rose bush nearest and a flurry of rose petals dropped away. The caretaker shouted, making the attendant scoot over.

"She can't be doing that. I don't know what ye are doing bringing this lot out here. It is a recipe for disaster. The man is coming in to cut the grass, so ye better move back inside."

Bertha reached over and snapped a rose at its stem. The caretaker shouted louder this time, making the gateman bolt down.

"We had better get these in, before they cause any more trouble," a nurse said. One of the attendants walked slowly in circles, her arms out, herding the women like they were sheep in a field. When Bertha refused to move, the caretaker and gateman grabbed an arm each, half pulling and half carrying her.

Mandy and Grace quickly stepped into their shoes and stuffed their socks in their pockets. "Pity the old bag had to make a scene, otherwise we could have stayed for longer," Mandy sniped as they were told to hurry towards the door.

Back on the ward, Grace sat by the window. From here, the rose petals looked like small dots on the green grass. Vikram had promised to sow grass seeds for her at their home in India: "I will order the servants to water three times a day, so you can feast your eyes on green grass."

Closing her eyes, she tried to make out in her head how it could have been different.

When she had come downstairs to the drawing room that morning, the judge was sitting bolt upright on the couch, his arms folded across his chest. Aunt Violet was perched beside him, leaning over her walking stick.

"Aunt Violet has told me. Is it true, Grace?"

Hardly able to answer, she pulled her silk dressing gown around her and sat in the armchair near the fireplace. "I was hoping to talk to you on your own, Martin."

Violet, snorting loudly, raised her stick. "You are still my responsibility, young lady. I am here to ensure that no more shame is heaped on our family."

Martin stood up and leaned an elbow on the mantelpiece. "I appreciate your concern, Aunt Violet, but I would like to talk to my wife on her own."

He stood and waited for Violet to excuse herself from the room, which she did, huffing and puffing and sighing deeply, knocking her walking stick loudly on the wooden floor. Martin Moran waited to speak until he heard Violet on the stairs.

"Grace, I wish I had first heard this from you. This is a right mess."

"You were home so late last night and I was so tired."

"I know of your condition, if that is what you are wondering. Who is the father?"

"Vikram Fernandes."

"The doctor?"

"Yes."

Martin Moran reached into his pocket and took out his pipe, placing it in his mouth and pushing down the tobacco with his thumb. He cracked a match and lit the tobacco, taking short, sharp puffs. After a few moments, he took the pipe out of his mouth and gazed directly at his wife.

"What do you intend to do, Grace?"

Grace stood up beside him. "You should never have married me and I should never have married you. I love Vikram. I am going to India with him and we will raise our family there."

The judge puffed on his pipe.

"You are forgetting, we married till death do us part."

Grace walked to the window looking out on to the park, where John McDermott was sitting with his wife, watching their young son play among the flowers.

"I want an annulment, Martin. You know I can apply."

He did not answer for several minutes. The room was so quiet she could hear the ticking of the grandfather clock below in the hall. They both heard the third stair down creak and they knew that Violet was trying to listen in. Outside, a man whistled loudly at his friend and shouted to him to get a pint of milk in the corner shop.

Martin cleared his throat. Grace sat down, a bar of sunshine crossing over her so that he thought she looked even more beautiful than usual. He spoke softly. "I have neglected you and for that I am truly sorry. I was giving you time to get to know me, even to love me."

He stopped, aware that Violet was eavesdropping.

"An annulment is completely out of the question. We will raise your child as our own. You will not see this man again."

A scuffle on the stairs and the sound of Violet's stick tapping indicated that Violet McNally had heard enough and was making her way to her quarters.

"I won't stay here."

Martin Moran swung around. Grace's face was strained, he thought, but he saw too a look of defiance and it angered him.

"No, best not for a while anyway. I will arrange for Aunt Violet to take charge and take you away for a period. Hopefully by the time you come back, this man will have given up and moved on to the next foolish woman."

"I am never going to change my mind about Vikram. I love him and I want to spend the rest of my life with him. I know he feels the same way."

"What absolute nonsense. You are my wife and you can be thankful I will bring up the child as my own. If God is merciful to us, we should be able to do that. Grace, this is a terrible situation, but believe it or not I care deeply about you and I won't let you go." He stepped towards her. "I won't let you ruin your life with a man who is going to throw you over at the first sign of bother. We will continue to be married, be man and wife, and do our best to be good parents to the child you are carrying."

Grace began to sob loudly, but he ignored her.

"This is terrible for you now, but in time you will see the sense of the decision. Violet will take you to a hotel down the country, where you can rest and take time to think. Maybe then you will be more willing to be a wife and mother."

He was so close she saw the nerve at his neck pulsing, the hand down by his side slightly shaking.

"You don't love me, Martin. You know that."

He sat down beside her. When he attempted to put a hand across her shoulders, she shrugged him away.

"You want me to bring up my child in a loveless marriage. I will run away first."

Martin jumped up. "I love you, Grace. I am sorry you have not been able to find some way to love me."

"You can't keep me prisoner here. Vikram is the man I love. Nothing will stop me going to him."

Martin clapped his hands together. "Grace, the fact is we are man and wife and nobody can come between us. I understand you are upset, but the truth is that this Indian gentleman has no intention of taking you to India. He has made a fool of you. I am telling you, we can put it in the past, try and move on together, as man and wife and soon-to-be parents."

"I am leaving with him and you can't stop me."

Martin Moran walked to the door and turned the key in the lock. "Grace, I don't want it to be this way. But until you can see sense, it is necessary to protect you from yourself. I have sent a message telling this doctor to stay away from you. In the next hour, you and Violet shall travel to a small place I know in the west. You will stay there until we can sort this mess out and, frankly, until you can see the sense of the situation. I am doing this for your own good."

"I won't go. You can't make me."

Martin Moran walked towards his wife. "That is true, but I can say to you I will do everything in my power to make sure that Vikram Fernandes is made to feel very unwelcome if you don't abide by my wishes."

The tone of her husband's voice stopped Grace saying any more. They stood beside each other in the locked drawing room in angry silence for several minutes before a knock at the door made them both jump.

Aunt Violet was standing, her coat already on. "I have called a taxi for the station. It will be here in ten minutes. Grace, I have packed your clothes. Go and tidy yourself up."

When Grace did not move, Violet marched into the room.

"Young lady, if you don't do as I say, I will force you and not even your husband will be able to save you."

She raised her stick and was about to strike out when, from behind her, Martin Moran reached across, grabbing the walking stick so fiercely Violet nearly fell over.

"Mrs McNally, you will do no such thing. My wife is pregnant and deserves the respect that entails. I will have it no other way. I have instructed my good friends at the Falls Hotel to report back to me on the health of my wife. I do not expect to hear reports of any unpleasantness."

Violet, who was leaning against the velvet couch, straightened up and shook out her coat. "The girl needs to see sense and to begin behaving like a wife should."

"She will see sense in time, I am sure of it."

Grace slipped past the two of them to her room. Aunt Violet had cleared most of her day clothes into a case and thrown her toiletries into a vanity case. Grace took a notebook and pen from her dressing-table drawer. She would write to Vikram and ask the hotel to post it. It was as much as she could do now.

As she saw the taxi swing in the front of No. 19, she grabbed the photo-booth shot from its hiding place under her mattress. For one moment, she paused. It made her stomach lurch to see the two of them in a twinkling of happiness. Hearing the taxi man at the front door, she hurriedly stuffed the photograph in her coat pocket.

Now, Grace scrunched her eyes, trying to conjure up the image. Vikram's head touched hers; they were laughing and she could see the width of his smile. Violet might have snatched the picture and torn it to shreds when it dropped out of her pocket on the train, but Grace could still feel Vikram's arms around her.

"Dreaming again, Gracie. A basket of hankies for you. The super says he wants them by noon tomorrow. That should occupy you nicely," the attendant said as she dropped a brown wicker basket with one hundred roughly cut squares on the floor beside Grace's chair.

Twenty-Two

Bangalore, India, April 1984

The phone rang through the apartment early the next morning. Vikram heard Rhya talking in hushed tones.

"Should we wake Vikram or let him sleep?" he heard her whisper.

Vikram called out to his sister and Rhya stuck her head into the bedroom.

"That was Rosa. She wants me to come over."

"It is too early. What is wrong?

"That stupid husband of hers has come home and is breaking up the place. I have called for a car."

"I want to come as well."

"Nonsense, man, don't be stupid. I will ring you from there. She needs her mother. Once I know what is going on, I will update you."

He knew he had to be content with that. He heard the caretaker scrabbling out of his bed to get the compound gate open in time for the car to swing out. Vikram followed the noise of the engine as far as MG Road, where it revved, beeping its way into the early morning traffic.

He and Rosa were due to fly in two days. He prayed that nothing would happen to change their plans.

He knew every sound of this city: every sound of the road; when old man Saldanha woke up and, unable to sleep, paced his balcony, clearing his throat; when the young child across the way woke in the middle of the night; and when the servants began moving around early, the sound of coarse sweeping as the concrete courtyard was brushed out. How he wished he could have shown this city to Grace. If they had come back and set up home, he would never have allowed the old compound house to be knocked down.

Grace would have loved the low bungalow with its wide veranda, where they could sit out in the evening and watch people go down their road, those who knew them well leaning on the gate to pass the time. She would have learned how to handle the servants under the expert guidance of her mother-in-law. What she would have done without her fine dresses, he did not know. When he raised it with her, she had told him he was silly. "I will find a good dressmaker and we will design our own dresses. That is a trifle," she said.

Vikram lay into the softness of the pillow and allowed his mind to wander.

*

They got the train to Bray and jumped in the cable car to the summit of Bray Head, where they sat close, looking out to sea. He could see her face, open, happy, her cheeks rosy, her eyes sparkling with excitement. She caught his hand tight and he knew she had something important to say.

"Vikram, I only know to say it straight out. You are going to be a father."

The sun came out and bounced off her auburn hair and he had to shield his eyes so that he could continue to look in her face. Excitement streaked through him, along with a great fear and responsibility. "My darling, are you sure?"

"I went to a doctor yesterday."

"You did not tell me. I would have gone with you."

"I wanted to be sure. I went to a doctor in Raheny. He did not know who I was. I think I am about ten weeks on."

He threw his arms around her and could only stutter that he loved her. "This is the greatest news. I want to dance about and shout. We will go to India together."

She placed a finger on his mouth to hush him. A man out walking his dogs stopped and stared before turning away, shaking his head.

"But darling, now is the time to travel to India, where we will look after you until our baby can be delivered."

"Vik, I am only ten weeks. I need time to think. I have to talk to Martin. He is a part of this, whether we like it or not."

Vikram jumped up and began to kick at a gorse bush. "Grace, you can't do that. I am afraid for us. We have to plan to leave. I don't care whether you are married or not, we have to go. Have you a passport?"

Grace came behind him and, putting her arms around him, leaned into his back. "I never thought of a passport. Can't I talk to Martin? I am hoping if he sees how unhappy I am he will release me from the marriage. There are grounds for annulment. He will know this can't be his baby."

"I don't care about any annulment, Grace, I just want us to be together. You can be my wife in India. We can have such a lovely life with our child. You will love India, my darling, I just know it."

"Vik, I am going to tell Martin. I don't want to run off in the night. I have done nothing I am ashamed of. I love you and I will love our baby."

She started to laugh and he kissed her. "Darling, you will be such a lovely mother."

Not caring who passed comment, she reached out and took Vikram's hand and they walked close to each other, along the promenade towards the train station.

Only as their train pulled into Connolly Station, Dublin, did Grace pull her hand from Vikram's. "I want to tell Martin when I am ready, not when some nosy parker decides they have gossip to impart."

Vikram shook himself awake. He had a dreadful headache and he still had not heard from Rhya.

*

Rosa was standing on her bedroom balcony, watching the road, waiting for her mother to arrive.

When the servant opened the door, Rhya swept in. Anil was sitting watching TV.

"I see my wife has called in reinforcements. She is upstairs, has locked herself in the bedroom for some reason," he said, without turning from the screen.

Rhya ignored him and made her way upstairs. Rosa was already out in the corridor.

"I want to come home with you. I am not staying in this house a minute longer. I have packed my bags."

"Hush, Rosa. Don't let the servants hear you, they will have no respect."

"What of the servants? They know too much anyway."

Rhya ushered her daughter back into the bedroom, closing the door behind them. "What is all this talk, Rosa? What is wrong?"

"I came home early to find a woman here with him. He was entertaining her in the sitting room."

"What did you do?"

"I caught her by the hair and threw her out of the house. What else would I do?"

"And the servants witnessed all this?"

"What do I care?"

"What rot you talk, girl, you should care. You are making yourself a laughing stock."

"Mama, how can you talk to me so?"

Rhya went to her daughter and took her by the shoulders. "Do you think any of us found it easy at the start? Admittedly, this man of yours has behaved badly, but you need to outwit him. You should have sat and been openly civil to this girl and offered her a drink and some snacks until she felt so guilty and so bad she left of her own accord. Then your husband would have respect for you and you could begin to call the shots in this marriage."

"How can you let him get away with it?"

"That is the last thing I am doing. I am making sure he will suffer for what he has done for the rest of his life."

"It is too late now."

"It is never too late to assert one's authority. Granted, your behaviour has made it more difficult, but not altogether impossible."

Rhya kicked the cases lined up on the inside of the bedroom door. "Get the servant to unpack all your clothes. Go to that husband of yours and tell him you will spare him the shame of leaving him. Tell him you will stay and, from now on, he will behave like a husband should."

"That is not going to work, Mama."

"It is, if you tell him his behaviour will directly influence his position as the operating manager of the city office of the coffee estate. Tell him he is on his last warning."

"But I don't speak with the authority of the company."

Rhya turned to her daughter. "You do now. I, as acting president, appoint you vice president. Maybe you should share the good news with your husband."

"You can't do that, Mama."

"I can and I have. When Vikram was ill he appointed me, and I will stay in that position until he comes back from his trip abroad." Rhya pulled her sari pallu tightly around her. "And before you go downstairs, tidy your make-up. Wear lipstick, clip on some expensive jewellery and change into the royal-blue sari. Represent the family well."

Rhya walked quickly from the house, not saying a word to Anil, who was still lounging in front of the television, his two feet tucked under him on the sofa, a bowl of nuts beside him.

Rosa took her time getting ready, calling the servant to help her with her pleats.

"Ma'am is going out?"

"No questions. Unpack the bags," Rosa snapped as she sprayed perfume behind her ears. Before she left the room, she checked herself in the mirror, flattening the taffeta silk of the sari so it did not stick out.

In the sitting room, she sat at the end of the couch without even addressing her husband. She picked up the *Deccan Herald* and scanned the headlines. She saw him sweep his eyes over her before he spoke.

"Are you going out, Rosa?"

"Why?"

"You are very dressed up."

"I was trying on this outfit, wondering if I should wear it to the coffee estate offices tomorrow."

"Why are you going there? There is no special occasion." He let his feet drop to the ground and stretched his arms to the ceiling.

"It is an occasion for me."

"What talk, woman? What is this?"

Rosa stood up, walked over to the TV set and switched it off.

"What has got into you, woman?"

"I would rather you hear this from me, Anil . . ." She paused to steady herself and saw him smirk, which made her intensely angry. "Anil, I have been appointed vice president of the coffee company. It is widely known that Uncle Vik, when he passes, intends me to take over and now I begin my training."

"What nonsense, you know nothing about the business."

"I will delegate to you, as operating manager, but you will report to me, starting tomorrow lunchtime."

"This is your revenge, isn't it?"

He jumped up and, for a moment, she felt afraid of him, but she stood firm. "Take whatever view you prefer, but this is the way it is."

"Rhya has put you up to this. She never liked me. What about your job?"

Rosa took a step towards her husband. "This position pays a great deal more. Anil, I want us to be partners, but to do that you will have to first stop this silly whining and accept the situation."

Anil, whose one great attribute was to know when he was defeated, smiled and opened his arms wide to hug his wife.

"There is so much to do," she said, passing him by, leaving him standing in front of the blank television screen.

Twenty-Three

Our Lady's Asylum, Knockavanagh, March 1960

Grace pressed the needle through the double edge of linen. Her thumb scraped and bruised, she ignored the stinging pain, distracting herself by examining a patch of sky where a kerfuffle of clouds was gathering.

Outside, the cherry blossom was spraying its flowers, the light breeze ruffling the circle of daffodils that somebody years ago had pushed in the ground so the poor things at the asylum windows could take in a splash of colour.

She remembered Vikram was slightly ahead of her as they walked through St Stephen's Green. He stopped and put his hand out and she slipped hers into his.

"I never want to let it go," he said, kissing each finger.

She had laughed and told him he was a silly, emotional man.

New voices below in the yard made her stop to look out the window. A man in jeans with a small child approached the gate. About two years old, the little girl, still unsteady on her feet, ran to the daffodils and pulled at a bloom. She said something and the man laughed, scooping her up into his arms. A breeze swirled the spent cherry blossom sprays and dust around as they danced away towards the director's house and out of Grace's sight.

A twinge of pain brought her back, the nick of the needle making her stop to suck the blood.

"Daydreaming will never get those handkerchiefs done. They are sending a boy around for them this afternoon. Matron says to hurry up," the attendant called out. She looked over to the nurse bent over painting her nails. "She has been lost since that Mandy one started working every day for the priest. Mandy and Gracie, like peas in a pod, those two. She only talks these days when Mandy is about. Mind you, not that either of them have much to chat about."

"I reckon they must know what each is thinking."

"That is easy. Poor Gracie, she would give anything to get out of here, even after all these years."

"A beauty still. She had the world at her feet, but it did not stop her going mad." The nurse looked at Grace, who had returned to her sewing. "She is always looking out the window. What does she look at every day?"

"Beats me. Sure, the garden is not even tended properly any more."

"Why is she even in here? Mandy too. They seem such nice ladies."

"And murderers never look like murderers. Their families had their reasons, I am sure. This is your first week: give it a month or so, you won't be bothered asking the questions, just looking forward to the pay packet at the end of the week."

"Gracie, is she the judge's wife?"

"That's the one, old geezer in the criminal courts, the one who would jail a fly for buzzing too close."

"He was older than her."

"Which is probably why she had a fling with a handsome Indian who left her in the lurch. She is a quiet one now, but in her day she was feisty, ended up in isolation a few times. There isn't much fight in her these days. Nobody cares about Gracie. She might as well be dead too, poor thing."

"She seems so quiet."

"I think you could open up all the doors and she would just stay sitting at that window until the tea trolley came round."

"Is it true what happened to Mandy?"

"Another feisty one gone quiet. The father committed her after she had a baby in the mother-and-baby home. That's their big new house on the hill: the brother took over the farm and sold off a lot of land for development. They are rolling in it, not that that poor thing knows anything of it. I am not saying anything about recent events with that one."

"Jesus, I hope they caught the men who raped her."

The older attendant looked fiercely at the new nurse. "Don't ever mention it. They didn't even tell the Gardaí. The chief at the time had the caretaker and the gardener call to the homes of those involved and threatened them that if they came near the asylum again he would have them arrested. Three of the young fellahs left Knockavanagh that night and the other two have given this place a wide berth since."

"At least she gets to work for the priest. It must be like a day out for her."

"Poor man, he does his best, says you can't give up on a human being. He believes a person can be rehabilitated even after decades in here. Sure, he is half mad himself. One of these fine days we will find him murdered in his bed."

"Not Mandy, surely." The young nurse, who was holding out her hands in front of her to dry her nails, looked shocked.

The older woman grabbed her by the shoulders, her face so near she could feel the force of the delivery. "Why not her or Gracie? They might not have been mad when they were brought here, but don't you think the last years have done something to their brains, slowed them down, dulled them? What are they? Only two fat slobs, their arses too big for the chairs by the window. Imagine all the pent-up frustration that is going to come out some day. Just pray it is not on our shift."

The young nurse shrank back and began tidying away her nail accoutrements into a vanity case.

Grace watched the road. Since they had lowered the asylum walls and called the place a mental hospital, people walked past slower. Sometimes they sat on the walls. Around this time each afternoon, the women with their young children walked by, some harassed and busy, others strolling, having time to stop and stare.

She would never be a grandmother sitting beside Vikram at the coffee estate or breathing in city life.

She did not hold it against him, that he had not come back for her. Did he even know she was here? The only thing she held against him was that he had made her love him so much, and that he loved her, because the pain of being apart was truly unbearable. There was not much they could say or do in here, to match the pain of losing Vikram and a chance of a family. What he would make of her now, she did not know. Her hair was too long, coiled into a bun. Her skin was flabby. She had pains too, along her fingers. One thumb was bent a funny shape, from all the times she had hemmed handkerchiefs into the night, to meet orders for people she did not know.

That last time they met he had held her close, whispering plans into her ear. She had said she wanted to give birth in Dublin and he was annoyed.

"Grace, we need to leave here. I promise I can look after you, trust me. I want to look after you, to look after our child. We have to leave."

She agreed to tell her husband as soon as she could.

If she had known she would be spirited down the country and kept away from Vikram, she would never have returned to Parnell Square. She would have said something important to sustain him until they met again. Vikram, too, would never have let her go back to No. 19.

Grace paused and shook out the handkerchief, like she was trying to eradicate what might have been. She put her head down and concentrated on the stitches at the corner of the white linen square.

"Grace is slowing down. They are beginning to complain that she is not doing next to enough hankies these days. She will soon have to be moved on to a quieter ward," said the attendant.

"I feel sorry for Gracie," the young nurse said, concentrating on her nails again as she applied a clear coat on top of the pink polish.

Grace conjured up the primroses, the day in Skerries when she picked a bunch. On a whim, they had jumped on the No. 438 bus to the sea. They had climbed up the dunes and into the fields beyond. Pockets of primroses were stuck into the raised ditches under the trees. She ran between them, gathering up clumps, picking until she had a huge bunch.

"I will bring primroses to India. We have to have primroses. So lovely and so fleeting," he said.

Pulling a ribbon from her hair, she wrapped it around the thin stalks and held the bunch in front of her. He kissed her and told her everything would work out.

She saw Mandy walk down the road, leaning into the wall as she passed a group of schoolboys. At the gate, she stopped and talked to the caretaker before making her way to reception.

Grace hoped she managed to smuggle in some sweet cake, so they could eat when everybody else was asleep. Mandy called it "moonlight cake" because the moon was the only light they had as they munched slowly on the dry, shop-bought fruit cake.

Grace put away the handkerchiefs and sat watching the door, waiting for her friend to arrive.

Twenty-Four

Parnell Square, Dublin, April 1984

Emma pulled on her jeans and rummaged in a box marked "Grace. Jackets/Tops". At the bottom, folded in tissue paper, was a cream silk blouse, simple with soft pleats at the front. Opening the window of the blue room, she hung it there so that it could air out the mustiness of decades, be pummelled gently by the fresh, cold breeze sweeping into the city from the Irish Sea. A blue-flecked tweed jacket she shook out, hanging it up at the other window.

Sitting at the dressing table, she smoothed on light foundation, wondering how many times Grace had sat by the long windows, planning her wardrobe for the day. Pulling a silk blue-purple scarf from the pile on the floor, she released it, watching the emerald-green thread rippling through the blue shimmer before wrapping it around her neck. It was not musty but had the faint hint of the soft perfume that made up Grace. Playing with the blue and green silk fronds, she felt a great trepidation rise up inside her about the journey she was about to embark on.

Slipping on a T-shirt before the silk blouse, she checked in the mirror that it did not take from her smooth line. The jacket was a snug fit, the scarf at her neck picking up the bobbles of colour in the tweed.

She was standing at the bedroom room window watching the street below when she saw Andrew drive his car up and park outside the house. He opened the bonnet to check the engine oil, wiping the oil stick with an old cloth when he was finished.

When the doorbell sounded, Emma jumped, even though she had seen Andrew make for the front door. On her way downstairs, she quickly stopped to check her reflection in the hall mirror. When she opened the door, Andrew was standing there with a big yellow tin jug in his hand.

"I had better put some water in the engine. Can I fill up the jug?"

"Go ahead."

Emma stepped out onto the stone steps. From here, she could see across the park, over the Rotunda Hospital to the city below. The breeze did not seem so strong at this level, but she stuffed her hands in her pockets to ward off the early morning chill.

"I won't be long. Get in the car, it is open," Andrew said, splashing water on the outside steps in his hurry. "Have you got your house keys?"

Emma nodded and he pulled the front door shut behind him.

Andrew chatted on for a while, but, sensing her reticence to talk, he quietened quickly, leaving her to her own thoughts.

It was a still Sunday morning in the city. Had Grace gone to the asylum on a Sunday? She had no idea. Had the judge accompanied her? Surely he had. Why hadn't he told her when she reached adulthood? Was he still so full of shame that he couldn't?

A trickle of tears burst under her lids and she looked out the passenger window so Andrew would not notice. If he observed her discomfort, he did not let on, but he switched the radio a little higher as they pulled out on the road to County Wicklow.

"Less than an hour to Knockavanagh from here," Andrew said, but he was not sure if Emma heard.

"If there is a grave, I should have flowers."

For a moment, until Andrew answered, Emma had not realised she had said it aloud.

"I suppose it would do no harm. Or you could wait until we know for sure."

"Primroses are out this time of year, aren't they?"

"We can pick them ourselves: there is a nice spot after we turn off for Knockavanagh."

"How do you know where to find primroses?"

"Andrew Kelly is a mine of useless information like that, you should know that by now."

Emma did not answer.

"You know, they don't last very long unless you plant them out," Andrew said gently.

"I just think it would be nice. That's all."

She had no idea why she was so set on primroses. Creamy yellow, delicate-looking yet surviving in the damp crag. The judge had never let her pick a bloom. Once she had asked to pick just one in St Stephen's Green, but the judge rushed her along, chastising her that it was a selfish thing to pick a flower for oneself and not leave it for others to enjoy. "Learn from an early age, young lady, there are more people in the world than just you."

They turned onto a narrow windy road, Andrew sounding the car horn at the bends in the road.

"There is a wood up a bit further. You will get bunches of primroses there," Andrew said.

"You will stop for me?"

"Why wouldn't I? What is it going to add to the journey?"

"You don't think we should leave the flowers for others to enjoy?"

"Like hell. In Ballycolla Woods only the mountain walkers on the Wicklow Way bother to pass. Sure, they would only grind them into the mud." Andrew pulled into a small gateway. "It is dry enough today, so we should be all right."

They got out of the car and he led the way down the narrow path into the thick of the trees, the sunlight piercing through in small blocks.

"It opens up lovely further on. There is a nice shady patch, usually smothered in primroses." Primroses peeked from splits in the tree roots as the track broadened into a wider glade. "I told you, pick as many as you like."

Andrew bent down, yanking them out in clumps, and she wanted him to stop. Slowly, she bent down and snapped a stem, letting the sap wet her fingers.

"Why primroses?" he asked, holding a wide bunch.

"Beautiful, fragile, like Grace must have been."

They carried on until between them they had three generous bunches.

"We should have brought a basket. I think I have something in the car," Andrew said as they traipsed quietly out of the woods.

He rummaged in the boot until he found an old box. They

resumed their journey, the fresh, woody smell from the flowers seeping around them.

"This is Knockavanagh," he said after a while.

The main street was quiet except for a few cars parked outside the newsagent's. The grey asylum was boarded up, the roof caved in at the centre. Some walls were black, as if there had once been the intensity of fire. Election posters and graffiti on the wall of wood around the site discoloured and dirty.

Andrew turned in to the church, stopping near the big house beside it. The air was damp. Shivering, Emma turned up the collar of her jacket. Crows cawed loudly, unnerving her, as she could not see the birds in the tall cypress trees. The path to the church was gravelled and clean, but those around the graveyard were more like trails, some more worn than others. Sinking her hands deep into her pockets, she trudged behind Andrew.

Father Charlie O'Brien, standing at the notice board, waved at them, pieces of paper in his hand, two thumb tacks in his mouth.

"I will be with you in a minute. A fine church for a wedding, isn't it?" he said, pulling the drawing pins down past his lips. Before they could answer, he disappeared around the corner to collect two rolled-up posters. "Just let me get these pinned up before we sit and discuss the wedding."

Emma giggled and Andrew looked out over his glasses and said stiffly, "We are not here about a wedding."

"Oh my good Lord, you are not here for the rehearsal of the Whelan/McInerney wedding, are you?"

"Afraid not."

Father O'Brien stuck out his hand to Emma. "I have made a silly blunder. Forgive me. How can I help you folks?"

"My name is Emma Moran. We are looking to find out about my mother."

"Your mother?" Father O'Brien looked momentarily taken aback, scratching his head in a loose attempt to hide his confusion.

"Grace Moran. We think she was a patient in the asylum."

"The asylum has been gone from these parts since it burned down ten years ago. After that, the patients were scattered to institutions all over the place."

"We don't know if Grace Moran died and was buried here. Could we check that while we are here?" Andrew asked.

"I can have a quick look now if you have a date, but it may entail a more forensic examination of the books later," the priest said.

The crows cawed rowdily, quarrelling in the trees. A child passing waved at the priest and he waved back. Emma shuddered as a breeze skirted past them, to pummel and disturb the plastic flowers on the grave before her.

"You can come with me, we have the records all in the one place." He led the way around the back of the church to a small door in a grey stone building with a deep roof. Unlocking the door, he held it open and they stepped in. There was a bare stone floor, rows and rows of shelves all around the stone walls, and long, wide books with dates printed on the spine stacked on each shelf.

"The asylum ran at full capacity until the early '60s. There is a lot to go through if you don't have a specific date." Father O'Brien swept his hand to indicate the extent of the work ahead. "I am not sure you will get your answer today." He took down one book and blew the dust from the cover before setting it down on a small table. "This might be a job for a local historian, but you are welcome to have a look through." He tipped back the cover and ran his finger down the first list of entries, for 1955. "If you were only sure of a date, it would make it easier," he said, waving his hand towards four different shelves.

"Sounds like more than half an afternoon's work."

Father O'Brien rubbed his hands together, as if anticipating the challenge. "I will leave you here, while I meet the wedding couple. You have to start somewhere. I am afraid the housekeeper has a few days off, but if you don't mind waiting an hour or so, I will make a pot of tea when I am finished."

Emma ran her finger down along the first page of the book. "Such a lot of names on just one page."

"I suppose nobody here remembers a person who was in the asylum," Andrew said.

"You are out of luck. Father Grennan was the chaplain here for years. He died two months ago." The priest looked uncomfortable and coughed to clear his throat. "There were a few fatalities in the fire. Those people are buried in a special part of the cemetery. Let me know if you want to check there."

Emma turned slightly away, so the priest would not see her upset. Tears blinded her eyes and the cawing of the crows intensified in her head. She wanted to run away, out of this cold, stone room with damp, wet walls, past the old blotched headstones to the car. She stepped out onto the gravel path, gulping in the cold air, which made her cough.

Andrew, who had quietly followed her outside, put an arm around her shoulders.

"Could it really be the case that she ended up in the asylum and died in a fire here? That is so hard to comprehend."

"We don't know anything yet, Emma. We will deal with each thing as it comes along."

"I should not have picked the primroses."

"We can place them at some lonely grave if we can't find one for Grace."

Emma took a deep breath and, steeling herself against the cold, stepped back into the icy room where the records of the asylum were stacked.

Andrew pulled at the heavy spine of one of the books. "We will take a book each and see how we go. We can cut down on the work by following the gender code," he said.

The cold seeped up through their shoes, their fingers were like blocks of ice, a band of chill crept up their backs and lodged there. Each entry was in the same swirling script, each person described as a lunatic.

The first few, Emma read every detail, but after a while she only picked out the female entries. After nearly an hour, pain flaring through her from the cold, the bones in her fingers grinding, she snapped her book shut, a puff of dust pushing into the air around her. "What is the point of all this? What is it going to be: only confirmation she was a lunatic who ended her days here and was buried in a lonely grave?"

"Maybe it is time for a break," Andrew said.

Emma moved out into the cold sunshine, shivering as she strode up the gravel path to the car. Andrew, unsure, loitered in the doorway, stamping his feet on the ground to keep warm.

Father O'Brien, seeing off the wedding couple, gestured to them. "I will make that tea. You must be frozen stiff."

"No, thank you. Maybe if we could come back later in the week, we can be better prepared."

"Why don't we move the books you are interested in to the house?"

"You wouldn't mind?"

"It will make it more comfortable for you. It is a hard enough task you are taking on without the cold biting into your brains. My housekeeper comes back on Thursday, so the prospect of a cuppa will be a much more welcoming proposition." He laughed at his own joke and marched into the stone records office and grabbed three of the ledgers. "I will come back for the others. Before you go, why not check the section where the ten poor souls from the asylum fire are buried?"

Father O'Brien led the way to the back door of the house.

"Come on Thursday and use the front sitting room. Don't worry, we will have the heat on from early. You never know, I might be able to persuade Miss McGuane to light a fire."

"We don't want you to go to too much bother."

Father O'Brien dropped the books onto the couch. "I only hope you find what you are looking for."

They walked down a narrow path to the far end of the graveyard, the long, uncut grass verges whipping against their ankles, old ferns washing water over their shoes, wet cobwebs sticking to their legs. At the end of a steep decline lay an area marked out by a small fence. A gravel path led to a tall cross with a plaque underneath.

Emma walked up the path, the length of five wide graves either side, to read the plaque and the names inscribed underneath. Her head was pounding, almost more than her heart.

To the Men and Women who lost their lives in a fire at
Our Lady's Hospital, Knockavanagh, April 18, 1964.
May they Rest in Peace.

Quickly, she scanned the names. Grace Moran: number five on the right.

Emma shoved her head into her hands. Andrew rushed to her side. They stood, the silence of the graveyard all around them. Emma, her shoulders hunched, let the tears flow into the silk scarf. That her quest had come to an end was both a shock and a sorrow.

After a few minutes, Andrew lightly pulled her at the elbow. "Do you want to find the grave?"

Emma nodded and they trudged between the graves, reading the headstones until Andrew called out at the far end near the wood.

GRACE MORAN.
Born August 21, 1935.
Wife of Judge Martin Moran.
Mother to Emma Moran.
Let the light shine on Grace, who died tragically on
April 18, 1964.

Emma wanted to scream, but instead she spoke in a calm, measured manner. "It has come to this: a cold headstone beside a craggy wood on a grey day."

Andrew, his hands clenched in prayer, head bowed, stood beside her and did not move.

Emma wiped a few leaves from the grave with her hand. She did not notice Andrew disappear back up the path to the car to collect the primroses. When he came back, Father O'Brien was with him, carrying three jars of water.

"These flowers will last longer if you dip them in water," he said, before they pulled back a respectful distance to allow

Emma to arrange the primroses at the top of the grave. "I should have recognised the name. It is one of the most visited graves in the plot. My housekeeper keeps the lot nice and tidy. There is never a day in the summer it is without flowers.

Emma didn't say it, but she appreciated his soft manner.

"I am sorry you should find out like this."

"You said it was a malicious fire?"

Father O'Brien sighed loudly. "A man in the village had some grudge against the place. Years before, there had been some incident, when a number of local men attacked one of the female patients." He stuttered in his telling. "There was a rape down by the well, but the Gardaí were never called. The director and a few of his buddies got together and warned the men involved to get out of town. When one particular young man returned a few years later, the director warned him again, but unfortunately this time the father took the matter into his own hands. He said afterwards he only wanted to give the director a fright, but when he set a rubbish bin ablaze, he had no idea the door to the basement would go up and the fire would enter the building. It was a windy night and sparks went all over the place."

Andrew kicked at the loose stones on the path. "I bet the bastard apologised to try and get a lighter sentence."

"He apologised all right, but it did nothing to ease his conscience. He took his own life in prison. He is buried at the far side of the cemetery." Father O'Brien waved his hand to the new section of the graveyard. "There are a lot of tragic stories here, but I am sorry you had to find your mother is one of them. Come up to the house for tea."

Andrew answered for them. "We are all right, Father, we had better get along."

He guided Emma away from the grave, out through the gate and up the hill towards the car.

"Do you think that is why he never brought me to the grave? Because he did not want me to know about the fire?"

"It would certainly have been a valid reason when you were a youngster."

"Do you think we could stop at the asylum?"

"You are a glutton for punishment, you are."

Father O'Brien waved them off. Emma closed her eyes for a moment, until Andrew pulled the car to a halt.

"I don't think we can get in."

"I am not sure that I want to. Maybe I could stand at the gate. I won't be long."

Emma stepped over the sodden rubbish on the ground at the old gates. The timber placed there to block out the outside, decades ago, had fallen away, exposing the brown, rough, rusted bars. The overgrown driveway could have been the entrance to a big house. The lawns that must have once been manicured were now sodden and mossy. A monkey puzzle tree stood tall and proud.

She pressed her face against the bars of the gate. The doorways of the old grey building were boarded up; every pane of window glass was smashed, as if there had been a grand stoning of the building. The walls that were still standing were scorched black. A chaffinch landed on a hedge at the side of the avenue and twitched its head, watching her. In the distance she saw a low grey building, the parking clearly marked out. From one window on the top floor, an old flag lay forlornly, as if somebody at one time had put it there in a burst of enthusiasm and completely forgot about it, through too many heavy winters.

A sweep of loneliness threatened to overtake her, so she turned away quickly and jumped into the car.

Andrew did not need to ask how she was. He could see the scowl of worry on her forehead, her mouth set stiff as she tried not to cry.

They were about a mile out of the village when she spoke. "Why did she ever have to come to a place like this?"

"We don't have the facts, Emma. There is no point trying to rationalise it until we do," Andrew replied.

"I think even if we do come across the facts, it is not going to make sense."

Twenty-Five

Bangalore, India, May 1984

Rosa, he thought, looked a little different: more confident maybe, her mouth set at a harder angle. "Anil, is he behaving himself?" he asked.

"A coward always does what he is told." She sat down and looked at Vikram. "Uncle, I want to hear the whole story."

He took her hand and squeezed it. "I will tell, but if you get bored, please stop me."

She shook her head, smiling. "It is a break for me, Uncle, from what has been going on these last few days."

*

"Grace was pregnant. It was such news, I wanted to take her away immediately and come to India, but she was afraid. She had to get out of her sham marriage with her husband. She waited until she was gone three months to tell him."

Vikram stopped as a stab of pain shot through him. He was

not sure if it was a new pain, because of the stress of talking out these past events, or the old one visiting in a different way.

"Grace said she was going to tell the judge, and we arranged to meet at four o'clock, when I finished work the next day. I wanted to go along with her, but Grace would not hear of it. She was going to ask for an annulment and tell him she was leaving for India with me. She was nervous but not afraid. She hoped that, him being a realist and a pragmatist, he would relent.

"We completely underestimated the evil of her aunt Violet, who did anything she could to stop our union. Neither was Violet going to allow Grace to walk away from the marriage." Vikram's voice was shaking, his eyes wide, as if even after all this time he found it hard to comprehend. "Rosa, it became a total nightmare. I never saw Grace again. The next day I was on duty on the women's ward. I was almost sick with worry. A woman came in complaining of back pain. When she insisted I pull the curtain fully around the cubicle, I did not think anything of it. Thinking she was a prudish sort, I pulled the screen round the bed. Next thing, she was shouting and roaring I had tried to feel her up."

He swallowed hard. Rosa, seeing how hard it was for him to call up such painful events, said, "Uncle, if it's too much . . ."

"I came back to India a broken man. I want you to know why. How does a man heal from something like that?" Taking a deep breath, he spoke faster, as if by rushing, he might avoid the necessary pain in the delivery. "Next thing, I was suspended from my work. Neither did Grace turn up at our meeting place that afternoon. When I went to Parnell Square, there was no answer at the door. I went home and hoped for word. The only visitors were two uniformed police officers who brought me to the barracks and charged me with the rape of one woman and the indecent assault of the hospital patient. A court appearance followed and I was remanded in custody."

"Uncle, what are you telling me?"

"Rosa, it was all a complete lie, I swear to you. Don't please for a second think I could do such a thing. I am sure Aunt Violet had something to do with it. No matter what my solicitor did, no matter what money my parents pledged, I could not get bail."

Vikram felt the words choke through him and he began to wheeze heavily, unable to stop.

"Uncle, please don't do this to yourself. Mama can tell me further." She squeezed his hand so hard that the trapped sweat between them squelched.

"I have to. Whatever I went through is nothing compared with my lovely Grace. She was carrying my child and was no doubt being told I was a rapist by Aunt Violet." He spluttered as he tried to calm the coughing. Rosa held a glass of water to his lips and he took a few sips. "The solicitor told me that Grace had been sent down the country. I did not know where she was."

Rhya walked in with a tray of coffee and stopped in the centre of the room. "What are you doing, telling her this? Don't you know even thinking about it destroys us all?"

"Mama, I need to know the full story."

"It is bad luck to be discussing these terrible events," Rhya said, shaking herself as if she was cold. "Enough, please, some secrets are best left buried."

Recognising the agitation in her voice, Vikram put his hand up to indicate he was done. Rhya, seizing her chance, pulled her daughter into the bedroom, where she immediately bombarded her with questions on what exactly she had been told.

Vikram, on his own, conjured up an image of Grace, resplendent in her gold pleated-linen Sybil Connolly gown. She had worn that dress the night she chanced it and stole off with him after she had been to the Law Society ball with the judge.

*

Martin Moran had spent the night deep in conversation with Judge Fitzpatrick, leaving his wife in the company of the other judges' wives. Grace told Vikram later she had wanted more than anything to be whirled across the dance floor, to see the lights reflect off the dress, to feel the fabric as it weighed across from one side to the other. On two occasions she went over to her husband and stood nearby, hoping he would pick up the signal, but he did not notice.

Claire Fitzpatrick, dressed in peacock blue, did not mind so much. "Darling, when these men go out, they see it as an extension of the day job. Once a judge, always a judge. You will get used to it," she said, and the other women around all laughed.

Grace shortly after excused herself and went to the bathroom, where she placed her head against the cubicle wall and allowed the tears to flow down her face and neck, wetting the top of the bodice. She only stopped when she realised that if her eyes were too red she would have some explaining to do to the other women, so she fixed her make-up before returning to the table.

Martin Moran was waiting for her. "I think we can safely leave now," he said, and they went to the cloakroom to ask for their coats.

As their car pulled up outside No. 19 Parnell Square, Grace had seen Vikram standing across the road in the shadow of a tree overhang from the park. She smiled to him as she ascended the steps, knowing he would wait until she came to him.

Inside, she went straight to her room, waiting until she heard her husband pass on to the next floor before daring to go to the window and signal to Vikram. She should have taken the dress off, but she was vain enough that she wanted Vikram to see her in what was probably the most beautiful dress she would ever own. She waited until she heard her husband's snores before padding downstairs in her bare feet to the front door.

Vikram silently ran up the steps to her.

"I have never seen you look so beautiful." He caught her around the waist and waltzed a few steps, making her giggle.

When she kissed him, he ran his hands over her, pressing the fabric to her, and he knew that night they would be together for as long as they could. He pulled her hands and they ran together to the park. Placing his coat on the cold ground, they lay together under the city sky, the windows of No. 19 Parnell Square watching them.

It was on their way back, as he led her to the front door, that Vikram carelessly stepped on the hem of the dress, tugging it too fiercely, so that a small section of linen came away. Grace laughed, teasing him that in years to come they would look at that small rip and know it was the evening she went to the ball but finished her night in the park.

Vikram now smiled to think of Grace fingering the pencil-like shimmering pleats of the dress, announcing it was a gown made to party and dance. Wearing the gold dress, she had insisted, was like trying on a waterfall.

Twenty-Six

Parnell Square, Dublin, May 1984

Emma could not sleep, so she padded down the stairs to her mother's room. The gold wreaths on the wallpaper twinkled in the dim electric light. The room was quiet, the city slumbering outside the window. She could not get the asylum fire out of her head. Had Grace tried to escape it or had smoke overcome her before the intensity of heat destroyed her?

A letter had arrived calling Emma to the reading of the judge's will. She wondered if she would even own this place afterwards. If she did, she would stay here. Maybe she could make a few bob taking the overflow from Angie, though she had not yet broached that subject with her neighbour.

She could move into this room and live among the vintage and only memories of her mother. A pain of loneliness swelled in her heart for the woman she did not know, the mother she would never know. Sitting at the dressing table, she twisted the cap of the remaining bottle of brandy and swigged a gulp from the bottle. With her right foot, she manoeuvred a cardboard box full to the brim towards her. Prising back the bulging flaps, she could see several silk pieces, wraps or scarves neatly folded.

Taking the first one, a gold paisley wrap, she shook it out. It unfurled in a shimmer of gold. Soft to the touch, it was wide enough to cover her shoulders, delicate hand-knotted fringes skimming over her blouse. Emma stood in front of the wardrobe mirror. The flashing gold of the wrap set off her auburn hair. She decided she must wear it the next time she went to visit Andrew.

Next was a cardigan-type shawl as light as gossamer in a soft grey lace-ply wool, the intricate knitting a pattern of flowers. Emma slipped her arms into it, letting it hang down her back. She straightened, pulling the small hood halfway up her head. It felt like a film of lace. There was no label on it, so she presumed Grace had women who knitted and crocheted according to her fancy.

How different it could have been, growing up with Grace at her side. Emma had only been brought clothes shopping twice a year, and never by her father. For some reason he never let her go out with Violet, who visited the children's department of Clerys twice a year, before Christmas and in May, ordering all the possible things a young girl would need. When the job later fell to a housekeeper, Mrs Esther Harris, she insisted on bringing Emma with her.

"You may think your father is made of money, missy, but Mrs Harris is not a spendthrift," she had said as she picked the best price in everything, once pushing Emma into sandals a half size too small because they were on sale. "Sure, it does not matter with sandals. Aren't your toes hanging out anyway?" she had said.

Emma's musings were interrupted by a soft knock on the

front door and Angie's unmistakable voice calling up at the window. Glad of the diversion, Emma ran downstairs to find Angie in a silk nightdress, dressing gown and slippers.

"I saw you couldn't sleep as well. I have brandy," she said, pulling a bottle from under her dressing gown. They went up to the drawing room and settled on the couch, their feet up. "I could never have done this to the judge. Only a woman understands the urgent need to talk."

Emma listened and Angie prattled on about this and that until she suddenly stopped and let the tears flow. Unsure of what to do, Emma waited until there was a break in the flow to ask what was wrong.

"It always happens on my third brandy. I had two before I woke you up. I had my coat and boots on and was going to walk the angst off. I thought, 'Stupid woman, you will be attacked and end up on page one of the *Evening Herald*.' Then I saw your light." She stopped to gulp another mouthful from her glass.

Emma wanted to laugh out loud, but instead she rubbed her hand across the other woman's back as a shudder of tears swelled through Angie.

"You are wondering what the hell is wrong with me. The truth is I don't know."

"Is it something with your health? Is there anything I can do to help?"

Angie looked stricken. "God, no, nothing like that. I am in love."

Emma burst out laughing and Angie half-heartedly joined in, giggling and crying at the same time. Gulping back the laughter, Emma asked what could possibly be wrong with falling in love.

"Don't you think it is some sort of betrayal of Christopher and Timmy?"

Emma did not know how to answer, but Angie didn't wait.

"Christopher was the love of my life. How can I think of being with another man? I have ably resisted it until now, but, Emma, I am lonely."

"Nobody would blame you. It is so many years on."

"I blame myself, Emma. I should have been more involved with the two of them. I should have been out on that boat. If we had all gone together, I would not be marooned like this. If it was not for Martin Moran, I don't know where I would be."

"What do you mean?"

"He is the one who came out to Greystones and took me away from there. He was a dear friend of Christopher's. When Martin was a practising barrister, Christopher was his instructing solicitor on a lot of cases. Martin said he owned the house next door at Parnell Square and the area needed a nice bed-and-breakfast establishment. He insisted I was the one to set it up and run it." She took a deep breath. "That man, you can say all you like about him, but he forced me out of myself. Five years later, as a gift, he signed the house over to me. He did not want anybody to know, but that is all a matter now."

Emma got up to make some tea. Confused, she leaned against the sideboard on the pretence of waiting for the kettle to boil. Why had she never seen this side of her father? The man she had known was aloof, snobby, stubborn and strict; the man everyone else knew was the exact opposite.

Angie rearranged herself and began to talk about Henry Fortune, who worked in Clerys department store and had been asking her out for a long time. She had relented last week, agreeing to go to a movie. She even allowed him walk her home afterwards. "I am in love, Emma, a woman my age. What am I going to do?"

Emma turned around. "What can you do? Only follow your heart."

Angie stood up, tightening her dressing gown around her. "So like your father: always the sound advice. Now, I won't keep you up any longer. I am afraid tea after the brandy would only be a let-down."

Emma listened until the front door thudded shut before sitting down. Discarding any idea of tea herself, she poured herself another brandy.

The more she found out about Martin Moran, the less she knew him. If only she could find somebody who had known her mother as well, then she could start to piece together the mystery of the marriage between her mother and father, a story with already too much tragedy.

The phone ringing drew her back. She wanted to ignore it, but she thought it might be Angie with a second instalment, so she went down to the judge's library to answer it. The room was chilly when she entered, the phone on his desk ringing, calling out to a naked room.

"Em, it's me."

"Why are you ringing?"

"Em, when are you coming back? We need to talk, get a divorce."

"I am not coming back. It is not as if I have anything to come back to."

"I have an offer on the flat. There is paperwork for you to sign."

"So?"

"Em, I can't finalise the sale without your permission."

"Can't all this be done through solicitors?"

He sighed loudly at the other end. "Don't you trust me?"

"What do you think?"

"I was not going to go to the bother of a solicitor. Can't we act civilised?"

"Civilised? You don't expect me to answer that after what you have done. Next time you call, have the name of your solicitor ready and we can exchange details. It is the only way I will do business with you from now on."

She heard the click of the phone and knew he had cut her off in anger. Pulling the lace wrap around her, she went back to the sanctuary of Grace's room, wanting to forget about the husband she hoped she would never have to meet again.

A few hours later, Andrew Kelly knocked on the door. He was not to know that Emma had only been asleep a short time. She thought of not answering, but she could not lie on the bed as the bell sounded, followed by a few heavy hammers of the knocker. She was surprised to see Andrew so early. He handed her a small loaf of bread, still warm at the base.

"I make the best brown bread on any side of the Liffey. Put on the kettle and we will have tea."

She did as she was bid, leading the way to the drawing room upstairs, where she switched on the small kettle on the sideboard. Andrew, she thought, looked slightly worried and she wondered why he'd decided to call on her. He sat on the edge of the velvet couch, his hands bunched as if he was in prayer.

Chatting away about nothing in particular, all the time both of them knew there was something in the background, something Andrew was almost afraid to mention. He made a big meal of cutting the loaf, removing small pats of butter, along with jam pouches, from his jacket pockets. "My one vice in life, I can't leave those things on the table when I have my breakfast in the courts café every morning. I tip well, so the waitresses say nothing. They are probably laughing up their sleeves at the rich lawyer who steals the butter and the marmalade."

Emma laughed and they sat munching the brown bread, which was crumbling-warm. She waited for him to bring up the reason for the surprise visit, but he seemed content to enjoy his breakfast. The bus to Cabra revving up the hill was the only thing invading their peace.

Andrew finished his tea and refused another cup. "I was hoping you wouldn't mind. I just did not want you turning up at the solicitors and seeing me there."

"My father must have thought a lot of you to mention you in the will."

Andrew laughed. "Emma, don't be worried. Your father has not left any of his wealth to me: that is why I am here, to allay any fears you may have."

She was slightly annoyed that he knew what was in the will, when her father had not bothered to tell her.

"You are put out."

She did not answer, so he continued.

"And so you should be. I am sorry your father never revealed any of his life to you. He is leaving that task to me. We have been special friends for over a decade. I loved your father very much. I miss him every day. There, I have told you. Your reaction is yours. Whether you approve or not is not a consideration, it is entirely your own business."

Emma did not know what to say. Andrew's delivery was precise and firm, as if he was addressing the court, but his face was contorted, nervous she may overreact.

"Why did he never tell me?"

Andrew shifted on the couch, crossing and uncrossing his knees. "Our relationship was in its infancy when you left for Australia. I don't think Martin would have put such a thing in a letter. Anyway . . ." His voice trailed off, as if he did not want to cause hurt by referring to the rift between father and daughter.

"Why didn't you tell me earlier?"

"That bit is easy. I wanted to get to know you. I didn't even know you were going to stick around."

Emma stretched and took Andrew's hand in hers. "His death, the funeral, it must have been so terrible for you. I am so sorry for your loss."

He sat, the tears rolling down his cheeks, letting her squeeze his hand. "Afterwards, I went to Connemara, back to Lough Inagh, and went out on the boat and drank a bottle of whiskey. I waked him well."

"On your own?"

He looked at her. "How could it be any other way? We always had to hide things. If anybody found out, Martin would have had to resign. That would have killed him."

"He must have loved you very much to risk . . . I mean, isn't . . ."

Andrew sat up straight. "Homosexuality a crime in Ireland? Yes it is, and because I loved Martin Moran then I am guilty as charged."

"Stupid law."

"Stupid, yes, but still the law, so we had to be careful. Only a few close friends were entirely sure of the situation. Angie knew. She used to keep an eye on the house here when Martin came to live with me."

"Are you saying the judge didn't even live here?"

Andrew laughed. "You know Martin, he had it all organised. My driver used to drop him back here at 6 a.m. and his driver would pick him up at 7.45 a.m. sharp, to bring him to his chambers at the Four Courts. The same in the evening: he came back to the square first and my driver picked him up and ferried him to Rathgar later."

"But he died here, didn't he?"

"That is the only lie I told you. He died in Rathgar."

"And the library of law books?"

Andrew guffawed. "He was quite tired of his life here. You must come to Rathgar and see his room. He was a very different man on that side of the city."

Emma stood at the fireplace, leaning against the mantelpiece for support. It was so much to take in. All the time she had been in Australia, she had imagined him sitting at his desk, poring over his law books. Instead he was living a life, building a home, with Andrew. Stabs of jealousy mixed with anger flashed through her, yet she was almost relieved he had not spent the time waiting for her to come back. She turned to Andrew.

"You were with him when he died?"

Andrew nodded.

"I am glad he had somebody who loved him so much by his side. Thank you."

Andrew stood up and made to put his arm around Emma, but thought better of it. "Emma, you have to know he felt very guilty that he had not been a good father to you. He loved you but in his own way. He only ever wanted you to be happy."

"Let's not have that conversation now, Andrew."

"I was thinking you might like to come to Rathgar when all

this has sunk in, maybe see his room. He loved painting, oil paintings mostly. He did a lovely study of you sitting waiting to talk to him in his study here."

"My father didn't paint, he never had time . . ." She stopped herself saying more, for fear of sounding silly or confrontational. "So the marriage with my mother was a sham."

Andrew shrugged his shoulders. "I don't know much about that part of Martin's life. He never talked about it, but he said once he felt bad, because it was for all intents and purpose an arranged marriage. He went along with it and so did she. We know what happened after that."

Emma looked out the window to watch the clouds curl over the mountains, bringing rain to the city. She felt cheated: cheated of a father, cheated of the knowledge that would have freed her of guilt all these years. And she was angry: angry for Grace, the collateral damage in an arranged marriage.

Andrew clapped his hands together, the noise slicing through the tension in the room, bounding off the walls. "I might leave you to it. You have a lot to think about."

Emma swung around. "You knew him well. He does not seem to me a man who would enter into a loveless arranged marriage. What do you think?"

Andrew looked uncomfortable. "I think there is a lot we don't know about even those closest to us. Honestly, I never quizzed him on it. That was a closed book for Martin. In some ways I wish I had, but I am satisfied that he loved me as much as I loved him, and for that I am thankful." He moved towards the door.

She wanted him to leave, and yet she didn't. "I might call over during the week."

His face lit up in a broad smile. "Let me know beforehand,

I will send my driver. Come early and we can spend the day together." He stopped, worried he had been too familiar. With a little bow, he said, "I'll let myself out."

She heard the front door click shut. She watched him walking down the steps and the side of the square to the city, a lonely figure, this big man who was grieving silently inside.

Twenty-Seven

Bangalore, India, May 1984

Rhya was lying down when the post arrived. The caretaker crept into the apartment and left the letter addressed to Vikram Fernandes on the table. He made sure, when he pushed the door open, to be silent, lest he disturbed Rhya. He might suffer for his consideration later, because no doubt she would have something to say about not alerting her immediately to such an important airmail letter.

When Rosa came in a rickshaw, the caretaker pulled her away from within earshot of the gaggle of servants squatting gossiping.

"From Ireland, you say?"

"A white envelope, beautiful stamps, ones to keep. Addressed to Mr Vikram."

"We don't know anybody that side." Rosa hurried upstairs.

Rhya was expecting her but had not even bothered to tidy her hair. She was sitting at the table in the same spot where she had flopped when she picked up the letter, taking in the postmark. She had spied it as she walked through to the kitchen and could go no further. She should have been making tea after her afternoon rest. Never had a letter come into this house from Ireland that carried good news.

Rosa, when she pushed open the door, saw her mother sitting stiffly, holding the envelope. Rhya did not look up.

"Is there something the matter?"

Rhya, sobbing, shoved the letter across the table. "It is for Vikram. Why didn't the man wake me?"

"Don't blame him, Mama."

"What can it be? Vikram won't be home until late. He said he had to tie up a lot of loose ends at the city office and he would get something to eat at a stall downtown."

"Leave it, Mama. Maybe it is something to do with the trip. Quite harmless."

Rhya rose from her chair, her clothes crumpled, her hair untidy and dishevelled, a wild look in her eyes. "Isn't that what always brought bad luck to this family? A seemingly harmless letter from a small place. We need to know what is in it."

"It is for Uncle to decide whether to tell us, Mama."

"Vikram Fernandes won't tell us and we will spend the next decades wondering what it contained and blaming every bit of bad luck on it." Rhya tucked the letter inside the waist of her sari.

"Mama, what are you doing?"

"Rosa, if you don't want to know, you should go home now." Rhya called out to the servant in the kitchen and told her to go to the gate and wait for the dhobi or the stupid fellow would start shouting to be paid.

"Way too early, not for another twenty minutes."

"Don't answer back, just go and wait by the gate."

The servant shrugged her shoulders, leaving the apartment,

lingering for a moment in the hallway in case she could find out why she had been sent away.

Rhya whipped into the kitchen and plonked a dekshi of water on the gas flame.

"Mama, Uncle will know if you have steamed it open. Please don't do it."

"Rosa, maybe you should go home."

"I can't let you do this." She moved to take the letter from Rhya, but her mother raised her hand.

"Rosa, do you think I want to do this? I am trying to protect a man who has been hurt too much in life already."

"If you do it, I will never speak to you again."

"Don't be so dramatic, Rosa. I am only steaming open a letter."

"Mother, I will walk out the door and not come back again."

Rhya, who had used steel tongs to grip the letter and hold it over the boiling water, stopped, the envelope still aloft. "You don't mean that. What way is that to talk to your mother?"

"What way is this to behave towards your own brother?"

"I am trying to protect him."

"Go ahead, Mama, if you think it is worth it." Rosa marched to the door.

Rhya slumped against the marble worktop. "I have not done it. Take the letter," she called out, a pain shooting up her neck and along the back of her head.

Rosa returned to the kitchen. "You have to remember, there is nothing that country can do to Uncle now, Mama." She walked into Vikram's bedroom and propped the letter beside his newspaper on his desk.

Rhya pushed her head into her hands and shook her head.

"Does the pain ever stop coming? I can't bear this." Her voice was low and shaky, tears puddling into the creases at her neck.

"We won't worry, Mama, until we have to."

"Easy for you to say, Rosa," Rhya snapped as she paced up and down, catching up the pallu of her sari, pulling it tightly through her hands, twisting it around her fingers. "That country tried to ruin Vikram." Rhya flopped down on the armchair she usually reserved for watching television. "If I can't open it, maybe we should throw it away."

"Mama, why don't you go and lie down."

"And hear the ghosts whispering in my ear, Rosa? I don't know what to do." Rhya picked up the *Deccan Herald*, flinging it across the room. "All that small country has done is cause trouble for this family. Do you know my mother went to an early grave because of it? You did not have to lie awake listening to her crying because of what they did to her son. You did not see the haunted look on grandfather's face after Vikram came home and accepted an inferior post in the hospital here."

Rhya, unable to speak further, turned on her heel back into her brother's room. There was an awful loss in her heart, so she did what she always did these days when she was feeling down: she sat at Vikram's desk. Here, among the documents and scraps of paper, she could conjure up the brother who threw himself into modernising the coffee estate and putting the Fernandes family back on the coffee map of India.

This had been her father's writing desk. Rudolph Fernandes liked to sit and work in the mid-afternoons, when the house went quiet as everybody rested. He forbade his children to go near his desk, but once a year, on their birthdays, they were invited to open the small drawer at the top left-hand side where Rudolph kept his mints. Beside the mints were several small boxes, each with a child's name on it. On a birthday, one box was taken down, placed on the desk and the birthday child was told to sit and write a wish for the future. It had to be written in neat handwriting before being put back in the box on top of the wishes from previous celebrations.

Rudolph told each of his children that when they married and had their first child, he would give them the box. "Only when you have a precious child will you know the importance of such keepsakes. When you are old, you will look through these notes and some will make you laugh, others will make you cry and there will be some which will leave you with a sense of satisfaction, maybe of a dream achieved," he solemnly told each of them.

Rhya opened the drawer. There was only one remaining out of the five: a small sandalwood box with the name "Vikram Fernandes" inscribed on top. She had never opened this box.

Vikram avoided this drawer, she knew that. He had endured too much pain already to be reminded of the dreams of youth. He had returned to India, his face bloated and darker, the stress in his eyes so haunting she could barely look at him.

She took the last little box out. All these years, she had never opened the trinket box. Vikram said he already knew what was in it, so why would he open it? Delicately, she pulled off the top, which was stiff and swollen with age. There were several pieces of paper, some written in a very childish hand. She smiled at those early wishes for the future: "I want a motor car", "I want lots of money", "Please can I have a maharaja's palace", 'I want to fly an aeroplane", "That Rhya will stop following me all the time".

"That I will be as good as father." "That I can be a fine

man." She looked now at the last one placed in the box by Vikram before he went to Ireland.

"That I make my family proud."

And she wept a final deep weeping for a life so torn apart and left so lonely.

Rhya lay on Vikram's horsehair mattress and closed her eyes. Vikram was never going to be free of that country which had left him a broken man. As their mother slowly but surely fell apart over what had been done to her son, it was Rhya who had to step in and run the family. Her father lost himself in his work; it was Rhya who bore the burden. She had to get up every night to try and persuade her mother back to bed. It was she who had to sit by her bedside until she fell asleep, often waking soon afterwards, afraid for her son, who had come back from Ireland a shadow of his former self.

Vikram, so caught up in his own loss, did not immediately see the devastation in his family. Within months, he too had cut his hours at the hospital to two days a week and spent the rest of the time working on behalf of the coffee estate.

"Mama, I brought some cardamom tea." Rosa was standing at the door, a small china cup of tea in her hand, her face soft with concern.

Rhya sat up and allowed her daughter to fuss about her, placing pillows behind her head.

"Why not rest in your own room? There must be too many memories here."

"Sometimes memories are kinder than the present goings-on," Rhya answered, reaching out to take her daughter's hand. "Let go of this foolishness. You must stay at home and look after your own husband. Anil will feel neglected, you have been spending so much time here."

Rosa pulled her hand away. "Anil feels neglected even when I am right beside him."

"You need to look after your husband, girl, not be chasing across the world to a country where there will be no welcome for you." Rhya took a few small sips from her cup before placing it on the bedside table. "Rosa, I have a headache, I can't talk about this now. Pull over the curtains. I will rest here in the quiet of the room."

Rosa did as she was bid. She could hear the stress in Rhya's voice, an indicator her mother was trying to stop a big argument blowing up, in which they both might say too much.

"Do you want me to wait while you rest, Mama?"

"No need, Vik will be home by nine. I will be up and about by then." Rhya made an effort to smile so that her daughter would willingly leave her alone. She heard the doors swing back and the lift trundle downstairs, relief flowing over her that she could finally weep uninterrupted.

Twenty-Eight

Parnell Square, Dublin, May 1984

Emma waited a few days before making contact with Andrew. He was happy to hear her voice and sent around a car immediately. When she got to the house he was on the phone but indicated to her to sit in his untidy sitting room. He pushed a glass of champagne in her hand as he finished advising a solicitor about an urgent injunction application.

"It pays the bills, but that solicitor wants me to hold his hand even though he is only preparing the simplest of documents. Enough of that nonsense," he said afterwards as he fussed about, clearing a small mahogany side table for her glass. "Martin liked to sit in that chair, said it meant his back was to the substantial part of the room and the greater untidy mess."

He made her laugh and she relaxed, enjoying his banter and chat. They had quaffed a second glass of champagne each and she was feeling slightly tipsy when he suddenly left the room and brought in a large framed canvas.

"Martin had this hanging in his study. I wanted you to see it."

When he swung it around, she gasped in surprise.

The young girl was sitting on the chaise longue, her face sad, her eyes downcast, her brow furrowed in concentration as she tried to work up the courage to talk to her father. The dress was the blue flowery one with the zigzag braid around the outline of the pockets, her hair wavy, tied up in a bow-like clasp. She was wearing her summer sandals with her favourite pair of ankle socks, a small lace frill at the top. At the table, the judge was bent over his files piled on top of each other on either side of him. The window was throwing in light at the back, the law books standing sentry on the scene, a stack of files spilled untidily on the floor.

Andrew placed the painting across the couch and tiptoed away, leaving her to sit and stare and wonder how her father could have remembered the scene so vividly when, at the time, it was as if he barely noticed her. An oil painting, the canvas was rough to the touch, the colours of the library sombre, the little girl like a primrose in a dark wood, the father busy and preoccupied. She never knew he had remembered it; she never knew he had cared enough to paint it as it was.

"It is yours. I would like you to have it." Andrew, who had stolen back into the room, was leaning against the wall, watching her examining the painting.

"I don't know that my father would have wanted that."

Andrew came to her and put his arm around her shoulder. "This is exactly what he would have wanted. So do I."

He beckoned her across the hall to another sitting room-cum-office. It was almost the same as the first sitting room, but it was tidy. The person who sat here liked everything neat. The colour scheme was muted greys and blacks. There was a wide mahogany desk across the window span. At the fire, two high-backed armchairs, small footrests for the feet, mahogany side tables glinting in the sunlight. Over the fireplace a painting, a young woman in a shimmering gold dress, her hands fingering the tiny pleats and folds of the fabric, a faraway look in her eyes. The woman was standing as if examining the dress in a fitting, unaware that she was being observed or recorded. Around her neck was a delicate gold and pearl necklace.

Emma felt her throat tighten, her knees grinding. There was a dry taste in her mouth, so when she tried to speak she could not until she cleared her throat loudly. She sat down on the couch spanning the width of the fireplace, so that she could continue to look in the eyes of this woman she was sure was her mother.

"Why did he paint my mother?"

Andrew did not need to answer: she was so lost in the picture, she would not have heard him anyway.

The dress in the wardrobe, gold pleated linen by Sybil Connolly. Emma felt as if the ghost of Grace was on her shoulder, whispering to her. Her head was pounding, her heart racing. The artist showed a compassion for the subject; even the small curls around the front of her face were executed with precision, detail and care. Emma felt angry and confused. She wanted to run away from this double life and back to Parnell Square, where her father lived in the library and travelled between his law books in Parnell Square and his judge's bench at the Four Courts.

Andrew, detecting her confusion, sat beside her and pushed a tumbler of whiskey into her hand. "It is a lot to take in, I know."

She gulped the whiskey, not caring that it burnt the back of her throat.

"I never knew he loved her."

"He loved her and respected her, never forgave himself for what happened to her. Any bit of pleasure he got out of life, he immediately felt guilty, thinking of her, how she died in that asylum. He never meant that to happen."

"But how was it going to end, tell me that?"

"I don't think anybody can answer that. We only know how it ended in the tragedy it became."

"Why didn't he ever talk to me about any of this? I wish I had known he cared for her, it would have meant so much."

"Martin, as you know, was never good at talking about his feelings. I think it is only in the paintings that we can see how much you and your mother meant to him."

She got up and considered the painting close up, noticing for the first time it was set in the Parnell Square drawing room. There was a hint of the mustard velvet couch in the background. "Do you mind this being here?"

"Do I mind that he cared so much for her? I am glad he did. A man who could not have affection for such a lovely woman and daughter would be half a man."

Emma looked around the room, the bookcases laden with paperbacks, shelves of records, mostly opera, two shelves of model cars, rows and rows of pictures of himself and Andrew on their travels, fishing, side by side wearing tuxedos at society events.

"Am I really the only one who did not know?"

Andrew, concerned at the sharpness of her tone, thought for a moment before he spoke. "Everybody knew, but nobody knew for sure, like so many things in this great country of ours. There was only one person who knew absolutely. Angie Hannon helped us keep it all under the radar and for that we are infinitely grateful. She advised me to tell you and I was glad, because I wanted to, from the day of the funeral, though to have told you then would not have been the right time."

Emma ran her fingers along a dark wood bookshelf. The model cars, a Ford T, a Cadillac and a grey Morris Minor, were in perfect condition, not a speck of dust. Halfway down was a silver tray with a decanter of brandy and gleaming tumblers. Martin Moran saw no need to hide his drinking here. Tucked at the end of a shelf was a framed communion photograph, she and her father standing in the photographic studio on Dorset Street, her veil simple with a crown of artificial flowers, her dress panelled with a front inset of lace, the pearl buttons shining in the camera flash. She looked out of place here, this secret place where he led his real life. She felt very much a part of his other life. He was happy here, content, a man she had never known.

Andrew had disappeared again and for that she was grateful. If she had been idly looking around this room at the array of books and music, the old teddy propped against a shelf, the little mementoes of travel like the small lacquer box from Russia, the fly-fishing box displays, she would think it belonged to a person she could get on with.

Yet the man she had known was so different. Loneliness came over Emma for the father she did not know and the mother who had lost out on a husband and family life. Walking quickly out of the room, she stole a glance again at Grace. The exquisite dress added to the tragedy of the woman who had had everything and nothing.

Andrew Kelly called her to join him in the kitchen, where he was frying two steaks to serve with pepper sauce and a green salad. "Martin was never much of a cook. He was quite a cheat, used to get Angie to cook up a storm for him and then transfer it across in foil plates and onto the plates before I got home. Silly man thought I was completely fooled and I never let on." He stopped when he saw Emma's face crumple and tears splash down her face. "I have to stop going on so. Sit and get this down you."

He plopped a whiskey into a small glass and pushed it towards her. She drank it in one go, embarrassed that she should collapse in front of this man who was so loved by her father.

"I am sorry. I feel strange, not about the two of you, but that I missed out on knowing the real Martin Moran. I think I would have liked the man who was your partner."

"And he would have liked you."

"I couldn't come when you wrote."

"It is all right. He understood."

She fisted the table, tears coursing down her face. "It is not all right. I could have come, I just did not want to. I did not want to be by his side when he was dying."

Andrew Kelly, if he was shocked, did not let on, though when he spoke again she noticed his voice had changed to a more formal tone, which is what he probably used in court.

"The past is a painful place to live, Emma. Maybe it is time to move on."

She wiped away her tears and, in an effort to please him, began to eat her food, though she had no appetite. He babbled on about this and that, but she barely heard him, taking in instead the warmth of this house, compared with Parnell Square, the friendly atmosphere, the fact the judge had not been a judge here but a man and a lover. Here, Martin Moran had been willing to accept the idiosyncrasies of others, something he could never do for his daughter. If Andrew Kelly thought letting her peep in on her father's real life would help, he was very wrong. It made her feel even more isolated and lonelier than ever before.

She lasted through dessert before she said she had an appointment in the city and must go. Andrew Kelly did not believe her, but she did not care. She needed to escape from this house; she needed to find calm. When Andrew ran to the car with the library painting, she declined, asking him if he would mind keeping it for her until she was ready to accept it.

She got the driver to drop her off at St Stephen's Green. Shunning the busy centre of the park, she headed down the outside path, where the wind wheezed through the trees. Here, she could pretend she was far away. Spying a small gazebo lost in a small clearing, she went there and sat down, the damp air creeping around her, the leaves rustling, the branches creaking. A blackbird fluttered in and, seeing her, let out a loud warning call. A child running ahead of its parents peeped in and saw her but was whooshed on his way. Closing her eyes, she felt the tears bubble up, wrenching through her. She wept long and hard, screaming in her head for the mother and father lost forever, screaming in her head for the lives lived and those kept secret.

Twenty-Nine

Parnell Square, Dublin, May 1984

Two days later, Andrew picked up Emma and they travelled to the city offices of the solicitors together. They were immediately shown into a tiny room on the second floor. Andrew settled into a chair in front of a large desk, but Emma, more restless, stood, her hands running over the chocolate pleated linen of her box jacket and skirt.

The night before, at No. 19, she had rooted through the wardrobes for something to wear. A part of her was afraid of the finality the reading of her father's will brought, but another part of her wanted to represent her mother, to be present, to hear his last decision for the family. The suit she found at the back of the wardrobe was right for the occasion. She was flicking through the rail when an outfit covered in tissue paper with a note attached by a straight pin caught her eye: "To be collected, Grace Moran."

Emma tore off the tissue paper. Chocolate-brown, soft, tight linen pleats in a separate jacket and skirt. The skirt was the same as before, long, horizontal pleats, the jacket a box pattern in the same fabric, a deep ruffle of pleated linen on the elbow-length sleeves. Carefully, Emma slipped the outfit from its hanger. Stepping into the skirt, she noticed the chocolate-brown colour shimmered in the light. The box jacket buttoned up to a round, collarless neck. It was soft and comfortable and moved with her, her hair set off by the dark undertones of the jacket.

The door opened and a woman bustled in. "Miss Moran, Mr Kelly, thank you so much for attending our offices here today. I am Natalia Redlich: we should get started."

Emma smiled at the solicitor's business-like manner and remained unflustered, waiting for the reading to commence. Natalia Redlich was fussing, so Emma took in instead the painting of a woman sewing, her child leaning against her mother's lap as she stitched a square of fabric. When the solicitor broke into her daydream, Emma flinched.

"I will now read the last will and testament of Judge Martin Moran, No. 19 Parnell Square, Dublin."

Slowly, she opened the grey folder and took out a large sealed envelope. Using her pen, she ripped open the seal, taking out a sheet of paper and two smaller envelopes.

"I, Judge Martin Moran of Parnell Square, Dublin, being of sound mind and body do make this last will and testament and leave my estate, including the following properties: No. 19 Parnell Square, Dublin; 21a Rue du Bac, 7th arrondissement, Paris; and St James's Terrace, London, NW8; and various bank accounts to my daughter, Emma Moran, to be distributed as outlined in the accompanying letter. I also ask that the second accompanying letter be handed to Mr Andrew Kelly, my best and loyal friend."

Neither Emma nor Andrew said anything, but accepted the letters when the solicitor handed them across.

Emma did not want to open hers. Maybe it would be better to stuff it in her pocket and read it at home. The solicitor coughed politely and drummed the desk with her fingers. Emma ripped the seal and pulled out the paper roughly, as if she was in a hurry.

"Maybe I should go," Andrew said, rising slowly from his chair, as if he did not want to disturb the quiet.

"You are entitled to stay, but if you prefer to go . . ." the solicitor replied impatiently.

Andrew sighed loudly, before turning to Emma. "Emma, I can wait downstairs."

"Can I meet you another time? I think I might need to be on my own for a bit."

The solicitor looked at her watch, tapping her fingers on the table. Andrew made to open the door, but appeared to hesitate and turned to the solicitor. "Miss Redlich, I am sure you do your job very well, but it might be best to remember in the future you are dealing with people with real live emotions, not just files and numbers."

Natalia Redlich's face turned sour, making Emma stifle a laugh as she concentrated instead on the letter in her hand.

"Do I have to read it now?"

"It is probably best that you do, to make sure you understand the contents," the solicitor said gently. "Would you like to be on your own or will I stay?"

"Maybe on my own."

Natalia Redlich gathered up her files and quietly left the room.

Emma was not sure what to do. Part of her wanted to read the letter, another part was afraid. A squall of wind shook the glass of the window, making it rattle fiercely. The wind pushed on to the river, curling up the Liffey, making the pedestrians on the quays move faster.

She carefully unfolded the letter and began to read.

19 Parnell Square,
Dublin
February 18, 1984

My Dearest Emma,

Your mother, if she had been able, would have loved you with every fibre of her being. In her absence, I tried to fill a gap, which was too deep and wide.

I know the last time we were in my study together, you said some things. I am sorry I didn't stand up there then and tell you how much I cared for you. I am equally sorry that writing it down can never compare to saying it, with all the emotion such a statement as "I love you" deserves.

I have tried to be a good father, but I was always a better judge and I wonder what that counts for now.

I must leave you, dearest Emma, other bothersome matters I should have had the courage to address much earlier. I know you believe when you were born your mother was very ill and later died. What I concealed from you, I stress for no other reason than to protect you, was that my Grace did not indeed die but had to be committed to an asylum. The poor thing was unable to function on her own and her aunt Violet suggested a short spell in the asylum in Knockavanagh. Reluctantly I agreed, but, unfortunately for Grace and all of us, it went on longer than it should. I am sorry to report Grace died in the asylum. She lost her life in a fire. I left her there and she suffered that terrible fate. For that, I will never forgive myself.

I profoundly regret that I had neither the strength nor the bravery to tell you the truth. I regret even more that I had not the strength of character or mind to take Grace from that asylum and look for alternative ways to help her. As you know, Aunt Violet has had a huge influence on our lives and it was only on her death bed that she admitted to me that Grace was never as bad as had been insisted upon by the doctors. Violet had paid them a monthly stipend to exaggerate Grace's symptoms in reports to me. These same reports kept her in the asylum. Violet had her own twisted reasons for that. That I got caught up in it and never questioned these reports is an incredible shame and sadness for me. I let Grace down and I will never forgive myself.

There is one other matter that I feel I should trouble you with. I don't do so lightly. I think you always felt I was your father only in name, and you were right. You were fathered not by me but by the man Grace loved all her life, an Indian doctor, Vikram Fernandes. Not only that, but you are not an only child. It was only when *she gave birth that we realised Grace had been pregnant with twins. It was impossible to tell back in those days and I understand that Grace was so overcome during the labour that I do not know if even she was aware of it. But the twin girls were born two different colours: white and brown. Tell me, Emma, how could we in Ireland of the '50s keep a brown baby? Not even my position as a judge could protect us on that. Vikram Fernandes, when he returned to India, took your twin sister with him. He did not know the details of the birth and as a result did not know you existed. I have to point out that at this stage I knew nothing of any of the things that led Vikram Fernandes to make the decision to leave this country. Aunt Violet told the man Grace was dead, which I think was a despicable thing to do, but then Aunt Violet always put her own selfish needs first.*

At the height of all the stress and anxiety surrounding the birth, I did what I thought to be best. You and your sister can pass final judgement.

You were right, Emma, I was not your father and, to my eternal shame, I never showed you how much I cared for you. Your sister and her father were constantly on my mind. Even judges make bad decisions, Emma. So do the most well-meaning of fathers. As you stand in judgement over me, I hope you will assess the mitigating circumstances that led to my decisions and the pain and loss I have had to live with all these years. If you can, please judge me half kindly.

I was married to Grace and regard her children as mine. Therefore, in my final will, I leave my property folio and bank accounts to you, Emma, and to the little girl who was sent to India I leave £100,000. It will leave you both with an ample legacy and maybe help in some small way to right the wrongs of the past.

With esteem, love and respect,

Martin Moran

Emma let the letter drop into her lap. Her mouth was parched dry, pain thumping at the back of her eyes. From where she sat, Emma could see out into the company car park, where the parking attendant was drinking a mug of tea, his feet up reading a tabloid newspaper.

She had a sister. A sister that maybe did not look like her, but a sister. Grace was dead, and now she had to find her sister.

Emma turned away to watch the late-afternoon sun flash across the wet bonnets of the cars. How would she find her sister?

When Natalia Redlich slipped into the room, Emma jumped up, pacing about.

"You know where my sister is, don't you?"

The solicitor looked flustered, fiddling with items on her desk.

"In the letter, my father says he left money to my sister. You surely have an address, something. I have to find her."

Natalia Redlich sighed deeply. "At the risk of being accused of being heartless, I can only tell you what I have been instructed to say." She held up a page, as if to create a barrier between them, and read out the sentences. "'My daughter Emma will want to know about her sister. I have only the information I have included here. The address of Vikram Fernandes is Residency Road, Bangalore, Karnataka, India, which I stress is an address from the 1950s. I have instructed my solicitors to write to that address and have also enclosed a letter to one Vikram Fernandes, telling him of Emma's existence and other matters which need not concern you. I have also instructed the solicitors on the reply to make contact with my daughter Emma and forward to her the address of Mr Fernandes or his next of kin, if that is relevant.'"

"Has there been an answer?"

"The letter was only recently dispatched. We have not yet heard from him."

"You are saying there is nothing I can do. I will have to wait for him to make contact."

"I am saying we will have to wait and see how things pan out."

Emma moved to the window. Small waves raced along the top of the Liffey, the seagulls flying low, squealing. She imagined she heard the birds squawk out the word "sister" over and over.

"Is there anything else we can do for you, Miss Moran? Probate should take a few months. We will be in touch."

Natalia Redlich made to stand and Emma, wiping a tear from the corners of her eyes, gathered up her handbag. "Thank you, Miss Redlich."

Ignoring the hand extended, Emma rushed from the solicitor's office and down the stairs to the street. She was shaking, a piercing pain stabbing through her head. Not knowing where exactly she was going, she made for the bridge. She made a lonely figure lingering on a windy day on a bridge over an angry river. Passers-by looked oddly at her as she leaned on the parapet for support, the power of the water rushing underneath making her skin tingle.

All the times she had wanted a sister. All the times she had wanted a mother. The man who was not her father had taken them away from her.

"Emma? Emma, where are you going? You will get your death of cold. Come on in, it is time for a hot whiskey."

Andrew Kelly had waited in a doorway opposite the solicitors but was too slow to stop Emma before she went on Grattan Bridge spanning the River Liffey.

"You knew, didn't you?"

He did not answer but steered her into the Clarence Hotel. He called for two Irish coffees as he guided Emma to the lounge area at the back.

"What sort of a man was he, Andrew?"

"Martin? An inept man trying to do his best, I suppose, like a lot of us."

"Hardly. He left my mother in that asylum and he let my twin sister be taken away to India."

"What?"

"My father wasn't my father, Andrew, and I am not an only child. My mother gave birth to twins. My twin sister was sent abroad because of her colour. She may have done better than me: she, at least, was with her birth parent."

"What do you mean?"

"My father was an Indian doctor." Emma gulped too much of her coffee when it arrived, burning the back of her mouth, but she barely noticed. "How can it be one baby white, one brown? Is this just some sick joke?"

"Martin would not do that to you."

"He put my mother in an asylum."

"I know Martin was a good man. His word always was true and it still is, in my books. I know a doctor, a medical expert we use in cases. Let me ring him and ask him about this. No names, of course."

Emma nodded and Andrew disappeared out into the lobby to make his call. She sat, her hands cupped around the glass. What would this sister think of her? Would the father turn his back on her? Why couldn't the judge have left it? Surely she had enough to contend with. Big tears rolled down her cheeks, one plopping into the creamy top of the Irish coffee, sinking to nothing.

Andrew came back in and sat beside her. "It is rare, but it can happen. Was there ever anybody who was not white in your background?"

"My grandfather was Pakistani, but nobody was supposed to know that. It was a big scandal at the time. Aunt Violet said at least Grace looked white."

Andrew threw his eyes to heaven. "Aunt Violet was a cruel and heartless woman with a tongue that was way too sharp."

Emma sipped her coffee. "What next?" She said the words, but she did not know if she wanted an answer. Andrew reached across and took her hand and squeezed it. She handed him the judge's letter, but he refused it.

"I don't need to read it, Emma, if I did I would have to hand you my letter from him, but I am not ready for that yet."

She didn't question him further. Refusing a lift home, she opted instead to walk alone along the rainy streets.

Thirty

Bangalore, India, May 1984

Rhya was in her own room, still upset, when she heard Vikram come home late. He slipped off his sandals at the door and padded quietly across to his bedroom, so as not to disturb her.

Feeling tired, he wanted to lie down straight away, but instead he sat at his desk to write up some last-minute instructions for Anil. He was halfway through when he saw a letter propped behind his ashtray. Annoyed that the girl should leave his post where he would not at first notice, he snatched it. His hand shook. He felt his chest tighten. Stress pains spanned across him. He started to breathe deeply, but his heart did not calm.

In all the years since he had come back to India he had not received any communication from Ireland. Neither had he made any enquiry of anybody or any organisation in Ireland. And now that he was ready to go back there, a letter arrived.

Using his letter opener, he carefully slit the edges, opening it enough so that a letter and another envelope popped out. His brow furrowed. He scanned the business-like words.

Why on this earth would Judge Martin Moran leave a letter for him to read after his death? Fear crept through Vikram as he pulled open the second envelope.

Skimming down through it, his chest tightened fiercely. A sweaty clamminess seeped through the roots of his hair. Squeezing his eyes shut, he hoped the pain would leave him. Clutching the paper so he scrunched it, he opened his eyes warily, fear gripping him as he flattened the page and reread the sentence that turned everything on its head and made a terrible mockery of his whole life. He jumped up, the chair clattering backwards. Sweeping his hand across his desk, everything crashed to the ground, the glass where he normally kept his pens shattering on the marble.

Rhya thumped on Vikram's door, shouting at him to let her in. Ignoring her, he kicked the pile of ironed and folded clothes beside his bureau, and pushed at the display of silver on top next until the heavy ornaments toppled on the floor.

By the time Rhya had run around to access the room from the balcony, Vikram had collapsed onto the bed, his body writhing with the power of loss and anger combined. Strange, mournful sounds emanated from her brother, who could not enunciate even one coherent word.

Rhya, surveying the room, shook her head. Walking to her brother, she placed a hand on his head and began to stroke him, like a mother does an upset child. He did not acknowledge her presence, though the gulping tears lessened. She sat down, reminded of her mother with her father after news came through of Vikram's plight in Ireland. What a tsunami of pain that small country had unleashed on the family. What more was to roll in on them now?

Vikram sat up and looked at his sister. "You know the contents of this letter from Ireland?"

"Vik, it came today, but I have not touched it, I swear."

Shrugging his shoulders, he kicked a silver bowl out of his way as he made for the outside door.

Rhya pulled at him. "Where are you going, Vik?"

Hearing the pain in her voice, he hesitated. "I don't know, Rhya. I just need space." He made his way through the apartment and stepped into the lift, pushing the button so the doors would close over before she had time to object.

Vikram did not even notice when the nightwatchman saluted. He stumbled his way, keeping to the near middle of the road in places in case he tripped or fell in a hole. He had no idea where he was going, only that he had to walk, because to stand still would mean despair would envelop him.

How could he not have known? Surely their love was such that he would have known if Grace was still alive. He would never have left, but that he believed she was dead. Why had the judge waited until now to unburden himself and place a load of such magnitude on his shoulders?

When he looked back at the apartment, he saw Rhya was pacing up and down the balcony. He rushed on so that soon he would be out of her sight.

How long had Grace waited for him? Pain stabbed through him to think of her believing in him, despairing when he never came for her. All these years he had consoled himself that there was no other option; all these years he had lived a lie. He had had to leave Ireland, there was no doubt at the time, but why had he left it a lifetime before seeking to return?

He was a coward who had let her down. Now he must

suffer, knowing not only had he walked away but he had taken their daughter from her too.

At Cubbon Park, he strode along the dark paths, his head down, not caring what he met. Inside he was weak, but he felt the strength of anger and outrage as he pushed on through the park, sweat pumping from him, mixing with the tears that were flowing down his face.

In his head, he shouted Grace's name over and over, beseeching her to come and strike him dead like a pauper lifeless on the path, to be found by the workers as they cut through the park on the way to work. She did not answer him, and who could blame her? He who had said he loved her, would never leave her, he who had knitted fanciful stories of their future life together.

Collapsing onto a bench, Vikram gasped for air. A man curled up under a grey shawl asked him if he was all right, but Vikram was unable to answer. The man called out to a friend under the tree, who came over to enquire if Uncle was ill. "Go home, Uncle, this is not a place for you. You should not walk through the park at night." Vikram moved on as the men settled themselves back to sleep.

He was pacing too fast, propelling himself along so that he was in danger of tripping. A pain crept up his arm and across his chest. He stumbled to a park bench, afraid he would have a heart attack, that he would not make it to Ireland to find her grave. If he were to die, let it be beside her, not in this dark unfriendly place. His forehead was clammy, his hands shaking, but he felt the pain abate. He sat up straight and tried to get his bearings.

The statue of Queen Victoria towered over him. The big busty lady with the stone brocade dress was a reminder of his younger days, when his worries were minuscule. In the full moon, he took the statue in. His good friend Rahul had once climbed it and, standing eyeball to eyeball with the queen, kissed her. Taking a small can of red paint from his pocket, he coloured her eyes red and drew a big, elaborate, hairy moustache on the imperial face. Afterwards they ran like the wind, afraid they would be nabbed by a policeman, basking in the glow of having done something silly and getting away with it. They only became slightly worried the next day when the newspapers carried a report of the vagabonds who had defaced the famous stone lady.

The pain was intermittent, so Vikram began to slowly trudge home. He was exhausted, his head full of Grace. He heard her whisper in his ear, stealing up behind him.

He jumped and she laughed at him, teasing him.

He pulled her into a gazebo almost covered with creepers and climbers, out of sight of the path. He kissed her, and she giggled, kissing him back. Afterwards, she leaned into him and he held her close, until they had to part. As they crept out of the gazebo, she turned to him.

"Promise me you will always love me."

"How could it be any other way?"

"Promise me."

"I promise to love you beyond forever."

Vikram shook himself free of his dream and, seeing a rickshaw, the driver asleep inside, pushed his feet to wake him up.

*

Rhya, when she heard the rickshaw slow down at the apartment block, listened intently for the lift. She was glad when she heard Vikram come in but decided to leave him alone. She heard him go to his room and begin to tidy up. Happy the servants would not have anything to gossip about, she stayed where she was, her sari cupboard open in front of her.

When Vikram had walked out, she had watched for a while from the balcony as he rushed up Residency Road and away. She refused to fret, instead taking her bunch of keys and unlocking the sari cupboard.

She had draped her hands across the neat piles, feeling for the sari of her youth, the one that brought her most comfort. A simple blue nylon-chiffon sari with a deep colourful border, she had worn it the first day she visited the family home of the man who was to become her husband. Unbeknown to her, Sanjay had been standing out of sight in the driveway of their compound, watching the Fernandes Ambassador car pull in off the road.

When she got out of the car, he told her later, he could not see her face. Neither could he remember the colour of her sari, always pleading a very good reason: he was smitten by the beauty of her slim ankle, revealed as she alighted from the car. She was spirited away and he did not see her again until their official meeting one week later, when they sat stiffly on chairs making polite conversation in the presence of their parents. The next time they met was on their wedding day.

Sanjay she had loved deeply, but she and her family were unaware the promising young lawyer was a chronic asthmatic. Barely two years into the marriage, he died horribly of a severe asthma attack in the hill station of Pune as his terrified wife attempted to open his mouth wide to force more oxygen into him.

Draping the sari over her, she swished across the room,

remembering his shy smile, the way he pulled her to him, the way he liked her sandals to have a heel to show off her ankles, even though most of the time he could not see her tiny feet under her sari and petticoat.

Taking off the sari, she folded it quickly and deftly, lest this daydreaming make her cry. Carefully, she placed the sari at the top of her special pile, leaving the sari cupboard open so she may air it out before she had to lock it, when the servants arrived in the morning.

Vikram, she knew, would not want to talk to her, so she lay in her bed, closing her eyes, conjuring up images of the time when she had a husband, young children and a home of her own. Her life had changed at the click of a finger, as fast as a cat pouncing on a mouse. Once her husband died, his family did not want to know her and her two children, so she came back and lived in the Fernandes home. This is where both she and Vikram stayed, nursing their old loves, not allowing anybody else into their lives. How things could have been so different, if only they had known what to do to make it happen.

She had had offers, but never could she contemplate another man in her bed. On these types of nights, she missed the companionship of sharing a problem, the support of a husband, the second opinion at the time of crisis. Rhya closed her eyes and hoped everything would be better in the morning.

Thirty-One

Parnell Square, Dublin, May 1984

Emma stopped in Wicklow on the way to Knockavanagh to buy pots of primula and a deep-red fuchsia for the far-right side of the grave, where the wind punched through like needles.

"Would you not get a few plastic flowers? It makes the maintenance much easier," the man in the shop said.

"I think my mother would not like that. I imagine she loved fresh flowers."

She had already got out the pots and placed them in a row on the bonnet of the car when she realised she had not brought any tools to Knockavanagh. Knocking on the presbytery front door, she hoped the priest was not saying Mass.

Mandy McGuane, when she opened the front door, took in the young woman with the bouncy brown hair.

"Miss McGuane, Father said it would be all right if I tended to my mother's grave today." She held out her hand and Mandy shook it gently.

"Do you need any help at all?"

"I should be fine, though I have just realised I forgot any tools."

"I think we can run to that." Mandy noticed a softness in the young woman's eyes. "I have everything in the shed out the back. Which grave is it? I will bring down what you need."

"Grace Moran's grave."

Mandy stopped and stared at the young woman standing in front of her. "Father O'Brien said you called." She wanted to say more, but her mouth was parched dry. Her throat was as if it was swollen.

"I thought it might be nice to tidy up around the grave, plant some flowers."

Mandy shook herself so that she could answer without giving any hint of her inner turmoil. "Go on, I will drop the tools down to you in a few minutes."

"Can I carry anything for you?"

"You are all right."

Emma turned away without detecting the teary shake in Mandy's voice.

Quickly, Mandy closed the door and scuttled to the kitchen, where she gathered up a tea towel and howled into it, her cries muffled by the thick cotton. She stayed like this, gulps of tears rushing out into the cloth, before she left to splash cold water on her face. Using a fresh tea towel, she patted her face dry, making sure to throw them for the wash afterwards.

After she had collected the shovel, she set off down the path to the asylum fire plot, where Emma was already on her hands and knees arranging the planting.

"I thought primroses in the centre and the fuchsia to act as a windbreaker. I did not know my mother, but they strike me as right for Grace."

"She would have loved this attention."

"You knew Grace?"

"We were friends."

"Do you mind if I talk to you about my mother? Could you maybe tell me what she was like?"

Mandy looked in alarm at Emma. Her knees were going soft; her head was thumping. "I can't stay long. Father O'Brien likes a big fry-up after Mass."

"How long did you know Grace?"

"We were friends for years. There was nothing wrong with her. Mentally, I mean. She had the same misfortune that I had: an interfering family who were ashamed of her. We were both abandoned by our families, lost our babies and were stuck in that awful asylum."

"Did you know about Vikram Fernandes?"

"She waited for him all her life, never gave up on him, though many told her she was foolish."

"It is so sad."

"The judge died?"

"Yes, he died not long ago."

"You said Grace was your mother. Yet she told me you died at birth. How can you be here?"

Emma gave a sharp laugh. "And my whole life I was told my mother was dead. We were both told lies. I am only getting to the truth now."

A shadow stretched across Mandy's face as she stooped to hack the ground, getting it ready for the primroses.

Emma stopped what she was doing and looked at the older woman. "You are not dressed for this cold wind. I can do this on my own."

Mandy, who had begun to shiver, was glad of the dismissal. "Please call up for a cup of tea, when you are done."

She walked back up the little hill. Before turning into the house, she stood and looked at the young woman carefully pushing her primulas into the soil and watering them with the can she had filled for her. She went to sit in the kitchen. She was not sure what she should do next, not sure if she should tell this young woman the whole story.

She jumped when there was a knock at the door. Emma stood, a big smile on her face.

"I am finished a bit earlier than I thought. The wind has risen and it is a bit chilly."

"Why don't you come in and have some tea?"

"I was hoping you could tell me a little bit more about my mother. I know a fair bit about what she liked – I found all her clothes and jewellery in the attic – but I know nothing of the person she was."

Mandy led the way into the kitchen, busying herself with taking the mugs down from the cupboard.

"Were you there the night of the fire?"

Mandy stopped what she was doing. For a moment, Emma thought she was going to ask her to leave.

Slowly Mandy turned around, tears shimmering in her eyes. "It had started off such a happy night. She had stitched a lovely dress for herself. I had got the fabric when I was out in the town. She made me put it on so she could judge the length. Next thing there was this awful smoke. Everybody started screaming. The ward doors were locked.

"She ran to a window, but when she realised I was not with her she came back to where I was hiding. She pulled me out from under the bed and told me I would definitely die if I stayed there. Next thing she had pushed me out the window. I was knocked unconscious in the fall. I broke my ankle, hurt my back. I don't know what happened to Grace, why she didn't make it."

They sat quietly until the kettle boiled, switching off with a loud click.

"I am raising ghosts, I am sorry," said Emma.

"It is only natural that you would want to know about it. She saved my life, but by the time they let me out of hospital she was already buried. I didn't even get to the funeral. Everybody in the asylum was scattered all over the place. There was no interest in rebuilding it. Father Grennan said he would take me in and be responsible for me, so I had a home."

"My father, did he ever visit the grave?"

"He paid for the whole plot. That is why it looks so nice. He sent a cheque every year for the upkeep, but he never set foot in the place after the funeral. You are the first of Grace's family to come here."

Emma traced a pattern on the oilcloth covering the kitchen table. "I should get back. I promised my friend I would help her with her patchwork quilt: she has to finish it for some competition." Emma stopped, rattling the car keys in her pocket. "Do you like sewing at all, Miss McGuane?"

Mandy looked taken back. "In my day, I was good at the stitches."

Thirty-Two

Bangalore, India, May 1984

Vikram did not sleep, so by the time Rhya woke up he was sitting reading his newspaper. His case was packed, his passport left on top.

"Are you still going, Vik?"

He closed his *Deccan Herald*, folding it with extra precision. "More than ever, I have to go now. Rosa rang. We will have lunch here and go together to the station in the evening, after our rest."

"Vikram, this is madness." Rhya's voice was low with defeat. "What has to happen to make you stop wanting to go to that country. That place is going to be the death of you."

"Rhya, don't you see? I have to stand at Grace's grave, to ask her forgiveness. I have to do it."

"I am so worried about you, Vik."

"Rosa won't let anything happen to me."

"Madness, unadulterated madness."

"It is the right thing to do."

"Right, wrong, what does it matter? It is not going to bring back the lost years or bring Grace back to life." As soon as she said the words, Rhya regretted it. The pain inflicted by her careless words crawled across her brother's face. "Is there any way I can stop you, Vikram?"

"Not even if you stand in front of me, Rhya."

Rhya threw her hands in the air. Everybody thought she was the stubborn one, but Vikram won hands down every time. "Your room, you cleared it?"

He did not answer but reached into his pocket and handed her a folded page of lined paper. "Read it to understand my mood. I have told my man to replace what is broken and fix the chair."

Opening the letter carefully, Rhya sat down, but when she heard Rosa downstairs she stuffed it quickly back in her pocket. "Call it off, Vik. No matter about the money."

He jumped up, striding out to the balcony. Rhya knew better than to follow.

Rosa arrived, her voice ahead of her as she instructed two servants where to deposit her luggage. Taking in the nervous twitches of her mother, the hunched figure of Vikram on the balcony, she asked what was wrong. Rhya threw her hands up in the air.

"Call it all off. That country is no place for our family, that is what is wrong."

Rosa burst out laughing. "Mama, you are nervous for us going on a long trip. We understand."

They heard Vikram sigh loudly as he went into his room, locking the door behind him.

"Rosa, I don't want you travelling to that place because of what it did to your uncle. It practically ruined our family. This family almost floundered after Vikram was arrested and charged with the most heinous crimes. What do you think it took to stop the news spreading? We managed, but at a terrible price. You going back just digs it all up again." She stopped, afraid she had said too much.

Rosa put her arm around her mother's shoulder. "Mama, nobody has ever told me exactly what went on. Isn't it time?"

Rhya called the servant girl and sent her on an errand before closing the front door and snapping the lock. She did the same with the door to the balcony.

"There are those who have their own theories, but they will never hear anything in this house." She dropped her voice and motioned Rosa to sit close. "Vikram appeared before a court and was charged. You know the charge, I can't bear to repeat it. It took several weeks for the letter to arrive. Imagine the consternation when my mother opened it.

"She fainted, fell on the floor in front of us. My father sent us all out and carried Mama to the bedroom. There, he also read the letter. I can still hear his weeping. We all stood beside the jackfruit tree in the garden, us children and the servants listening to Rudolph Fernandes weeping like a child. We all thought Vikram was dead." Rhya stopped to swallow hard. "They told us Vikram was very ill and Father would have to travel to Ireland. We all cried as he prepared to take the night train to Delhi. I was a married woman at this stage, but my parents told me nothing.

"When my father came back from Ireland, he was a broken man. He was not the man he had been and he did not bring any hope with him for Vikram." Reaching for the end of her pallu, Rhya dabbed her eyes as she continued. "My father offered everything we had to get poor Vikram out on bail, but the court would not accept any terms, so he had to leave him there in a jail, where he had already been attacked and was now in solitary confinement for his own protection. Father employed a solicitor, but it was still nearly six months before Vikram was released and the charges against him dropped.

"Nobody apologised, nobody did anything about the false allegations, nobody cared that Vik's job and reputation were gone. He was left with no option but to return home." Rhya began to pace around the room. "It was the worst of times, Rosa."

"Wasn't I born around then?"

Rhya stopped patrolling. "You came into our lives at a very strange time. When Vikram returned to India, he could barely talk. If it wasn't for the good standing of our father he would never have got work again, even if it was a much inferior position than he had hoped for. There was that and the fact that nobody knew the truth of what went on in Ireland. They still don't. If that happened even now, we would not be able to hold our heads up."

"It was a false allegation. Did nobody do anything about that?"

"What to do? We looked after Vikram, that's all we could do, and our poor mother went slowly but surely mad. It started the day father set off for Ireland. She was certain we had lost our two men to that country. She barely ate, paced the veranda, up and down, all night long. She aged in front of our eyes, and then after father came back, it continued. She was constantly going checking on Vikram, almost as if he was her baby again. This went on for months, before she took to her bed.

"The only time she got up was at night, walking the house looking for Vikram, shouting that bad people had got him.

When she started getting angry with us, the doctors tried to find out what was wrong. The only conclusion was the stress had triggered something that should have happened much later in her life. Poor mother was losing her mind."

"I don't remember Grandmother."

"Mercifully, she died before you were three years of age, but those years ground us down to nothing. She could not be left on her own and we had to get in extra servants to help at a time when the coffee estate was in trouble financially."

"Uncle Vik turned around the coffee estate, didn't he?"

"He hated the job he had in the Bangalore hospital and begged father to let him take over the coffee estate. Father, feeling defeated, thought it could do no harm and Vikram moved to Chikmagalur and took over operations. He made a surprisingly good fist of it. He buried himself in the mountains, working all hours until our coffee estate was one of the foremost in the area."

Rosa noticed that Rhya's shoulders had straightened with pride.

"Vik wanted to make up for the pain and hardship he had caused the whole family. He was gutted about what happened to our mother. When the day came, she did not recognise him. He said it was for the best, maybe she had forgotten, too, the awful shame he had piled on her shoulders."

Rhya went to the kitchen to run a small towel under cold water, squeezing it out to swipe it along the back of her neck.

"You surely understand why I don't want you to go to that place."

"Times have changed, Mama. What can happen to us now?"

"You are beginning to sound too much like Vikram," Rhya

said as she unlocked the apartment door. A small breeze passed through the room.

"Two weeks only, Mama, and we will be back."

"I know, Rosa, but what will happen in the meantime? Tell me that."

They were both quiet when Vikram unlocked the bedroom door and opened it wide.

Rhya called out to him and he walked over to his sister. Gently running a hand along her cheek, he spoke to her in a low, comforting murmur. "Please don't worry, but understand this is something I must do."

Rhya let tears coast down her face as she hugged her brother. Grasping her daughter's hand, she spoke in an almost cross voice. "Come home safe, both of you. I insist on it."

It was late evening when Vikram and Rosa called a car to bring them to the station to catch the sleeper train to Delhi. Rhya did not go downstairs to say goodbye but stood on the balcony, watching the car until it was out of sight.

All day she had fingered Vikram's letter in her pocket and now she had time to read it. Settling on her bed, she took it out, flattening it to the edges. Curse the Morans and their small country, she thought as she set about reading. Soon she would have to tell Rosa the full truth, but at least now she could wait until she came back from Ireland and until Vikram was stronger.

19 Parnell Square
Dublin
February 18, 1984

Dear Dr Fernandes,

This is a very difficult letter to write and I won't insult either of us by enquiring after your health. Time, I find, is snapping at my heels and due to a cancerous tumour I do not expect to be alive for very long. I know by the time you are reading this I will have passed on. At this moment, when the pain of cancer consumes my body, it is indeed a comforting thought.

As happens when an approximate date to leave this world is flagged, I have been assessing my life on this earth and moving to right any perceived wrongs .For obvious reasons, your name has come back in focus, and I feel I must alert you to something important. I believe you loved my wife Grace and I know she loved you, something she could never offer to me. Ours was an arranged marriage. It is something I will regret beyond my dying day. Yet there is another matter that is altogether more serious and has over the years troubled me greatly.

When I told you to take away your daughter, I led you to believe she was the only survivor of a terribly difficult birth. That is not, however, the case. Another girl, who I have brought up as Emma, was born that night. When the two were born, we were faced with a difficult dilemma and to split them up seemed the appropriate and only solution.

I saw no need to consult you then and neither do I offer an apology now, merely an explanation and information you may want to act on. The other baby was for all intents and purposes a white child and I brought her up as my own daughter. Emma had a good education and, while she suffered because of the lack of a mother in her life, she has turned into a fine young woman. It is with regret I have to say I have not spoken to her in several years, since she left home in something of a fury at what she perceived to be my interference in her life. She emigrated to Australia and my reports from there say she is married. I hope beyond anything she has found some happiness. No doubt, having brought up a daughter, you will understand the difficulties a parent experiences trying to steer them on the road to success and achievement.

This information will come as a shock to you. The following information may also be of some assistance. I put it in your hands to pass on as you see fit.

As you know, I am a wealthy man and I have given much thought to the following. I intend to leave my house in Parnell Square, Dublin, my apartment in Paris and my London apartment to my daughter, Emma. However, I feel that I must be fair to the other little girl who, through no reason other than her father's origins, missed out on the same upbringing as her sister.

I leave also to this girl, who is the daughter of Vikram Fernandes and Grace Moran and a twin sister of Emma Moran, a significant amount of cash and have instructed my solicitor as such.

There is another matter that requires to be addressed. I know Violet McNally took you aside and told you Grace was dead. I know

now, but I swear I had no knowledge at that time, that she was the one who arranged for the charges against you to be dropped, providing you leave the country. I tell you most sincerely I knew nothing of any of this. When you came to me after the case had been withdrawn, I honestly thought the wheels of justice had been turning. It made sense you would want to return to your home country. It also made sense you would take away the little girl, who had no future and would not fit in here in any way.

Violet McNally, before her death, told me you thought Grace was dead when you came to my house that night. She also admitted she was behind the vile and false accusations made against you.

To my eternal shame, I did nothing about either admission. In these regards I have done wrong, and I sincerely apologise. I have my own cross to bear. Grace died at the asylum, a fact that tortures me every hour of every day.

I realise the above will come as a shock to you and no doubt to your daughter. All I ask in return is that I am not thought of too unkindly. I wish you and your daughter well.

I suppose I have to refer to the nasty business that went on between the two of us. All I can say in mild mitigation is that, at the time, I believed it necessary. There were extraordinary excusing circumstances which led to the decisions made. That they caused you pain and will again now, I profoundly regret. If we could all look back and *say with alacrity that we stood by every decision we had ever made, we could indeed be regarded as superhuman. Unfortunately none of us can lay claim to that badge, not even a judge.*

Yours sincerely,

Martin Moran

The letter dropped from Rhya's fingers, floating to the ground. A white child? What would they do with a white child? What sort of man was the judge to separate twins? Maybe it was a sick lie, a joke made by a man insane with the prospect of death.

How could a woman give birth to one brown and one white baby? Scooping up the letter, she balled it tight and fired it across the room. A white girl, a daughter he knew nothing about: no wonder Vikram wanted to risk everything by returning to that place. She should have read the letter before he left, talked it through with him. What was he going to do? Try to find this white woman who was his daughter? What would they do if she came to Bangalore?

Rhya put her head in her hands. Ireland had thrown so much at them and this, she felt, was the last straw, shame, decades after the event, decades in which she had worked so hard to present a cool outward appearance, decades in which she put her brother and Rosa, the girl she called her first child, before herself. Was this now to be trampled on by a white woman who would want a stake in the thriving coffee estate? She hoped above anything that her brother would keep his wits about him in Ireland this time round.

She heard the servant leave and she lay down, all alone in this big old apartment. There was little she could do until they returned. She could pray, but for what?

Thirty-Three

Dublin, Ireland, May 1984

They were both wearing heavy coats, but still they felt the damp creeping up inside their clothes as they walked along O'Connell Street. The cold wind against them as they paced up to the junction of Parnell Square made both Vikram and Rosa wonder if they could survive two weeks in this climate without catching a chill.

Vikram had insisted, after checking in, that they dump the bags and go to Parnell Square. He refused to let them rest, maintaining he had arranged a meeting with a solicitor later on. "Rosa, we have to do everything. I am sure the solicitor can help us. She passed on a letter from the judge and may be able to help us track down Grace's grave."

Rosa, too tired to object or to raise a question about the letter, trudged along beside her uncle, her hands deep in her pockets.

Stopping at the junction, they could see the houses at the top of Parnell Square perched on the small hill, as if the builders intended the occupants to get the best view over the city. The front of No. 19 was at first obliterated by a double-decker bus. When the traffic moved, the tall red-brick building that was like any other on the square was exposed. It looked jaded and worn, the good days long since gone. Both wondered if they should knock on the door or chance peeping in the letter box.

"We should at least see if anybody is home," Rosa said almost impatiently, and they climbed the steep stone steps. No good might come of it, but above anything she wanted to know what this place looked like inside. When she pressed the brass buzzer, the bell sounded through the house, bouncing through the rooms, as if seeking out an answer as it echoed through empty rooms. Rosa pressed again.

The postman shoved past her to plop three letters in the box. "Sorry, luv, I am a bit late today. Are ye looking for somebody?"

"I wondered who lives here now. My people know the place from years back."

The postman threw his sack on the ground. "Just been taken over by a young woman. They say she is going to do it up."

"And before that?"

"Some judge, but I never saw him here."

Giving up, Rosa and Vikram wandered down the side of the square. A woman struggling with a big box bumped into them and apologised.

"I only wish I could carry it on my head, like you lot," she said, and immediately looked embarrassed. "I haven't insulted you, have I?"

Rosa laughed, and Angie Hannon thought the sound was familiar.

Wandering into the park, they sat, as it was too early yet to go to the solicitor's. A man in a long black coat approached them.

"Are youse fussy where you sit or can I move ye?"

Rosa stared at the long empty benches spanning to each side of her and shook her head. Vikram shifted uncomfortably.

"You think I am pushing in on you, don't you?"

"Not at all."

The man stood in front of them both. "I know I am as odd as two left feet, but can I tell you why?"

Vikram sighed loudly, his head hurting. He wished he could find some way to make this intruder on his thoughts go away.

"It's my Maisie. We always sat there, you see."

"Your wife?"

"My everything."

Rosa looked about, but they were the only ones in the park. "Are you from here?"

"Lived all my life in a flat at the far side of the square. Maisie always wanted a house, but I wouldn't hear of it. I am sorry now. She wanted it so much." He sat down beside Rosa. "We sat here every day before wandering down to the Gresham for a cup of tea. Imagine, the likes of us in the Gresham, but, you see, my son worked there for a few years, had a pot of tea and a few biscuits ready for us. It was right nice."

"We are staying there."

"Good luck to you. You are right to spend it, if you have it." He stretched out his legs and examined the sky. "Maisie died last year. I come here to remember her. She used to sit where you are now. Sometimes, I close my eyes and imagine it as it was. Do you know what I mean?"

Rosa jumped to her feet. "We can sit somewhere else. Tell me, did you know Judge Moran or his wife?"

"The lovely slip of a thing and the solemn judge. I saw them; I never knew them. The house has a new owner now."

"So I believe."

The man looked at his watch. "Almost on the dot of nine. She died at nine in the morning, I like to remember her, especially at that time. I feel closer to her somehow."

"We will leave you to it."

"Before you go, I sort of knew Grace Moran. She used to wave to me from the high-up window. The woman who has the place now, she stands at the window as well. I might wave to her. Now, I must give some time to my Maisie."

They wandered off, not sure if the man, who was leaning back praying, noticed.

Vikram stopped again on the path outside No. 19. There were no curtains on the upstairs windows, but the window on the ground floor had nets, yellowed with age. A vase full of fake flowers on the windowsill was dulled with dust. Rosa called him and they made their way down the hill to the hub of the city, the solicitor's their next port of call.

At the solicitors, the phones were ringing and they had to queue at reception.

"We are awfully sorry, but you will have to wait. Miss Redlich is very busy and over-running on every appointment today, or we could fit you in on Thursday at 4 p.m."

"That is two days from now," Vikram said firmly.

The young woman behind the counter frowned. Natalia Redlich, walking through to her office, noticed the young Indian woman and the older man.

"Is there a problem?"

The receptionist explained in whispered tones.

"Mr Fernandes, I am the solicitor who made contact. I

handle the estate of Judge Martin Moran. I can spare a few minutes, if you don't mind stepping into a side room we have on this floor."

She led the way into what looked like a small conference room. Rosa perched on the edge of a chair. Vikram sat beside her.

"It is one of those weeks for us, I am afraid. There was a riot on Monday in the city and a lot of arrests. As a result, the practice is very busy."

"I won't take up much of your time, Miss Redlich. I want only to find the grave of Miss Grace Moran," Vikram said

"You came all this way to visit the grave?"

"It is of utmost importance and significance to me, and I want to visit the grave. If you could help us with the location . . ." Vikram answered quietly.

Natalia Redlich twirled a pencil between her fingers. "I really don't think I can help you in that respect. I know very little about Grace Moran."

"I have come a long way, Miss Redlich."

"That may be so, but it does not change the facts. I do not know where Mrs Grace Moran is buried." She pushed out her chair to indicate the meeting was over, and Vikram stood up.

"You were my last hope. I only want to stand there and pay my respects."

"If I could help, I would, Mr Fernandes. Can I call a taxi for you? It is raining heavily outside."

Vikram sighed loudly. "We only want the location of the grave, nothing else."

Natalia Redlich looked sternly at her watch.

"We are staying at the Gresham," Vikram said, his tone low and defeated. For the first time since landing in this country,

Vikram regretted his decision to travel. Maybe Rhya was right, it was a waste of time and money.

After a while, the receptionist put her head around the door. "Your taxi is outside, Mr Fernandes. Miss Redlich says don't worry, it is on the account."

When Vikram got back to the hotel, he let Rosa go to the room to lie down. Unable to waste time in a hotel room, he set off again to Parnell Square. Ironic that he was staying in the Gresham, he thought. Sometimes he and Grace, if a story of a Hollywood star had got around, had stood there to see them arrive or leave in their limos. No stars today, just a doorman cupping his hands and blowing into them to alleviate the cold. At the bottom of Parnell Square, he stood for a while to take his breath. Whippy's ice cream was gone and the hardware store was no more. A nostalgia rose inside him for the old street, the happy days when he and Grace had tripped along, the days before it all went wrong.

The hill was not steep, but he took it slowly, slightly losing his breath as he rounded the corner at the top and saw No. 19. Immediately he was transported back to watching her window, an old hope in him that he could glimpse her. He thought he saw a shadow pass by the glass and he shook his head to dislodge the hopeless fantasy. Should he call on Emma Moran now? Rosa would never forgive him if he sprung a twin sister on her, though her forgiveness might be in doubt anyway when she knew the full story. He needed time to mull it over, and yet he felt compelled to rush, to find answers. There was also Rhya to consider. Leaning against a bollard, Vikram knew there was only so much stress he could deal with these days.

The last time he stood in this exact spot he had had a

sleeping baby, Rosa, in his arms and a bottle of milk in each jacket pocket. How was he to know that another child was kept from him? He had spent months in prison when suddenly he was told he was being released.

Rushed before a late sitting of the District Court, he stood while the DPP withdrew the charges and the case against Dr Vikram Fernandes was struck out. It happened as quickly and quietly as that. Thinking his father had turned up something, Vikram dared to hope he could work to clear his name, expecting Rudolph Fernandes or his representative to be waiting for him. Instead, a man he recognised as the judge's driver offered him a lift.

"They want to talk to you at No. 19. Violet McNally sent me to fetch you. I don't know what any of this is about, so don't ask me."

He said not another word to Vikram until they reached Parnell Square.

"Good luck," he said, and Vikram thought he detected a hint of sarcasm in his tone.

The car had only just stopped when the back door opened and Violet McNally instructed the driver to get out and let them have their privacy. She slapped Vikram on the shoulder to make him shove over on the seat.

"Dr Fernandes, I want you to listen carefully. My beautiful niece is dead. Died in the agony of childbirth. I hold you personally responsible, do you understand? This is what you are going to do." She stopped for a moment. "You can take your head out of your hands, we all know you were only using the silly girl. Crocodile tears will get you nowhere. Grace Moran had the world at her feet until you came along and turned her head. A child is still alive. She is your responsibility now. You will take the child and leave. You will agree with the terms the judge puts in place. He knows nothing of this conversation and that is the way it is going to stay.

"I tell you most sincerely, if you set foot in this country again or try to do anything to interfere in any way with this family, I will make sure the charges against you the next time stick like glue. Leave while you have a chance and be glad of it."

She left the car, banging the door so hard the sound bounced through the quiet of the square.

Hardly able to walk, but desperate to compose himself, Vikram pulled himself up the steps to the front door. The house seemed quiet. He rang the bell, the sound vibrating through the rooms, highlighting the sense of agitation and fear rising inside his heart. He heard a heavy step in the hallway. The door was barely pulled back.

"Dr Fernandes, come in."

Martin Moran walked ahead into his library and Vikram followed.

"I hear the charges against you were dropped. A very messy business. I am glad it has ended well for you," he said, sitting behind his desk.

He did not ask Vikram to sit down.

"I know you want to know about my wife and I will tell you. Grace gave birth, but there is a situation with the child." Martin Moran coughed, unable to fully articulate his concerns about the child.

"I want to see Grace."

"That is not possible. Don't you think you have done enough to this family?"

Vikram made to walk out of the room, but the driver stood in his way. The judge stood up.

"My driver is also a Special Branch detective, so I warn you to stay quiet and listen."

"I only want to see Grace. I won't believe anything unless I see her."

"Dr Fernandes, whether you believe or disbelieve me is of no concern. I merely state the facts." He put up his hand, as if trying to stop Vikram interrupting. "These are the relevant details. You will leave Ireland straight away. I have here the tickets and an emergency passport for this little girl. You will both leave this country and not return. The child is more Indian than Irish and will do better with your people. You have been registered as the father."

He picked up the phone and asked for the baby to be brought to the library. A few moments later, Aunt Violet came in carrying a baby wrapped in a wool blanket. She handed the baby to Vikram.

"She is sleeping. We gave her the name Rose," Martin Moran said. Looking down on the baby, he shook his head. "She may be that colour, but she has the look of her mother. Rose was a name Grace liked," he said, almost as if he was talking to himself.

Vikram could barely hold the child, he was shaking so much.

"Steady yourself, man, there is a long journey ahead. My driver will bring you to the airport."

"What if I don't go?"

"It would be a stupid man who would put the future of his own child at risk. Please leave us be, it is such a difficult time for all of us."

Violet opened the library door. Vikram, clutching the baby tight, walked through to the hall.

Martin Moran, Aunt Violet by his side, watched the two of

them go down the steps to the waiting car. The driver took the baby to let Vikram get into the back. Handing the bundle back to Vikram, he nodded to a case on the front seat.

"I went over to your place earlier and packed your things. I thought you could do with them."

Vikram did not say anything. Not a word passed between them on the journey to the airport.

Vikram shook himself, as though to slough off the bad memories. Smartly, he walked over to No. 19 and, without taking too much time to think it through, knocked on the door. Angie Hannon, coming out of her door, immediately recognised the old man who had helped her earlier. "Can I help you?"

"I am looking for Emma Moran."

"I am afraid you have missed her. She went out early. Will I tell her who called?"

He felt his test chest tighten and he leaned against the door jamb.

"Sir, is everything all right?"

"Maybe. I am a little tired."

"Come in and have a drink."

"I don't want to inconvenience you."

Angie reached out and took Vikram by the elbow. "Have a sit-down and I will call a taxi for you. Write your name and address on the piece of paper and I will see that Emma gets it." When she saw Vikram was staying at the Gresham, she shook her head. "The taxi driver will try and rob you blind, but it should not be more than a fiver." She helped Vikram to the car, promising him she would pass on the message to Emma as soon as she arrived back.

Thirty-Four

Parnell Square, Dublin, May 1984

Andrew Kelly, sitting with a pot of tea and a whiskey on the side in the Lord Mayor's Lounge at the Shelbourne, was keeping a keen eye out for Emma. He had asked to meet her here because he wanted somewhere neutral and discreet, so they could have the conversation he intended to initiate.

Emma, wearing a turquoise linen dress under a tweed coat, looked suitably dressed for a pleasant afternoon tea as she walked into the hotel. Andrew noticed she appeared nervous, tugging at her hair as she asked directions. He waved to her from his spot on an armchair by the fire.

She smiled when she saw him and he was glad her step became lighter as she approached.

"Sorry I am a little late. I was out in Howth; I needed to think about things. I am afraid I miscalculated the timing of the journey back."

"This was a pleasant place to wait. It is not as if I was on a street corner."

"I had a think about things. I have decided to stay on in Dublin; Australia does not hold anything for me any more."

"Great news, I am delighted."

She thought Andrew appeared distracted, though he was very attentive when the waitress came to take the order. He recommended Earl Grey tea with some biscuits on the side, if she was not going to partake of alcohol.

"It is a relief to have made the decision. I went to Knockavanagh in the morning, put some more flowers on the grave. Met a woman who knew my mother, though I think she will have to get to know me better before she gives away anything."

"You are a good daughter."

"I wish I'd had a chance to be."

Andrew fiddled with his left cufflink, rotating it round and round, so that Emma thought it might pop out.

"Your father had an awful lot to contend with. I am only beginning to realise that myself."

"I don't hate him, if that is what you are worried about." She stopped for a moment. "Neither do I love him."

"Indifference is never a nice place to be."

Emma poured the tea from the silver teapot. Andrew fidgeted with a chocolate biscuit, nipping crumbs from its side. He took a snip of the biscuit, hoping the sweet taste would distract him.

"I asked you here because I wanted to give you some more information. It was in Martin's letter to me at the time of the will. He said it was up to me whether I tell or not." Taking another nibble of the biscuit, he let the sweet chocolate momentarily distract him.

"What good is all this going to do, Andrew? It is not going to bring back either of them. I have had it with all the bits of information. Maybe I want to start putting it behind me now."

He shifted closer to her. "Admirable as that is, I think you need this last nugget. In the days before he died, Martin told me he had written a letter for me which was to be included in his will, and he asked me to carry out the instructions contained in it. All he would say was one sentence: 'Some things are best left until we can feel no more and death has called.' I will never forget those words."

"I don't see what this has to do with me."

"That is true, and that is why I won't be showing you the letter, but a major part was an explanation as to why your father was the husband and father he was."

He waited for Emma to say something, but she didn't. Instead, she cradled the teacup nervously. Andrew took the letter from his pocket and scanned it before clearing his throat to read out the relevant parts.

I am sure Emma is blaming me and she is right. I was a coward all my life and now I know it has brought pain and suffering to so many others, particularly lovely Grace, who at all times was such a beautiful young woman. I am writing to you because I want Emma, when she finds out the following information, to have somebody with her who can be a comfort to her. The kindness of a solicitor watching a clock is never the same as the attention of a friend. There are, at this stage, so many questions that Emma must have and this letter is an attempt to answer some of them.

I was so fond of Grace. I did her a terrible injustice the day I married her. Not only did I condemn her to a life without a proper love to sustain and cherish her, I put her at the mercy of Violet

McNally. The root of this problem goes back to when I was a young barrister and best friends with Violet's husband, George. We studied law together and were in the Law Library at the same stages of our careers. We were very close. Too close, I suppose. I need to acknowledge on paper: I loved George and he loved me. Violet had taken in the baby, Grace, and, for a time, she was well occupied.

Two years later George and I were doing well in the law and spending most of the weekends here at Parnell Square. I am afraid we also got in the habit of writing letters to each other, often about silly things in the news, notes on cases, but sometimes they were deeper, more emotional. It was one of these letters, I was much later told by Violet, that she found. She confronted George. He stormed out of the house, supposedly coming to live with me. He never got to Parnell Square, but was found in the canal three days after he went missing.

An inquest found he may have slipped into the canal and that his death was accidental. Both Violet and I know George would not have ended up in that water if he had not intended to. He was also an excellent swimmer.

Violet never said anything to me. I lost quite a bit of contact with her and concentrated on my work. By the time I took silk I was the highest earner at the Bar. There was speculation in the newspapers on the next High Court appointments and sure enough I was summoned to Violet's house in Drumcondra.

She was polite and civil, the house the same as

before, though more faded and worn-looking. She put a proposal to me that I was unable to refuse or, rather, not brave enough to turn down.

She had in her possession the letters I had written to her husband, which confirmed the existence of a homosexual relationship between us. I will never forget her words: "They won't put a man on the bench who has committed such a dreadful crime. You won't get around that, Martin Moran." She threatened to go to the worst British newspaper, which would be delighted to print the scandal about me.

I should have walked out of her house and told her to go to hell. I will regret my inaction far beyond my dying day.

She told me she had reliably heard I was in line to get on the bench, but government ministers were worried I was not married. I had no reason to doubt what she said. I knew she had quite a lot of contacts at a high level. She said the worry was that there was something wrong with me, that I had not married. She, of course, offered a solution - Grace. If I provided nicely for Violet - a sum of £130 a month and allowed her her own quarters wherever I lived with Grace - she said her silence would be secured.

She was vicious in her choice of words: "We were rowing about you, when George stormed off, probably to go to you. We all know he did not fall in that river. He jumped, and you with your carry-on and love letters as much as killed him. My husband was never a homosexual, but you made him that way.

I will make sure the world knows that. However, you have my silence for as long as you and Grace remain married and the monthly sum is paid."

I knew I had to have a wife to be in line for the job on the bench and that part of me pushed me to sign a contract that Violet had conveniently drawn up. It tied me to her for the rest of my life. Unfortunately, what it did as well was lock poor Grace into this plot.

She was a beautiful young woman and I loved her, but in a different way. If she had not met Dr Fernandes, we might have been able reach a reasonable accommodation, but she fell in love. In truth, I was jealous of her love, but only because it reminded me of my own sweet love for George.

Violet dominated our lives, even though I insisted she live in separate quarters. I knew Grace was taken with Dr Fernandes, but I hoped it would fizzle out. When she said she was pregnant, there was nothing I could do. I knew Violet would expose me and we would all be ruined. The biggest mistake I made was trusting Violet when she told me Grace was behaving like a madwoman who was steeped in depression after the birth. The doctors in the mental hospital told me the same lies. They had been bought by Violet. By the time Violet died, it was too late for Grace. She had perished in a fire at the asylum.

I have behaved badly and put my career, status and good name above everything. In the process, I allowed a wicked woman to have a hold *on me and for a beautiful young woman to lose out on what should have been a good life.*

If it is any consolation, this whole thing has left me a broken man in every way. I am thankful every day for our partnership, Andrew. It is truly one of the best things to come out of this sorry life of mine.

Andrew's voice was shaking, but he continued.

My regrets are huge and weigh me down. I want Emma to know I have always loved her and I sincerely apologise for not being a good father. I sincerely apologise to Vikram Fernandes and his daughter and to my lovely Grace, who was cursed the day I walked into her life.

I won't ask for forgiveness. I merely offer an explanation.

Yours,

Martin

Emma did not say anything, but she shifted on the chair, noticing a little girl hovering near the piano, hoping to push one of the keys, a stylish lady hissing at a man in the grey suit, and a waitress, bored and buffing up her nails.

"That is it, then?"

Andrew did not need to answer. They sat, each lost in their own thoughts. Emma watched the little girl, remembering when Aunt Violet used to bring her to the Gresham every Sunday for tea. It should have been an outing to look forward to, but Emma hated every minute of it. It nearly always started badly, with Violet insisting she wear white gloves. Once, Emma managed to strip them off and conveniently forgot them. Violet frogmarched her back up the hill to the house and stood over her while she fitted the gloves back on.

A pot of tea and two ham sandwiches was the order, but never biscuits. The Hendersons from Mountjoy Square were always there on a Sunday. Maggie Henderson was allowed a meringue with a cream filling.

Violet would knock back a few glasses of sherry and have to lean on the young girl during the journey home. It was at these times that she berated the child the most, giving out too about the stupid father who had not knocked any sense into her. As they turned the last corner up into the square, Violet demanded they stop and look the height of No. 19.

"Aren't we the lucky ones? We have the luxury life living in the judge's house." Violet chuckled at her own private joke, like she always did.

Andrew called the waitress for the bill. Reaching over, he took Emma's hand. "Please keep in touch. Someday, I hope you will ask me for that fine painting Martin did of yourself and that other beautiful study of Grace in her gold dress. When you do, I will rush over and even hang them for you."

"You would give me the painting of Grace?"

"It is yours. You just tell me when you are ready."

After he had slipped a twenty-pound note to the waitress inside the leather bill binder, he shyly kissed Emma on the cheek as he left.

She waited a while before she got up to leave. As she made for the main doors, the footman offered to flag her down a taxi, and she accepted, for some reason anxious to get home to Parnell Square.

Thirty-Five

Dublin, Ireland, May 1984

Vikram waited until Rosa was fully rested and looking her old self.

"Rosa, I need to talk to you about something important."

She had her back to him, clipping on her gold jewellery at the dressing table. "Can't we talk at dinner, Uncle? I am starving."

He wanted to agree but knew that once he told her she may not like being in such a public place.

When he did not answer immediately, she swung around, her face anxious. "Uncle, what is the matter?"

Vikram shifted on his seat, his fingers fiddling with the lace curtain.

"You are having second thoughts about this whole trip?"

He laughed, but he saw irritation rise in her, so he blurted it out. "Darling Rosa, hear me out, please: I am your father, Grace is your mother and you have a twin sister."

He was so angry at himself for the vulgarity of the delivery, his heart breaking when he saw Rosa's face change from relaxed and happy to bewildered. He reached her in a stride, grabbing both her hands.

"I have been selfish and uncaring in the way I have told you. I was only thinking of myself. Forgive me, dear Rosa."

Rosa jerked her hand away. "What do you mean, twin sister?"

"I am your father, Rosa."

"What talk is this?" Rosa's face was contorted in pain.

Vikram searched for her hand again, but she pulled away from him. "Rosa, listen to me. I brought you from Ireland all those years ago. I was told Grace had died and that they could not keep you because of the colour of your skin. I only found out recently you were one of twins."

"But what about Mama?"

"Grace gave birth to you, but it is Rhya who has been a mother to you, Rosa."

"Where is this twin sister? Is she brown or does she fit in more with this landscape?"

"I only found out in a letter from the judge sent on after his death by the solicitor. Your twin's name is Emma and I imagine she is white."

"Twins?"

"Yes, Rosa."

"Lucky for me they got rid of me to India, where I could feel at home."

"I am glad that I at least had you, and that you, Rosa, grew up with a loving mother."

Rosa stopped, tears replacing the indignation. "Mama knew this."

Vikram ran his hand along Rosa's face. "Rhya has been the best mother to you."

"When was she going to tell me? On her deathbed?"

"Rosa, if you are angry at anybody, it has to be me."

"This is all rot."

"It now appears that your twin sister survived and was brought up by Martin Moran."

Rosa flopped on the bed, tears coursing through her thick make-up, making her mascara smudge under her eyes. "Vik, this is really too much to take on, too much. Mama would not approve of you telling me."

"I will have to worry about that another time. Rosa, please don't turn your back on me. We can get through it together."

"Am I going to meet this twin sister?"

"I sincerely hope so. I left a note for her in Parnell Square."

Rosa stood up. "I would like to go for dinner now."

Vikram nodded, and he waited while she fixed her make-up, letting her go out of the hotel room first, which she did with an angry swish of her sari pallu.

At first they said nothing over dinner and ate little, but they sat side by side, each deep in thought.

It was Rosa who broke the silence.

"I am sorry Vik, this must be so hard on you. I just don't want to lose my best friend when I gain a father. You are too important to me."

He squeezed her hand. "Never, darling Rosa, never."

*

Emma rushed in the door of the hotel, not altogether sure what she was going to face. The handwritten note from Vikram Fernandes had been brief and polite, informing her he would like to see her and could she call down to the Gresham at her convenience.

Angie had come in on top of her, holding the note aloft, once she got out of the taxi on Parnell Square. "Don't take off your coat, I think you will want to read this," she said, gabbing on about the polite Indian man who had nearly collapsed on the steps.

Emma set down the street straight away. She rushed, sweat forming on her temples. Why did a journey so short now seem so long? What would she say to this man who was her father? She opened the belt of her coat, running her hands along the turquoise linen dress she had decided to wear that morning. It was one of Grace's dresses. She had picked it because she liked the swing of the skirt, the softness of the linen and the way it kicked out from under the tweed coat, which was also her mother's.

Emma asked the receptionist to call his room, but there was no answer. The woman behind the desk smiled and beckoned to an Indian woman buying postcards.

"This is his niece, she will be able to help you."

Rosa, dressed in a royal-blue sari with a red and gold border, came over to her. "Can I help you? You are looking for Mr Fernandes?" Rosa took the woman in: the soft grey eyes, the auburn hair curling around her neck. So like Grace in the photograph she had seen.

"I am Emma Moran."

"Grace was your mother?"

"Yes."

"Vikram will be so glad to meet you. You look like her."

An Indian man was watching them from across the lobby. He did not need to be told who she was. Every bit of her was Grace: the way she stood, the turquoise dress, the tweed coat. It could have been his Grace. Emma turned slightly, flicking her hair, the movement making the aurora borealis stones of her necklace glint. Vikram's heart lunged and he could not move. The necklace had cost him a huge amount of his pay packet: the necklace Grace had adored. He could only stare at these two beautiful women, his daughters. Rosa swivelled, looking around for him, but he found himself stepping back so he would not be seen. For this moment, he wanted to be alone, so he could look upon these two women and remember his Grace. They both had so much of her, so much of the loveliness that made up the woman he adored and who he had let down so badly. Could these two ever forgive him for what he had done?

A waiter passing by saw Vikram lean against a pillar and stopped to ask him if he was all right. Vikram allowed himself to be assisted to a chair.

Emma saw him first. He noticed she half smiled and nervously tugged at her hair before tapping her sister on the shoulder, pointing across the lobby to him.

Rosa rushed across, her voice high in alarm. "Vik, what is the matter? Look who is here."

He made to stand up, but Rosa pushed him back into the chair.

"Rest, Vik. Miss Moran will not mind."

He took her hand, so like her mother's, her touch soft and gentle. Emma was speaking to him, but he did not hear the words. There was something about her, the way she looked at him, her clothes, her standing. He heard his own voice, but he was not sure of what he said until she shyly called him Vikram. Rosa made to go, saying she would leave them to talk, but Vikram called her back.

"Anything I have to say is also for your ears. Please stay, dear Rosa."

Emma looked at Rosa, who bent close to Vikram and kissed him on the cheek. Fussing, Rosa asked a waiter to push chairs together and bring tea for three. Emma took her in. Her long black hair was glossy, her skin soft brown, her eyes like her father's. If any of the sisters was to wear the gold dress, it should be this sister who stood so straight and carried with her a dignity that could only enhance such a beautiful gown. All the times she had wished she had a sister, all the times she had wanted to turn back the clock, to rewrite history, when all along this girl was celebrating the same milestones but growing up with their father. Emma felt a stab of jealousy of this exotic woman, but before it flared deeper she sat down and asked the question that had been burning through her. Speaking slowly and firmly, she directed her question at Vikram.

"What took you so long?"

His head hanging, his shoulders down, he began to cry. "I was told Grace was dead, I never knew anything else."

"Violet told you that."

"She was a poisonous woman."

"I am sorry if I sounded harsh."

"You have every right. It does not matter what you say, there is nobody harsher on Vikram Fernandes than Vikram Fernandes." He wiped beads of sweat from his forehead. "I regret every day that I did not break my way upstairs in that damned house in Parnell Square. I should not have believed them, I should have roared and shouted the place down until I got as far as Grace. I am sorry, Emma."

He reached out and took Emma's hand.

"I would like to get to know you, Emma. Maybe someday you will look on me as a father." He kept his hold on her hand, while reaching for Rosa's hand. "I swear, if I had known you existed, I would never have left you. Twins should not grow up apart."

Emma was not sure what to do.

"We must find Grace's grave and show her we three have at least been reunited. We have all suffered so much because of the damned lies of others," Vikram said quietly.

Emma spoke quickly. "She is buried in Knockavanagh, Wicklow."

Vikram squeezed his daughters' hands tightly. "Can we go first thing?"

"Why didn't Mama tell me all this time? Why didn't you?" Rosa asked, tears blotting her words.

"Rhya is so afraid you will hold it against her," said Vikram.

Emma, not sure she should be listening in, made to stand up and leave, but Vikram put his hand on her shoulder and gently pushed her back in the seat.

"It is going to take us all time to adjust," he said, holding out his hands again to his two daughters. They took one each. "This is a special moment, darling Rosa and Emma. We have to get to know each other." He placed Rosa's hand in Emma's. "Sisters and twins, you should never have been kept apart for this long. Now you must make up for lost time."

They were both embarrassed, but neither pulled away. Rosa was the first to reach further, pulling her sister into a tight hug.

"I never knew you existed until today, but I would very much like to become friends."

Emma felt the tears seep through her, but she made no attempt to stop them and let herself be taken in the warm embrace of this woman who was so like her but looked nothing like her.

Vikram watched his daughters and thought the only thing

that could make him happier would be if Grace could be there to bear witness. He could not rewrite the past, but maybe from today he could help write the future with these fine women who were his daughters.

Next they sat as Vikram told the full story, with Emma filling in the gaps. At various stages, Vikram stopped to sip tea, the strain of the new information evident on his face as well as the retelling of the old scandal. Vikram, as he told his side of the story, was a gracious and kind man, very particular in his telling, fair even when Violet's name came up in the mix.

"I believe your father did not know of Violet's scheming."

"He says he didn't, but who knows? Maybe he chose to ignore it, for his own reasons," Emma said.

"Often the good person can never see the bad and that is as damaging as the bad man intent on doing wrong. Emma, I want to travel to Knockavanagh first thing in the morning. Will you come with us? We can go together."

She hesitated, and Vikram, knowing the women in his household, felt she was holding back on something.

"Please Emma, don't hold back. I can take everything. What else could cause pain? I am stronger than I look."

Rosa, realising it was getting late, said, "Maybe we've heard enough for tonight. Tomorrow we can talk more."

But Vikram was insistent. "Emma?"

She shuffled her feet as if she wanted to leave. Clenching her hands together, Emma spoke in a low voice.

"There was a fire. I am sorry to tell you Grace died in a fire at the asylum." Emma, after blurting it out, felt her throat dry. Her face was swollen with tears.

Vikram let out a cry and fisted the coffee table hard so that people sitting nearby looked at them. Rosa put her face in her hands and began to sob.

Vikram reached out to his two daughters when he saw the raw grief in their faces. For now, he set aside his own pain and loss.

"What is another boulder on our shoulders? We are strong enough to carry them all, if we carry them together," he whispered, patting their heads as if they were children once again.

Even now, he thought, he was a lucky man: the father of two fine women. They were the same height, had the same softness in the eyes, their voices the same pitch. Their skin colour was different, but in everything else they were as one.

After a few minutes, he tapped gently on the coffee table to make an announcement.

"We will travel together tomorrow to visit the grave. I want to stand with our daughters on either side of me to pay our respects to the woman I loved all my life, your mother."

The two girls, both wiping their eyes, nodded, unable to say anything more.

Thirty-Six

Knockavanagh, May 1984

Father O'Brien asked Mandy twice if she was all right, and she smiled at him, saying she might be a bit out of sorts.

"There was no need to get up. I can get my own breakfast after the Mass. Why don't you go back to bed?"

"I might as well be working as lying in bed, not able to sleep."

"Is there something bothering you, Mandy? You don't seem yourself this morning."

"There is a lot to do, preparing for the communion on Saturday, and the garden needs a tidy."

"On top of that, I forgot to tell you, that woman from Dublin, Emma Moran, rang and said she would be down some time this morning to visit her mother's grave."

"When did she ring?"

"Late, after I got back last night from the Monsignor's dinner. You might have to schedule a chat with her on her own. I can drive you up to Dublin someday."

"I will play it by ear."

"You have to tell her."

"I don't have to do anything. Anyway, what good would it do?"

"Trust yourself and trust her."

Father O'Brien noticed Mandy was tugging at her hair, hunched at the table, a mug of tea in front of her, untouched.

"I will leave it to yourself, but don't leave it too long or you may regret it for the rest of your life."

Mandy sighed. "As if I don't have enough regrets already."

"You don't seem well. Maybe have a little rest, even if you don't sleep. Emma Moran said she was bringing a few friends but they know where to go."

"Maybe I will go back to bed," she said, but he knew she was only pretending to stop him going on.

"Do you think we should call the doctor?"

"No need, I will be all right."

"All right then. I'll go and buy the paper," he said. He grabbed his keys from the counter and was out the door.

Mandy stayed at the kitchen table.

Emma Moran was going to be asking more questions. The judge was dead. Mandy did not know about Vikram: maybe he was dead or had got married over there. There had to be a reason he had not come back. He was to be given the benefit of the doubt, because to do otherwise would mean the waiting of all these years, all Grace's yearning, had been for nothing.

She heard the sacristan arrive to prepare the church for Mass and felt relief wash over her that he did not call in for a chat.

If Emma had people with her, she would not be able to sit her down and tell her the whole story. The girl deserved that and she desperately wanted to let it out.

She wanted to get organised but felt compelled to dither, taking care with her make-up, pressing the powder firmly into her face. Her stomach was sick and a tremble came in her hands to think of Emma Moran and how fine she looked.

She did not know how to dress: should she be formal or casual? She pushed through the clothes in her wardrobe, not satisfied with any of them but eventually deciding on a navy-blue tweed skirt with a little bit of kick at the hem, and a light-blue blouse with a wide collar. Sweeping up her hair in a tight bun at the back of her head, she checked and rechecked her make-up. Emma Moran might not even bother calling in, but Mandy dressed as if they had a date for tea.

She had no idea when they were due to arrive, but she could not put her mind to anything. Instead she paced the front sitting room, stopping every few minutes to check the long driveway. It was some time before eleven when she saw a car turn in from the road, and she went to the kitchen so it did not appear as if she was waiting. She did not know why, but she started to wash up the breakfast cups, watching the road through the side kitchen window.

An Indian woman, her hair long and black, got out of the car, and Mandy waved to indicate she would come to the front door. She dried her hands as she made for the front hall and was still holding the tea towel when she swung back the door.

Rosa and Emma both turned around when the door was pulled back.

"Miss McGuane, this is my twin sister, Rosa. She is here to see our mother's grave."

Mandy stared at the Indian woman. She was wearing gold jewellery. Her hair was glossy black. Pain shot up the back of Mandy's neck and over the top of her head.

The woman held out her hand. "Hello, I am Rosa."

Mandy could not answer. She fell back against the wall, unable to utter a word.

"Ma'am, are you all right?"

Rosa reached out and caught Mandy by the shoulders to steady her.

"Is there somewhere you can sit?" Emma asked as she opened a door to a front sitting room and they helped Mandy in.

"I am all right, there is no need to fuss," she said.

Emma filled a glass of water from the tap in the kitchen and brought it back to her.

"Who exactly are you?" Mandy asked the Indian woman.

"Vikram Fernandes is my father."

"From Bangalore?"

"Yes, how did you know?"

"I don't understand." Mandy jumped up, tears gushing down her face. "What are you saying?"

"We are Grace's daughters: twin sisters."

Mandy screamed at the top of her voice and ran from the room.

Father O'Brien, making his way back home to cook his own breakfast, nearly slipped on the path when he heard the commotion. Thinking Mandy was being attacked, he rushed into the house to find Rosa and Emma standing in the middle of the sitting room.

"What is happening? Where is Miss McGuane?"

"Father O'Brien, we have done nothing wrong. I have found my twin sister, we are Grace's daughters," Emma said.

The priest shook his head and ran, shouting Grace's name. He found her in her room, sitting on the edge of the bed, staring at the wall.

"Twin daughters, alive all this time. Tell me, what do I do now?"

He did not answer immediately, because he had no answer. He sat beside her. Gently, he tugged at her arm.

"Come and meet your daughters, Grace."

"Those fine ladies don't want to know the likes of me."

Emma stood in the doorway, Rosa at her shoulder.

"You are Grace? All my life I wanted a mother, all the times I dreamed of it. Don't give up on us now, Grace."

"They told me you were dead." Her voice faded away, tears gulped out instead of words. Emma and Rosa ran to their mother. Grace leaned into them.

"We thought you were dead, buried in the graveyard," Emma said.

Father O'Brien cleared his throat and said, "I'll go and put the kettle on," but Grace pulled him back.

"Explain it to them," she said, and he did not argue.

"Mandy McGuane, God rest her soul, died in the fire, and Grace survived it. Nobody in the village knew Mandy back then. The poor thing who died in the fire was not in any way recognisable."

"How did it happen?"

"Mandy had no family left. Her parents were dead; her brother had sold the farm and emigrated years before. Everybody thought it was Mandy in the hospital. She was admitted under that name. She was there for a month, and by the time she came back out everybody in the asylum had been transferred off to different hospitals. Mandy had been buried as Grace, and Grace knew she was now free. She told old Father Grennan the truth, and he and I have kept her secret until now."

"Didn't the judge ever visit the grave?"

Father O'Brien snorted loudly. "He sent a cheque every year for the upkeep of the memorial plot, but after the funeral he never came back here."

Rosa spoke for the first time. "What about Vik? We must tell him."

Emma made to stop her.

"Give Grace a little time, let's see if she is all right first," Father O'Brien said.

Grace, shaking, her hands clenched, spoke quietly and firmly. "Please, tell me of Vikram."

Rosa looked at Grace. "I thought you knew. He is with us. He went straight to the grave."

"Oh God, my grave."

She pushed past her daughters and bolted for the back door, stopping only at the top of the small hill. Vikram was standing, his head bowed. She wanted to shout to him but no words would come out; she wanted to run but could only stumble. She wanted to say something but no words could represent the love and fear bursting inside her. Slowly but deliberately, she walked towards the lonely figure.

⋆

Vikram stood, looking down at the well-tended memorial.

How had it come to this? A beautiful woman in a cold, damp hollow in the shadow of the asylum walls. Slowly, he made his way down the gravel path.

He bowed his head. The crows seemed to caw out Grace's name, as if they were mocking his presence. There was a flurry of steps down the hill and then a quieter footfall behind him. He thought it was Rosa.

"I let her down so badly, Rosa."

There was no answer, but he felt a hand reach for his.

"You never let me down, Vikram Fernandes. I knew you would come back."

He froze. His limbs were heavy, his heart hurting. He turned and looked in her eyes. Reaching out, he grabbed her with both hands to make sure she was not an apparition come to haunt him. He pummelled with his hands along her arms, then let his fingers glide over her hair.

"Grace. Grace."

He wanted to ask so many questions but could only mutter her name. He thought he might collapse, but he fought the weakness that was creeping through him.

"You came back, Vik. I knew you would."

"How can this be, Gracie? Everybody said you died."

"They put me away, Vik, but the fire freed me."

Gently, he put his hands to her face, tracing from her eyes to her nose to her mouth. "Grace, is it really you?"

"I knew you would find me one day. You were not to blame, Vik." She reached out and took one of his hands.

"What do we do now?" He pulled her to him and she pressed her face into the nape of his neck. Overhead, the crows cawed louder and the wind swirled about them, making the trees creak.

"Our babies, Vik. I never knew."

He gulped big wet tears into her hair. Reaching into her pocket, she pulled out a small grey embroidered handkerchief.

"Wipe, Vikram. There are no need for tears now."

They heard Emma and Rosa walk down the path, one girl so like her mother, the other more like her father.

"We are a family, finally," Vikram whispered.

She nodded and he held her. When he pulled back so he could talk, she put her hands to his lips.

"Hush. We have a lifetime left for talking." She took his hand and gently pressed a small piece of white marble to it, closing his fist around it. "I knew you would find me."

"I love you to eternity and beyond, Grace."

"I know."

He took her hand and they walked hand and hand up the hill, their daughters following behind.

Epilogue

The Fernandes Estate, Chikmagalur, India, July 1984

Vikram sat out on the balcony listening intently. The insects hummed and in the distance a bird whooped, but he remained focussed, waiting for the Range Rover to growl as it pushed up the hill and around the steep bends, past the waterfall and the small stream that spilled out on the road to the bungalow.

He had left Grace sleeping, hoping Rhya and his daughters would arrive before she woke up. This would be the first time he had met his sister since returning to India with Grace. He knew when he told her over the phone that they would go straight to Chikmagalur that she was disappointed.

"Am I a nobody now?" she asked. "I have served my function." And he had to strangle a laugh, turning it into a cough so she did not notice.

"Rhya, Rosa and Emma are coming straight to you. Grace and I need some time alone, you surely understand that."

"What does it matter? Plans have been made," she said and he could see a picture of her pouting tightly in her indignation. She sighed and he asked, "What is wrong, Rhya?"

"Rosa for sure is angry at me. Emma won't like me."

He laughed loudly until he heard her snuffle back a tear. "Rosa understands, Rhya. She loves you: you are her mother. Emma just wants to meet you, get to know you."

"Grace is my girl's mother, we all know that."

"Rosa is lucky to have two mothers. Grace is grateful to you. Did you ever think of that?"

There was silence for a moment, before Rhya croaked, "No, I hadn't."

They both fell quiet again before Vikram said, "I must go."

With that, Rhya regained her strength. "You can't bring a woman who has only stepped out in India to the coffee estate. What will she think of your rough-and-ready style? The boy in the kitchen won't know what to cook for her. It will be too quiet, too rural."

"Which is exactly why I am bringing Grace there: all we ever wanted was to be in Chikmagalur together."

Rhya sighed loudly and he took the opportunity to run off the phone.

The clouds were falling off the hills, rolling about, making the air grey. A peacock called out and in the trees some birds sounded an alarm of something approaching through the thickness of the coffee plants. The old dog sat up for a moment, watching the grey, but he settled quickly back down, placing his head on Vikram's foot.

Vikram did not sense Grace come up behind until he felt her finger his hair.

"You should have woken me. It is way past four. I need time to get ready to meet them all."

He looked at her in the floaty kaftan she liked to wear when it was just the two them and he thought she looked so lovely, the simplicity of the sweep of the cotton garment highlighting the beauty of her face.

"You appeared so peaceful, curling up for your afternoon sleep, I could not wake you. Soon, the car will be here."

She looked agitated and he got up and put his arms around her.

"My sister is loud, a little annoying, but inside she is a woman who loves fiercely, and she will love you, I know it."

"I hope so."

When, soon after, he heard the revving of the engine as the Range Rover dipped into the shallow stream flowing too near the road, he whispered to Grace, who ran off to get dressed.

The old dog stood up, on alert, listening before ambling to wait at the gate for the car to arrive. The boy in the kitchen got a tray of cold drinks ready and the workers passing by stopped at the side of the road to watch for the visitors.

Grace, wearing a pale-blue shalwar kameez embellished with beads and silver embroidery, made it out onto the veranda and sat down on the swing seat, making it creak as the car pulled up in front of the bungalow.

Rosa was the first out. "I think these clouds see me coming and come down specially to greet me," she said as she helped Emma from the back of the car.

"It is so beautiful here. I never want to leave," Emma said, and Grace smiled, nodding her head.

Rhya was the last to emerge, but they had heard her first. She had called to the boy to bring drinks and snapped at the driver in Kannada to unpack all the food from the back.

"There is so much to be done and not a moment to spare," she said, and Vikram smiled at her fake, business-like voice. When she got to the bottom of the steps leading to the veranda, she stopped and looked directly at Grace. "Grace, you are welcome to India. I doubt if that brother of mine had the manners to say that."

Grace stood up and smiled at the tall woman who looked so like Vikram but was so different in temperament. Rhya was the first to speak.

"I have brought you a present, a very nice silk sari. I guessed the blouse size and the sandals, so hopefully all will be well for tomorrow."

"What about tomorrow?" Vikram asked.

Rhya stared at her brother. "Surely we can all dress up and have a feast to celebrate Vikram and Grace Fernandes and the love that endured so long."

Grace gently patted Vikram on the back. "You are being very kind, Rhya. Of course we can celebrate." Grace walked over to Rhya and enclosed her in a hug. "You will always be Rosa's mother. I am so jealous of you, but I thank you for giving her a mother's love, for bringing her up and making her happy."

Rhya felt herself slump and a well of tears began to rumble inside her, so she quickly hugged Grace back and kissed her lightly on the cheek. "Nonsense, I did what any other woman would do. Now, have you spoken to the boy in the kitchen? Does he prepare the food you like?"

Vikram laughed out loud. "Sister, Grace has had more to be thinking of than sorting out the servants. Come, have some homemade lemonade."

Rhya ignored her brother and put up her hand to wave away the tray of tall glasses. "That is our first task, Grace. Once you sort the servants and they know who is in charge, you will command this whole coffee estate and it will not matter what Vikram Fernandes has to say."

Grace allowed herself to be pulled along to the kitchen as Emma and Rosa sat together on the swing seat, making it screech loudly.

"Mama is quite something. Do you know she has been telling everybody Emma is Grace's daughter and you have met a lovely woman in Europe? She won't tell anybody the truth."

Vikram, sitting into his favourite rattan chair, shook his head. "Rhya has a lot to contend with. We must accept what she can and cannot cope with. What does it matter what others think? We know the truth. If it keeps Rhya happy, then so be it."

Emma paced across the veranda, leaning on the steel balustrading. "So like home, yet so different when the clouds fall off the mountains, swirling down to the trees, making everything ghostly."

"You like it here?" Vikram asked.

"The coffee estate and India, I love them both."

"Maybe you will come to India and live here."

Emma smiled at her father. "Maybe I will, but first I have to decide what to do with the Dublin house."

"You will sell it?"

"I could, or I thought Angie might like to rent the space for more bedrooms for her business."

"It could finance your life here."

"That is what Andrew, my father's— I mean the judge's partner said."

She looked embarrassed and Vikram stood beside her and took her hand. "Each one of us has a complicated history, Emma. Don't be afraid to call the judge your father."

"You will have to meet Andrew. He is a lovely man."

"Which proves there is someone for everybody," Vikram laughed as he turned to Rosa. "And you – are you happy, my Rosa?"

Rosa curled up her feet under her. "Now, yes."

"What of Anil? He has handed in his notice."

"We were not happy. I can't say I missed him when I was in Ireland. I grabbed the bull by the horns – that is what Emma said I should do – and I kicked him out. Really, it finished between us a long time ago. I threw him out, gave him one hour to pack his bags. The sorry fellow is living with his brother in Delhi."

"Maybe it is for the best, my Rosa. Real love could be around the corner."

"In this faraway location, I very much doubt it." Rosa laughed and Vikram thought there was so much of the woman who had raised her in this girl.

*

Vikram got dressed in his silk kurta early. Rhya shooed him away as she walked into the bedroom.

"You must give us time to dress, Vik, and tell the boy we will eat early."

He heard her talk gently to Grace and he felt complete joy to hear the hum of happy conversation emanating from the room as Rosa and Emma joined them.

It could all have been so different. Grace did not blame him at all. She had not told him what her life was like in the asylum, and he doubted she ever would, but he saw it in her every day: her childlike delight in being able to walk from room to room, stepping out on the grassed lawn in front of the bungalow, letting the dog lean into her, her hand gently caressing the dog's ears, her inability to order the manservant about, the way she jumped when anybody walked up behind her, the way she cried after he made love to her. All he wanted to do now was stay here, in this quiet place, surrounded by the coffee plants, the trees and the mountains, amidst the sound of the birds, the waterfalls and the wildlife, to just sit together and be.

So caught up was he, he did not at first hear Rosa call him.

"Vik, may we present Grace," she said, sweeping her hand wide as if she was introducing somebody on stage.

Nervously stepping onto the veranda, Grace stood in front of him, her white and gold sari perfectly draped across her light frame, her blouse with sleeves to the elbow edged in a deeper gold. Her hair was wrapped into a tight bun at the nape of her neck, and there was a shy smile on her face that he remembered from decades earlier. As he held out his hand to her, she stepped towards him. It was then he saw his mother's thick gold jewellery around her neck. He had once seen her, a vision in a gold ballgown. Now, cloaked in white and gold Indian silk, the sari draped in soft pleats, he could honestly say he had never seen Grace so beautiful, so serene and so happy. His heart soared to see her so lovely in front of him.

Emma, in a deep-blue sari with a red border, followed, her walk a little more awkward than her mother's, her shoulders hunched, as if she was unsure of how to hold herself in a sari.

Rosa caught her hand. The two sisters, one in blue, the other in purple, walked to Vikram.

Rhya, wearing a new sari in deep-green silk, hung back. Vikram turned to her.

"Rhya, you will always have the right to stand with us, you surely know that."

Her step was light as she quickly walked across to the rest of the family.

Vikram turned to Grace. "I promised a long time ago that we would be together in Chikmagalur. I wanted you to come with me. Here, in this beloved place, I will make that promise again in front of those who matter to us most and in front of these hills which have waited so long for us and which now shield us, in this cocoon away from the rest of the world."

The clouds had lifted, so he took her hand and they walked to their favourite spot, where, through the tall trees shading the Robusta plants, they could see the roll of the mountains as they stood on lookout over the estate. At their height was a rich blue-green against a blue-grey sky, where small scuffles of clouds lingered.

Vikram called to the servants and the older one shouted to two boys, who ran over, holding a bench between them, placing it for Grace to sit.

Vikram sat beside her and took her hand.

"Grace, nothing I will ever do will make up for the wrongs done to you, but I pledge here in this place of my heart, I am yours, to eternity and beyond. Let our family bear witness and let the hills bear witness to this simple but heartfelt pledge to you, that not a day will go by, in all the years I hope we have together, when I will not try to make it up to you."

Tears puffed up inside her and she stroked his face, her fingers lightly caressing his wet cheeks.

"You do not have to make up anything, Vikram, but I accept your love and return it thousands over." Gently, she kissed him. "Vikram, you, and this place especially, have set me free."

"Even when the clouds hem us in and the trees resemble ghostly soldiers standing sentry?"

She reached over, taking his two hands. "This is it, Vikram, the place and dream that kept me going. Now, it is our time to live it."

He hugged her and Rhya pursed her lips in dissatisfaction, to think any woman would want to stay in this wilderness full-time.

A breeze rose up through the Robusta plants, rumpling the feathers of the birds and tousling the leaves on the trees, swirling across the hill, scattering towards the mountains.

"We are all home," Rosa whispered, taking Emma's hand.

The twin sisters turned together and walked towards the old estate house, letting the others follow behind.